Dream Searchers

Part Two
The Borders of the Unknown

T0306468

First published by O Books, 2009
O Books is an imprint of John Hunt Publishing Ltd., The Bothy, Deershot Lodge, Park Lane, Ropley,
Hants, SO24 0BE, UK
office1@o-books.net
www.o-books.net

Distribution in:	South Africa
	Alternative Books
UK and Europe	altbook@peterhyde.co.za
Orca Book Services	Tel: 021 555 4027 Fax: 021 447 1430
orders@orcabookservices.co.uk	
Tel: 01202 665432 Fax: 01202 666219	Text copyright Andrey Reutov 2008
Int. code (44)	
	Design: Stuart Davies
USA and Canada	
NBN	ISBN: 978 1 84694 233 4
custserv@nbnbooks.com	
Tel: 1 800 462 6420 Fax: 1 800 338 4550	All rights reserved. Except for brief quotations
	in critical articles or reviews, no part of this
Australia and New Zealand	book may be reproduced in any manner without
Brumby Books	prior written permission from the publishers.
sales@brumbybooks.com.au	
Tel: 61 3 9761 5535 Fax: 61 3 9761 7095	The rights of Andrey Reutov as author have
	been asserted in accordance with the
Far East (offices in Singapore, Thailand,	Copyright, Designs and Patents Act 1988.
Hong Kong, Taiwan)	
Pansing Distribution Pte Ltd	
kemal@pansing.com	A CIP catalogue record for this book is available
Tel: 65 6319 9939 Fax: 65 6462 5761	from the British Library.

Printed by Digital Book Print

O Books operates a distinctive and ethical publishing philosophy in
all areas of its business, from its global network of authors to
production and worldwide distribution.
This book is produced on FSC certified stock, within ISO14001
standards. The printer plants sufficient trees each year through
the Woodland Trust to absorb the level of emitted carbon in
its production.

Dream Searchers

Part Two
The Borders of the Unknown

Andrey Reutov

BOOKS

Winchester, UK
Washington, USA

CONTENTS

Chapter One

Entering the Flow

The setting sun painted the sea in crimson color. Maxim was looking at the water, carefully listening to the soft rustle of the waves and thinking about how nice this place was. When he was a little boy, he dreamt of becoming a sailor and got completely engrossed in the sea novels by Jack London. But his dream, just like a lot of other things in his life, remained just a dream…

'What are you thinking about?' Boris got up and asked with a smile. 'Move over…'

'Nothing special. Just looking at the sea.' Maxim moved aside, making some room for Boris on the beach towel. 'It's beautiful out here. Even better than in Gelendzhik[1].'

'Yes, it is,' Boris agreed. 'We come out here almost every year. It's only last year that we haven't been here.'

'Actually, it is my first trip abroad.' Maxim picked up a pebble and threw it in the water.

'Don't exaggerate. You can hardly call Abkhazia[2] "abroad", even if you really wanted to.'

'But it is officially another country?'

'Officially maybe, but practically, he who controls a place – owns the place. Take, for example, the same Kosovo; officially, it belongs to Serbia, but who cares about that? The one who is stronger is right, and that says it all.'

'You like talking about politics,' Maxim grinned. 'Rather, about geopolitics.'

'I just like observing what's going on in the world. First of all, it's interesting and second of all, it allows you to discern a few emerging patterns…' Boris looked back. 'Oh, our witches are coming. They are probably going to drag us into the water again.'

1

Maxim too looked around. Indeed, Iris, Rada and Oxana were walking towards them. Iris was talking about something, Oxana was gently laughing. Rada was smiling timidly, as usual. It was strange to realize that no one at that beach had a clue about what these young women really were. While he was looking at them, Maxim sadly realized that there are probably a lot of incredible secrets passing us by in much the same way. They are here, close by, at arm's length, but we simply don't know anything about them.

Maxim, Boris and Iris came over to Sukhumi eight days ago. They tried to avoid talking about what happened in Gelendzhik. Yes, Kramer got what he deserved. But it nevertheless left a bitter taste in their mouths; not in everyone's, though. Already, the first day in Sukhumi, Iris had her say about Kramer's death:

'Have you seen the signs: "Don't climb the post – danger of death"?' she asked, looking carefully at Maxim. 'Kramer climbed a post just like that. If he had stopped bugging us, he would have been on the beach, and not in a coffin.'

Having thought about it for a little while, Maxim was prone to agree with her.

Oxana and Rada joined them three days ago, once Roman and Dennis returned to Klyonovsk. Maxim perceived Oxana's arrival with controlled emotions of happiness. He already knew that he was in love with this young woman. Besides, she was the only one he felt comfortable with. You could always expect a prank from Iris, and Maxim was even a bit afraid of Rada. It's just that he knew what kind of power that lovely, modest young woman was hiding. In comparison to these two, Oxana looked like an inexperienced silly little thing, as Iris called her once, and she still had a lot to learn. In this sense, Maxim and Oxana were quite alike, and that automatically brought them closer. In his heart, Maxim cherished the dream of returning to Rostov, hoping that Oxana would join him. They would have to create their own group there – practically from scratch.

The young women were getting closer and closer, and they were being noticed. Mostly Iris – her perfectly shaped figure and a soft graceful walk involuntarily attracted the eyes of the tourists.

'I bet you anything that she'll say something nasty,' Boris said quietly, obviously talking about Iris. 'You can tell from the way she is smiling.'

Indeed, that was exactly what happened. Having come up close, Iris took a quick look at Maxim and shook her head.

'You look much better with your clothes on,' she said. 'There is simply nothing to look at. Boris, once you get home don't forget to show him the way to the gym.'

'By the way, your hair is falling out,' Maxim echoed. 'And you snore in your sleep.'

'That was bad,' Iris shook her head. 'Primitive. Besides, you know yourself that there is nothing wrong with my hair, and I am quieter than a mouse when I sleep. I give you a "D".' Iris threw off her clothes and laid out her beach towel. She gracefully placed herself on the towel and shook her head – a cascade of luxurious hair ran down her shoulders. Having adjusted her sunglasses, the young woman lay down, perfectly aware of how many eyes were looking at her. Needless to say, she looked great – Maxim had to admit that.

'She is in a bad mood,' Oxana said, laying out her towel. 'She broke her nail.'

'On who?' Boris asked lazily. Everyone started laughing. Even Iris smiled.

'You see?' she asked Maxim without turning her head. 'That's the way you do it.'

'I'm going for a swim,' Rada exclaimed. 'Who is with me?'

Maxim looked at Oxana, silently urging her to go. 'Are you coming?'

'We are,' Oxana answered. She grabbed Maxim by the hand, pulling him up with a jerk, and dragged him towards the sea.

Kramer's death wasn't a big blow to Dags. People come and go, but the business remains. The loss of several documents that Kramer apparently took with him to Gelenzhik promised to bring much bigger trouble.

'It was foolish of him,' Dags sighed, once he found out about the loss. 'I should have snapped his neck myself. By the way, how did he die?' Dags glanced at the tall, round-shouldered man, who was about the age of forty-five, standing in front of him. Valentin Karetnikov, also known as Rat-catcher, was the Legion representative of the Krasnodarsk Terriotiry, and came personally to report on the incident to the boss.

'Here...' Having taken a step, Rat-catcher put a video tape on Dags's table and then immediately took a step back. 'It's all there.'

'You managed to tape it?' Dags looked at Rat-catcher in surprise.

'Not us.' The Rat-catcher cleared his throat; he was obviously embarrassed. 'You see... our man, responsible for the holiday village, had cameras put up in the various rooms. We only just found out about it, as we were searching through the room. This knucklehead says he was making these tapes just in case. You never know what can happen.'

Dags frowned. For a couple of moments he sat, tapping his fingers on the table then he looked up at Rat-catcher.

'So, what you are saying is that he was taping me too? I was on vacation here too, and I was not alone. You know that perfectly well.'

'Mr. Dags, we seized more than a hundred video tapes from him. And I swear to you that I haven't watched a single one of them. I have them with me; they are yours now. I haven't even looked at the labels. I just put them in a box and brought them with me.'

'What did you do with the owner of the village?' Dags asked, having taken the video tape off the table.

'Nothing yet. He's under arrest. Would you like to have a word with him?'

'Not really, thanks.' Dags became thoughtful. 'Here's what you'll do: take him out to the sea, far away from the shore, bind his legs and push him overboard. And then let him swim, until he drowns – I want him to suffer. Don't forget to make a tape of this outstanding event.'

'It will be done.' Rat-catcher cheered up, feeling that the storm had passed him by.

'You've already watched this?' Dags tapped the tape against the table.

'Yes,' Rat-catcher nodded. 'We had to watch it.'

Dags drew a sigh, rose from his chair and approached the TV installed in the closet. He put the tape into the VCR slot, grabbed the remote, returned to the table and got himself back in the armchair. Having pressed play, he began to carefully examine the screen.

'The quality is not the best,' the Rat-catcher explained. For some reason, he was whispering. 'The camera lens was very small.'

On the screen, Kramer was still alive and getting ready for bed. Now he got himself in bed, picked up a book and started reading.

'Now...' Rat-catcher whispered once again. 'You see, the mask has cracked? He brought it with him... And now look at the back of the bed... There, do you see it?'

'Be quiet, why won't you...' Dags cut him short, intensely staring at the screen. The steel tendril that crawled out of the bed railing had already grasped Kramer by the throat then a man appeared in the shot. He took off his mask, but Dags didn't see his face. And he didn't need to – he could hear Kramer utter the man's name with a frightened voice.

'Sly again,' Dags whispered. 'Damn it!'

Rat-catcher remained discreetly silent, understanding full well that the boss was in low spirits.

Meanwhile, the bed railing released another steel tendril; it froze in front of the victim's face. Dags didn't pay much attention to the dialogue between Sly and Kramer – he simply knew that he would watch this tape more than once. All his attention was glued to the steel sprouts; it occurred to Dags that all of this was already very serious. And even his vaunted mask didn't help. Dags frowned and twitched as the steel tendril pierced through Kramer's forehead. Dags's own forehead was covered in perspiration. Yes, it was already very serious.

Meanwhile, on the screen, it was all over – the bed railing drew in its tendrils, Sly exited the shot.

'That's it,' Rat-catcher said, and then added very quietly: 'Can you tell me what that was?'

'That was death,' Dags answered just as quietly. After a short silence, he sighed: 'This is very valuable material, Valentin Alexandrovich. Very valuable. You've done a good job, I'll think about your transfer to Moscow. There's plenty of work. Go home and don't forget to bring me the tape.'

'Yes, Sovereign. Will do.'

Maxim really enjoyed his vacation in Abkhazia – warm sea, nice people, good company – what else do you need to have a good time?

But everything comes to an end, and so even this fairy tale. Still, he was looking forward to going back to Klyonovsk; he had things to do. And if something did unsettle him, it was the role of a freeloader; Maxim wasn't used to living at someone else's expense. That's why already in the beginning of September, on the third day of their homecoming, Maxim decided to have a word with Boris regarding his possible return to Rostov.

Boris was understanding. Having listened to what Maxim had to say, he smiled:

'Basically, you can return to Rostov. But you would have to completely change the way you look. Not one of your former acquaintances should be able to recognize you.'

Maxim frowned. He didn't want to change; that caused a burning feeling of protest in his heart.

'Is that necessary?' he asked.

'If you want to go back to Rostov – yes, it is. Don't forget that the Legionaries have your photographs now; they know almost everything there is to know about you. And in order not to fall into their clutches, you'll have to turn into a different person. That's the only way of defense right now.'

'All right, but what do you mean by change? Different clothes, different image?'

'That too,' Boris agreed. 'But to become someone else is bigger than that. You must take off the mask you wear now and put on another one.'

'I wouldn't say that I'm wearing a mask,' Maxim said.

'You do,' Boris confirmed with a smile. 'Just like the rest of us. Remember, magicians trace themselves – their habits, their reactions, their way of perception – it's just a part of the art of stalking. A good stalker has a perfect understanding, not only of the behavior of other people, but also of his own. And he thinks nothing of replacing one guise with another. You do not have that kind of experience yet, so it will do you a whole lot of good to practice it.'

'Fine,' Maxim agreed. 'I'll try.'

'No,' Boris shook his head. 'You can't create a new image all by yourself just yet. Let's entrust this to our girls. I'm confident that they'll be more than happy to do it.'

'Ok, sure,' Maxim agreed, thinking to himself how happy he was that Iris wasn't with them – she left for Belgorod to visit Danila – they've been together for quite a while. 'I don't mind.'

Rada and Oxana gladly agreed to work on Maxim's image. And Rada immediately put forward one condition – they work, he obeys. Maxim had to accept. First Rada brought scissors and a hair clipper. Maxim dreaded the inevitable.

'You always wear your hair long,' Rada explained, sitting

Maxim down on a chair, 'now you'll wear it short. Grow a little mustache – it suits you. And don't worry, I know what I'm doing,' Rada smiled, plugging in the hair clipper.

'I sure hope so,' Maxim answered in a depressed voice.

The hair cut took about half an hour. One cannot say that Maxim liked what he saw, but he couldn't call it bad either.

'You're quite good,' Maxim told Rada, having examined himself in the mirror.

'There was a time I studied to become a hairdresser,' the young woman replied. 'In another life. And now we're going shopping. We're going to dress you up.'

Maxim couldn't do anything else but agree.

This project dragged on for three hours, and all of that time Rada explained to Maxim all the peculiarities of his new image in detail. Oxana almost didn't interfere – she simply knew that Rada was a true expert in these things.

First of all, Rada forbade Maxim to even think about jeans wear, having declared that that style was from now on unacceptable to him.

'We are going to create an image of a young businessman,' she said. 'Self-confident, business-like and well off; a man that knows his worth. The former jeans boy is gone, you can forget all about him.'

Rada chose the suit and the shirts herself, and that made Maxim frown even more. It was not the clothes that made him feel uncomfortable, but rather the price – he thought it simply indecent to spend that kind of money on clothes. On top of it all, Rada chose a whole dozen ties for Maxim, and not just some ties, but very expensive ones. When Maxim asked her, why all these neck clothes – which he doesn't even know how to tie – Rada only smiled.

'You cannot walk around in one and the same tie. Make it a principle to change your tie every day. See it as a little assignment.'

The next stop on their tour was the shoe shop – of course, one of the most fashionable shops in the city.

'Don't even think about sneakers,' Rada declared at once. 'Only good quality shoes, and several pairs of them.'

'Sneakers are comfy,' Maxim drawled in a sad voice, having already realized that arguing is pointless. And so it was.

After the shoe shop they visited a couple of other shops. Rada bought for Maxim a rather expensive digital watch – not made out of gold, but very functional; a leather belt for his pants; a lighter; a hair brush; and a couple of tie-pins. Finally, the last item they bought was a middle-sized leather suitcase.

'That's it for now,' Rada finally said. Maxim sighed with relief. 'If there's something we forgot we'll buy it later.'

Maxim was dressed in new clothes back at the house. Having arrayed himself in the suit, he felt strangely awkward. Everything seemed extremely uncomfortable; Maxim felt like a scarecrow, but Rada was pleased.

'Wonderful,' she said, tying a tie around Maxim's neck. 'Even better than I expected. Go on; take a look at yourself in the mirror.'

Maxim looked in the mirror – the reflection showed a completely different person: tall, slim and very ungainly.

'I look like a proper fool,' Maxim muttered, turning in front of the mirror. Oxana gave a quiet laugh. Rada softly smiled.

'Ever heard the expression "a round peg in a square hole"?' Rada asked. 'So far, that's about you. It's not enough to just put on a suit; you also need to learn to feel comfortable wearing it. Now each day you will spend a couple of hours walking around town. And not just walking, but going into shops and visiting different companies. Ask about their merchandise; ask to see their price lists; look for non-existent people – all of that will help you grow into the character of a businessman.'

'But I'm not a businessman,' Maxim objected.

'Who knows,' Rada smiled. 'Perhaps you'll become one.'

Maxim didn't want to argue.

'What do you mean by looking for non-existent people?' he asked.

'It's just a good excuse to enter any establishment. You can even write down on a piece of paper some information about this person in advance. If you want, you could come up with a whole story. For example, you are looking for your dear girlfriend, who is working here somewhere.' Rada smiled again. 'These too are elements of stalking. You are putting on a show, but not to fool other people. You are putting on a show for the Spirit. If you are not too tired, you can go for a walk right now.'

'Tomorrow's better,' Maxim replied. Rada barely noticeably smiled.

He went out to town the following morning, right after breakfast. He felt very ill at ease; Maxim thought everyone kept staring at him. The suit irritated him and restrained his movements; the shoes made too loud of a tapping sound against the sidewalk – could they ever be compared to the soft walk of the sneakers? And on top of everything this hideous noose of the tie...

Maxim didn't look for any non-existent people. Having spent an hour in the city, he returned home. He was in a terrible mood. Maxim didn't like the new clothes and he crustily thought that he would have to continue walking around like a hobgoblin. Only when he got home and changed into his precious jeans and a simple shirt, did he feel better.

His mood didn't pass unnoticed. At lunch the searchers kept making fun of him, but when everyone had left the table, Boris invited Maxim up to his room.

'Spit it out,' he said with a grin, when both of them had made themselves comfortable in the armchairs. 'What happened?'

'Nothing really,' Maxim answered sullenly, shrugging his shoulders. 'I just don't like my new look. I don't like suits and ties; it's not my thing. I don't feel comfortable in them. I don't think that I can ever get used to wearing them.'

'Man is not a dog; he gets used to everything,' Boris grinned. 'Seriously though, you just made a small mistake: instead of focusing your attention on positive things, you noticed only the negative. It's not surprising that the whole world started to seem repulsive to you.'

'But the suit is really uncomfortable,' Maxim objected.

'You're wrong. You just forgot the main rule – the world is the way we want to see it. Remember, we've already talked about flows. You know that the whole world is made out of flows, but so far you know that only on the level of your mind. Your knowledge doesn't give you anything in practice. And if you had remembered what I've told you, you would have realized one simple thing: with your active aversion, your irritation, you've got yourself into a negative flow. The elements of the flow are bound by attraction, so your discontent causes the world again and again to throw you events that can trigger your annoyance. You've entered the flow; you are driving on a negative chain of events and you're not even aware of it. Even now you are still in that flow, because my words annoy you as well.'

Maxim was silent. True, Boris definitely had a point. But the suit was really uncomfortable.

'You need to learn to trace the flows you are in,' Boris continued. 'If you've realized that you are in a flow, getting out of it is already easier. The idea is simple: you need to perform an action that doesn't match the suit of the events of the flow. For example, at this moment it's enough for you to simply smile. True, it will be a forced action; after all, you do not want to laugh. But you'll make the first step towards getting out of the negative flow that carries you. Go on, try it. Show me the saber-toothed smile of a cool businessman.'

Maxim involuntarily smiled. Not because Boris said so – the words about the saber-toothed smile amused him.

'Good,' Boris complimented him. 'You're already on the mend. More precisely, an ill person is more alive than dead. Now, in order to leave the negative flow all together, you need to strengthen your success. Tell me a joke. Come on, don't be shy.'

'I have a bad memory for jokes,' Maxim replied. 'I hear one, I laugh, and then I forget it.'

'Then I'll tell you one. I just heard it yesterday. It's short, but smart: two little mice are nibbling on a tape in a film storehouse. One mouse stops nibbling, looks at the other and says: "You know, the script was better".'

Maxim smiled.

'Another one, before I forget,' Boris continued. 'A bumper sticker on a car: "Is there life after death? Hijack this car and find out".'

Maxim grinned again then laughed.

'Now it's your turn,' Boris said. 'Come on, start remembering – anything at all.'

'All right,' Maxim became thoughtful for a couple of seconds. 'A guy sits on a sofa in his flat. He hears someone knocking on the door. He gets up and opens the door and there's an old lady with a scythe. He asks: "Who are you?" – "I'm death." – "So what?" – "So that's it."'

Boris grinned.

'Not a bad joke,' he said. 'Although a bit depressing. And now evaluate your state – honestly and objectively. Analyze your feelings. There are two flows competing in you now – the old one and the new one.'

Maxim knew what Boris was talking about. On the one hand, he still wanted to grumble, be angry and complain about life. At the same time all of that had already fizzled out; it didn't have the same strength. Jokes didn't appeal to him either, but the idea of them didn't put him off. Practically speaking, Maxim had a choice – to continue being angry or choose laughter and joy.

Boris was looking at him with a smile.

'Castaneda said that all our thoughts and what we are, are defined by the position of the assemblage point. If we were to use his terminology, we could add the following: we may shift the assemblage point, consciously entering one flow or the other. And if you've got an aversion to suits, then there's a position of the assemblage point where you're just crazy about them. So for a magician, to love or not to love suits is a matter of choice. So far you've chosen to hate them. But the possibility of the other choice is not less real; it's in very close proximity. Next time, having put on a suit, focus on the positive aspects of it. They don't have to have anything to do with the suit. It's enough if you notice everything that's nice and beautiful around you. Such a focus will drag you out into a favorable flow, and once there, the suit will no longer seem that bad. With time, the new position of the assemblage point will become stable; you'll feel in a suit like a fish in water. That's what stalking is about – the ability to glide in the flows around us, choosing those that we like. At the same time, a magician is always aware of what flow he is in at the moment. We cannot free ourselves from flows, it's impossible. But we can choose the flows that we like.' Boris went silent for a second. 'There is another subtlety,' he continued. 'You see, we can use the power of those flows we are involved in. These may be all kinds of flows – for instance, religious, political, social flows – the array is almost infinite. You enter a flow and introduce your intention to the flow. How to do that properly we'll talk about later. You get the desired result, after that you exit the flow – before it hooks you up and you'll have to pay with your energy, or even your life. Depending on the quality of the energy you need, you may connect to all kinds of flows. For example, in big cities like Moscow you can use the energy of the subway. If you've been to the metro, you've probably felt all of its power. In this case, it doesn't matter to a magician what kind of flow it is; it's simply enough to activate its power for his purposes. The flow fulfills your wish and once that's done you exit it.'

'And how does one activate the energy of the metro?' Maxim smiled. 'Jump before the coming train?'

'Jumping before the coming train is not necessary. But it is actually a complicated topic; let's leave it for a separate discussion. Now we're talking about flows in general. Remember your exercises with the PM – practically, you were guiding not one but four flows at the same time. And if you wanted to win the lottery, that's the flow of diamonds, then the remaining three flows – the flows of hearts, spades and clubs, turned into weights on your feet. So the next stage, after the PM, is to learn how to work the flows without any patience. If you want to win the lottery, just try entering the flow of diamonds. And how you go about that – try to figure it out for yourself.' Boris softly smiled. 'Tomorrow you'll tell me about yet another walk in the city, and then you can let me know what you came up with. Agreed?'

'Ok,' Maxim nodded. 'I'll give it all some thought.'

'That's another story. By the way, where's your annoyance?'

'Gone,' Maxim answered.

'Exactly,' Boris agreed. 'Or rather you left it.'

The next day did turn out to be much more pleasant than the day before. Now even if Maxim did get angry, he got angry only with himself – for letting emotions carry him away. Yeah, it's a suit – and so what? There are plenty of people in suits. And this one is quite fancy too.

This time around Maxim didn't feel as constrained. And even thought the suit still made him self-conscious, Maxim tried not to fixate on it – why would he with so many wonderful things around him? – the sky, the clouds, a young woman in a light colored skirt, children with ice-cream in their hands, a funny looking dog with just as funny female owner – the world is wonderful; you just need to know how to notice it. He went into shops and asked the prices of things. At the same time he was even amused by the shop assistants treating him in a pointedly attentive way. Before, when Maxim walked around in jeans and a jeans jacket, salespeople just followed him with their gaze; he was of no interest to them. Now they thought he was a wealthy buyer, so it wasn't surprising that they hovered around him, praising their merchandise to the skies. In the end, Maxim arrived at the conclusion that looking wealthy is not that bad.

He only managed to have a talk with Boris around midnight. Boris and Roman had disappeared somewhere – the mayor elections were approaching, and counteracting Legionaries took way too much time.

Boris was obviously pleased with Maxim's report.

'You did everything right,' he said. 'Now you know how little you need to enter a good flow. The important thing is to realize that you've been captured by a bad flow then moving into a good one is much easier. By the way, did you come up with anything on how to enter a diamond flow?'

'As far as I see it, you need to focus your attention on everything that has to do with money, right?'

'Close, but not quite. Remember, we talked about the Net. And the Net consists of many flows – big and small ones. Let's say, there are rivers, and there are tiny streamlets. If you just start focusing your gaze on elements that have something to do with money, you enter one of the tiny streamlets – in fact, you create one. But a streamlet like that is very weak, and if you are trying to win the lottery then, in the best case scenario, you'll win a hundred or something rubles. The force of the flow you find yourself in will be too small to secure a substantial win for you. So, you need to move to the flows of a higher level. How do you do that? Find the elements in the real world that reflect this higher level. And here we are approaching a very important topic – the geographical expression of the Net. I suggest you conduct the following experiment...' Boris got up from his armchair, opened the door of a cabinet and started digging in papers. 'Ah, there it is...' Having retrieved a large piece of paper folded fourfold, he closed the cabinet and got back into the armchair. 'This is the city map.' Boris unfolded the map and ran his palm on the fold lines. 'It's a bit crumpled, but it doesn't matter. In the hall, next to the phone, is a phone book. In that book are the addresses to all city organizations. Your task will be to mark some of these organizations on the map. But you shouldn't choose them randomly, but according to suit, like in the PM. For example, mark all the big stores on the map. Then mark cinemas, churches, defense and law enforcement structures – like ATC, ROVD, FSS, military enlistment and registration offices and so on. In a word, mark all of the most important city objects. What's important is not to just mark them, but to arrange them into a Net, connecting the dots. You can get color pencils from Oxana and mark out the different areas of the Net with different colors. As a result you'll get the reflection of the Net on the local area. If you then analyze the obtained scheme, you'll be able to mark out certain special patterns. This could be triangles, rhombs, pentagrams or hexagrams – they could be even, regular and not so much. Your next task would be to introduce a similar geometric figure into your chain. And if your chain is a diamond chain, then you need to look for, for example, triangles made out of banks, large stores – that is, some kind of commercial structures. The more regular your triangle or rhombus is, the better. Then, when carrying out the chain, you'll have to visit all of the connecting points of this triangle or rhombus in order. By doing that you enter yourself into a diamond flow of a higher level; you connect to the power of these structures. There are many more subtleties in this, but now you know the general scheme and can sort out all the details yourself.' Boris smiled. 'Knowledge has power only when you sweat for it. So take the map and do it!'

'But isn't structuring according to the four suits artificial?' Maxim asked and drew the map to him. 'It doesn't reflect the entire variety of elements.'

'True enough,' Boris confirmed. 'But what stops you from creating your own classification system? Have ten suits, twenty or just two. After all, it's a field for research – the more thoroughly you work through the elements of the Net, the better. Basically, everything we see is part of the Net. Now you perceive the world the way you are used to; there is no place for magic in your perception. By exposing the Net in the local area, you start changing the standard cosmography, replacing it with a magical one. There are no longer just roads or sidewalks, just banks or shops – all of these are the elements of the Net. Having carefully worked with the map, you'll be able to mark out junctions and main routes, find out about the hierarchy of the map's elements. Ultimately, the new perception will force out the old one and the Net will gradually start revealing its secrets to you. That's when real magic will start happening in your life – for example, you'll see that any element of the world around you could be made into an entry point into the system. And an entry point is the main element of your favorite portals. Imagine you are walking along a sidewalk, focusing your attention on it. At the same time you know that on some street in Rostov there is a very similar sidewalk. Your attention connects these two dots, and the Net opens a portal for you – an instant, and you realize that you are walking down the sidewalk in Rostov. Or you enter an elevator in one city, and exit in another city. You can find dozens of entry points, but all of that will work only once the Net has assumed a firm place in your representation of the world.'

'That's something to think about,' Maxim agreed. 'By the way, how did you open your first portal? And when?'

'About seven years ago...' Pensiveness appeared in Boris's gaze. Nevertheless, he immediately smiled. 'I lived in the Moscow area at the time and took the el-train to work. I had to get up at five am, while it was still dark, and then walk for about twenty minutes to get to the train. There was a road, lined with maples. In the autumn it was all covered in leaves; I really liked that place – during the day, of course, not in the dark. Just another autumn day, I was walking down this road – it was dark, cold, leaves rustling under my feet. I remembered that in Moscow, on my way to work, I go through a park with the same maples and the fallen leaves rustle in the same way. For a moment I even thought I was in Moscow. I grinned and immediately walked into a fountain – a fountain in the Moscow Park.'

'And?'

'And nothing. It took a while for me to come around. I glanced at my watch; it wasn't even six in the morning. Usually, I would arrive in Moscow an hour later. After that incident I spent almost three months trying to open the same portal, but I couldn't manage. I left the place in January and then I had other portals.' Boris smiled. 'That's how it usually starts. Almost by accident at first and only later you do it consciously.'

'Okay, but how do you open a portal consciously? Surely there are some technicalities involved?'

'Of course. Portals will remain fairy tales to you until you learn how to create a point of entry. There are different methods, but I'd recommend you the following one: try paying attention to the stirring of the air. For example, try meditating on the air in a door opening, preferably against a dark background. You'll notice a slight vibration, heaving. Continue watching; your task is to locate the observed area of space, to notice its peculiarities. At the same time, the most important thing is to detect the stirring of the air in the door opening not only with your sight, but with your whole body. If you're doing everything right, the chosen area of space will start getting darker and eventually turn into a dark spot. This spot makes out the basis of a portal. Having expanded the spot to the right size, you may enter it. Again, the important thing here is the complex sensations you experience with your body. Say, I opened my first portal, having caught on to the rustle of dry leaves. In the case with the spot, you'd need to catch on to the sensations of the spot – your feeling of it. At the first stage, your task is to learn how to create an entry point in any place and in any environment in a few seconds. Then you can learn how to use the portal, but you need to be very careful – uncontrolled transfers through portals may get you into a nuthouse. Again, it's recommended that portals should only be used in case of flagrant necessity. And if you'll jump back and forth like a yoyo, then one day, when you really need to open a portal, you won't be able to do it – you simply won't have enough strength. That is, with portals, like with everything else, you need to stay within reasonable limits. Generally speaking, try working on the entry point; that will surely prove interesting to you.' Boris demonstratively glanced at the watch.

'I'll try it,' Maxim smiled. 'Thanks, Boris. Good night.'

Chapter Two

A New Assignment

Dags appointed Yana instead of Kramer. Perhaps that did raise some eyebrows, but no one dared to argue with the Sovereign.

Yana took her promotion for granted. It was bound to happen someday – it's not like she could stay subordinate to a nobody like Kramer for the rest of her life. Now, looking at the shots of Kramer's death, Yana was barely noticeably smiling – one might as well say 'thank you' to Sly.

'So, what do you think?' Dags asked when the recording stopped.

'Only Rada could have taught him that,' Yana answered. 'She has always been interested in these kinds of things.'

'Did you know they could do this?' Dags gazed intently at the young woman.

'No.' Yana shook her head. 'But I have a pretty good idea of who does what. That's how they do it over there – each of them specializes in some area then teaches the rest. And the same goes for between the groups. It's a very efficient approach; it gives good results. Rada has always been interested in using dream techniques – IRL. Now we see that she's been successful in that pursuit.'

'I don't get it,' Dags mumbled. 'We've got six research groups; we pay them so much money – and all for nothing. These fools can't even master any of the known methods, not to mention coming up with something new. I'd break up the sodding lot of them.'

Yana was silent. The boss was not in the mood, and she had a pretty good idea why. Legionaries have been trying to win over to their side a rather well-known Siberian clan of magicians, hoping to use the clan in the game against the searchers. They promised big money and just as big prospects – in response, the magicians politely told the Legionaries to get lost. True, you could declare war on them, but Dags refrained from taking such an ill-advised step. He's got his hands full with the searchers; he'll still have time to get even with the Siberians.

'How are we doing with Internet?' Dags asked sullenly. 'The new forum is already up and running?'

'Not yet,' Yana replied. 'We can't just open a new site. We need to organize a well thought-out full-scale attack on the searchers. I've picked a team of guys; they have dispersed among all of the more or less known forums. They are now settling in, gaining authority and trust. I provide them with a little information now and then, so that people will be drawn to them. When needed, they'll have their say.' Yana smiled, yet her eyes remained cold. 'As for the main forum, we are now looking for a leader. We've got a few candidates, but we want someone more impressive.'

'Fine,' Dags sighed. 'I'll wait.' He went quiet for a second then looked up at Yana. 'Now let's get back to the most important thing… Yesterday I spoke to the Supreme Hierarch; he's seen the tape with Sly and Kramer. He was impressed. We're asked to deal with this problem as soon as possible, before it develops into new trouble. The Hierarch needs Sly's head. He recommends us to get the others alive. What do you need to make it happen?'

'I'll get you Sly's head.' Yana gave Dags an intent look. 'But in return I ask you to place the analysis department and the fifth department of the security service under my authority. I need these structures.'

'You ask too much,' Dags snorted. 'I can understand why you need the analysis department, but why do you need the fifth department?'

'I need experts, and not the rejects you've handed Kramer. Remember what happened when Kramer tried to capture Sly? Remember Dana's death? If I had experienced people with me,

21

and not the rabble like Venya, I would have taken her. Finally, remember the car explosion – any idiot would have known that they were being lured into a trap. But those idiots died idiots; they didn't have enough brains to realize simple things. Every time a more or less decent man appears, you immediately take him in under your custody, into the security service, or appoint him curator of some project. After that you ask for results, forgetting that you can't get a result out of nowhere. Forgive my sharp words, but that's the truth.'

'You're not like Kramer,' Dags solemnly smiled. 'Maybe you've got other requests?'

There was threat in Dags' voice. Still, Yana didn't plan on backing off.

'I do,' she agreed. 'Some while ago, you lured me with power and knowledge – and where is it? Had I stayed with the searchers, I would probably be able to do everything Rada or Iris can by now. But I came to you, and what do I have?'

'But I've appointed you a curator. Do you mean to say that a curator has little power?'

'I'm talking about a different kind of power.' Yana fixed her eyes on Dags. 'You know what I am talking about. Ordinary power is not worth a nickel.'

'What do you need, specifically?' he asked.

'I need access to the Legion archive.'

'Access to the archive?' Dags involuntarily grinned. 'Aren't you asking a bit too much?'

'Who said I was asking?' Yana inquired. 'I am demanding. You've seen what happened to Kramer, and I do not want to share his fate. I need knowledge, Sovereign. I need the archive.'

'Very well, I'll think about what I can do,' Dags grinned. 'And now – go. It's time for my lunch.'

'Bon appetite, Sovereign.' Yana forced a smile, got up from the armchair and headed for the exit. Having closed the door behind her, she nervously opened her handbag and groped for the cigarettes. 'Son of a bitch,' she muttered, lighting up. 'And he's gay too. You can't trust anyone.'

She hid the lighter in her bag, glanced at Dags's office door with disgust, then turned around and quickly headed for the exit.

The next talk with Boris happened about a week later. By that time Maxim was quite at home with his new image, the suit no longer troubled him. Now all of this made him laugh, Maxim couldn't believe that he could get angry and upset because of something as trivial as a suit.

'It's just that there is a lot of nonsense that sticks to people,' Boris explained, when Maxim shared his thoughts with him. 'All of this can be viewed from all kinds of different perspectives, but the fact remains the same – even a wise man could be brought to tears if you find a vulnerable string in him. And that's why magicians recommend you to get rid of the weight of the junk that accumulates in our consciousness, to change your worldview. Man cannot belong to two worlds at the same time, one day he will have to make a choice between the world of magic and the ordinary world that we are all used to. Or rather, not even make a choice, but be aware of it. One day he suddenly realizes that the only thing left in his life – is the world of magic. Where all the usual human thoughts and ambitions resided once, there is only emptiness now. The weight of human ambitions is no longer holding the magician – and that's when real magic starts.'

Maxim involuntarily smiled.

'You keep telling me that only after this-and-that real magic starts. And each time it is something different.'

'It's just that magic is a complex discipline,' Boris answered with a smile. 'Not one of its separate elements in itself will make you a magician; they work only when combined. Let's take an ordinary computer – recall how many different elements there are in one of those things. Some are more important, like the processor, others are less important, but you still need them, without them your computer won't function. The same with magic skills – there are dozens of different techniques, each of them is seemingly not that important on its own. But only when combined do they produce the required result.'

'Yes, I understand.' Maxim went quiet for a moment. 'I've been meaning to ask you – when can I get back to Rostov?'

'You don't like it here?'

'It's not that.' Maxim shook his head. 'You know, I can't just sit around; I have to keep myself busy.'

'Well, that's what we are getting to,' Boris grinned. 'Didn't you notice?'

'What do you mean?' Maxim didn't get it.

'What would you like to do in Rostov?'

'I don't know yet. Maybe I'll grow flowers.'

'Yes, that's interesting,' Boris agreed. 'But have you already made a rough calculation of how much this project will bring you and how much it will cost? As far as I know, there's a sea of flowers being imported from the Netherlands and other countries, and with their level of know-how, you'll have a very hard time competing with them. Again, you need to take into account the existence of the flower mafia. The flower market has long been divided and is now well-controlled; they are not too fond of strangers. In practice, you'll immediately get under the care of the criminal structures, and they will be the ones to set the price on your products – not you. That's the reality of Russian market economy.' Boris demonstratively smiled.

'But I'm not planning on opening a factory,' Maxim objected. 'It will be a small home conservatory.'

Boris smiled again.

'You see, Maxim. I've been doing business for some time now and I am able to correctly assess the situation. At this moment, for instance, I see that your project has lots of minuses and very few pluses. True, seemingly you are going to do what you enjoy doing.

But let's dig a little deeper: do you just like flowers or you like selling them?'

'I just like flowers,' Maxim answered.

'Just as I thought. So, let's try to rephrase the problem: you want to fiddle with flowers for the sake of your own pleasure. Question: what stops you from doing exactly that? Go ahead and analyze.'

'Lack of money,' Maxim admitted. 'I have to make money somehow.'

'That's right. You tried combining the two, but in today's Russia that option is basically undoable. But there is another option: making a living a different way and fiddling with flowers just for the sake of your own pleasure. How do you do that? Set up some kind of business, then hire a manager and enjoy life, doing what you like doing. Take me as an example – I am the owner of a couple of companies, but my ownership comes down to making money off these companies. Everything else is the concern of the company management. That is the alternative I suggest you go for.'

'But I am not a businessman!' Maxim objected.

'And who stops you from becoming one?' Boris enquired. 'After all, that too is an art of stalking. So, why don't you practice it? It will be useful in all respects. Your image is already quite respectable; you only have to find your niche. And don't forget the main principle: your role must come down to organizing the process. Let other people do the job. If we live in a market economy, we have to use its opportunities.'

'I'm not really used to having people work for me,' Maxim frowned.

'That's nonsense. Look at it differently: there are so many unemployed people out there and there are so many swindler businessmen, cheating their employees. You have the opportunity of providing people with a safe, well-paid job. Now, is that a bad thing?'

'No, but...' Maxim stopped short. He couldn't come up with anything else say to justify his unwillingness to get into business.

'But you are afraid,' Boris suggested. 'You don't think it's your thing. You think that you are a creator, and not a salesperson. I can go on forever.' Boris settled back and looked at Maxim with a soft smile. Maxim was quiet. 'Maxim, we've just talked about the templates of our consciousness, about all of that nonsense that is in our heads. All your doubts are determined by that specific human side of your consciousness. But to a magician, who got rid of all that junk that's common to mankind, any opportunity is simply a result of his choice. Just like in that joke – I can dig and I can stop digging[3]. It doesn't matter to me. Try formulating the same attitude towards business. Most businessmen are hostages of their strive towards success; they put too much on one card. A failed project is a disaster to them; many commit suicide after such an ending. That is the greatest foolishness imaginable, that's what you get when you are being too serious about yourself. Try treating business like a game, like an interesting puzzle, with a lot of unknown variables. Lighten up, meet every situation with laughter. If it works – great, if not – to hell with it.'

'But I really don't know what kind of business I could do,' Maxim answered. 'I simply don't have the slightest idea.'

'You've got some time to think it over. I could give you about ten different alternatives off the bat, but I'd like you to come up with a line of business yourself. Besides, you'd feel much better if you achieve success on your own, and not because of me.'

'Okay,' Maxim agreed. 'I'll give it some thought.'

A couple of days later they had another chat about business. Making himself comfortable in the armchair, Boris asked Maxim if he had come up with anything.

'Programming,' Maxim exhaled. 'I could set up a company; put together a staff of programmers. There's plenty of work for them now.'

'Quite a sensible suggestion,' Boris agreed. 'I'd even say – very sensible. Its advantages are that there are many talented guys out there right now – guys who are capable of solving the most complicated programming problems. Again, these guys already have computers, so you wouldn't even have to spend money on equipment. They could work at home, that's convenient both for them and for you – hence, you wouldn't need to rent a place. Your task will only be to make things work. It's a very good option.'

Maxim sighed with relief. He was actually afraid that Boris wouldn't accept his proposition.

'I'm happy you liked it,' he answered. 'Now I'll have to come up with a strategy for setting all of this up.'

'You will, don't worry,' Boris agreed. 'But that's details and, to be honest, I'm not interested in them. You don't need my guidance and advice; you are quite capable of handling the whole thing. But there is one aspect we need to discuss, namely – the magic constituent of business. Not even business, but any undertaking.'

'What do you meant?' Maxim inquired.

'The technology of achieving success,' Boris answered. 'The knowledge of magicians tells us that any undertaking involves three stages before it's realized: the stage of intention, the stage of action and the stage of obtaining the result.'

'I think that's pretty clear without any magic,' Maxim couldn't refrain from commenting.

'True,' Boris agreed. 'But people don't know what these three elements should be like and what the important bits are. In a graphical representation, the three above-mentioned elements represent an equilateral triangle. In real life, two of its sides are always strong and the third is weak. But the order of the strong and weak lines could vary. What does that actually mean? Say, our first line is strong, the second one is strong and the third one is weak. In real life that would correspond to a strong intention, strong effort and weak result. A situation like that could be described with the expression "a mountain has brought forth a mouse".

'The second alternative,' Boris continued. 'Weak intention, strong action and strong result. That's the best way of doing business: you have a weak intention, that is, you are not chasing results, instead you are just doing an honest job – that would thus be the second line. Then the last line – the third one – would by definition be strong, and you'll get a good result. The third alternative corresponds to a strong intention, weak action and strong result. That's the option often used by magicians. More specifically, to reach a goal you simply formulate a strong intention, and then you let go of the situation, allowing it do develop on its own. Giving up control would correspond to the second line being weak. As a result, the configuration of the matrix of events will come together in a way so that you'll get the result you bargained for – the third line is strong.'

'All right.' Maxim thoughtfully looked out the window then shifted his gaze back at Boris. 'Say, I really want to go fishing – the first line is strong, right? I enthusiastically dig for earth worms, then grab my fishing gear and go fishing – the second line is strong. I get to the river, catch me some fish and go back home – the third line is strong. All three of these elements are strong, but there is a result. I could give you thousands of examples like that – when a person has the determination to achieve something, applies some effort and in the end gets what he planned for. How does that scenario fit into your scheme?'

'Stars incline but do not impel – ever heard this expression?' A ghost of a smile slipped across Boris's lips. 'The schemes I've cited reflect the main principles of achieving a result. True, you can get results in different ways. But I dare claim that the easiest way of getting a result is by having a weak intention and strong action.'

'Could you expand on the weak intention bit?' Maxim asked. 'To intend weakly means not to intend at all?'

'Not quite. Proper intention in this scheme should be delicate, unnoticeable. You know what you want, and you simply start working on realizing your plan, without any kind of foolish speculations. A scheme like that corresponds to the laws of the universe, it's in harmony. Simply try applying it in practice and you'll see that it's working just great. When using this approach, you are not wasting your strength on empty philosophizing, talking business, discussing whether it will work or not – you just act, transforming your potential into actually doing work, and not into an imitation of that work. When realizing a project, it's important to catch the flow – if you did everything right, you'll feel the flow pick you up and carry you. Everything will happen automatically; events will happen the way that's best for you. And all of that only because you know what's important. I know a guy, Ilya, he's a self-made man. A master with a God-given talent. He can construct anything; he's done dozens of unique constructions, anything from a light airplane to a remotely controlled underwater robot to a windmill and a cross-country vehicle. And he almost doesn't care about blueprints. This is roughly what his approach to construction looks like.' Boris collected his thoughts. 'First of all, he identifies in the most general terms what exactly he would like to make. An engineer would immediately start drawing up blueprints. Ilya goes off to examine his bins, namely – a yard with all kinds of scrap metal; he's got mountains of it. He goes through his iron, in the meantime estimating which pieces he could use. And already at this stage, some details start coming together in the strangest way. I'm sure that not one engineer could ever come up with the solutions Ilya uses in his home-made constructions. Basically, what Ilya does is he creates a flow. That flow picks him up and carries him onwards. As a result, another masterpiece of a technical mind is born in a relatively short period of time. Ilya will already be driving around swamps on his cross-country vehicle, while an engineer in his place would still be poring over his blueprints. And it's very likely that the engineer would have never realized his idea, all of his activity would have turned into steam already at the stage of making blueprints.'

'But you can't really build anything worthwhile without blueprints, can you?' Maxim objected.

'I'm not saying that you should build things without blueprints. And Ilya is very competent in technical matters, so he does draw some blueprints. The point is not the blueprints, but the approach – Ilya simply starts doing something, and then everything comes together on its own. While an engineer in his place will waste tons of paper and in the end arrive at the conclusion that he doesn't have any money, the right materials, equipment and so on. Then he'll put away the blueprint rolls on the top of a closet, and that would be the end of that. In this case, the engineer would have a strong intention, strong activity and a weak result. And Ilya would have a weak intention, strong activity and a strong result.'

'Okay, I agree with that. Then how about this: say, I have a strong intention of becoming a president, but I don't do anything about it. That is, the first line is strong, the second is weak. So what? I'll become a president anyway? After all, the remaining third line should be strong?

'Yes, but here you've touched upon a magical way of realizing intention. Your connection with intention should be very pure, then the configuration of the matrix of events will change and you'll somehow get noticed, and on the tide of public adoration or some other way you'll be elected president.'

'So, the second method is not for all?' Maxim asked.

'Basically, no, it's not. But sometimes even an ordinary person could unconsciously realize this scheme – sometimes miracles happen and our strong desires suddenly come true. It's as if something comes together, comes into agreement, the cogwheels of the universe start rotating, sorting people and circumstances, and we suddenly get what we dreamed of. In this case strong intention plays the role of a catalyst, launching an appropriate chain of events. The configuration of the matrix of events changes, and you get what you planned for. An ordinary person, in a situation like that, will say that it's luck, but he won't even suspect that he accidentally launched a mechanism that realized his wish.'

'Got it. It's not the first time you mention the matrix of events – could you tell me more about it?'

'It's just a term,' Boris smiled. 'Imagine how many chains of events that happen around you at the same time. Say, you are walking in town, and around you everything is moving, everything is stirring. Hundreds and thousands of people, and each of them leads not one, but a great number of chains, and he takes part in the chains of hundreds of other people. Say, you decided to set up a company. You start acting; you collect the right documents, run from one official to another, pick your staff. By doing these things you are launching a chain of events, which, in turn, starts having an effect on hundreds of other chains. It's like a stone you throw in the water, which sets off rings in all directions. Your activity gives rise to a change in the current configuration of the event field, or the event matrix. As a result, the event matrix changes – your company appears in it.'

'Yes, I understand,' Maxim nodded. 'That's pretty much how I pictured it. Only now I must give it a lot of thought. There's so much information that it's all just a big mess in my head. Now I have to sort it all out.'

'You do that,' Boris agreed, getting up from the armchair. 'And I have an important meeting to attend in a half an hour.'

While everything was going more or less smoothly with the stalking, Maxim still hadn't managed to make any progress mastering the dream world. His first successes no longer seemed as important to him, Maxim didn't feel that he was getting any further. It was rather the other way around, he sensed a decline. He had one or at most two very short lucid dreams a week, and that despite a huge desire and serious meditation practice. It seemed that all his efforts were in vain.

And now, after Boris's explanations, things started to clear up. Maxim's attempt to burst through to the world of dreams corresponded to the scheme 'strong intention – strong action – weak result'. So, he had to adjust it somewhat, having replaced strong intention with weak intention. Boris said that intention in a scheme like that should be delicate, neat. That meant he had to forget all about his attempts of trying to break through the barrier of the dream world by force. That is, he shouldn't think about success and concentrate on the real aspects of his work. Then, in theory, the third line would become strong and ensure a successful business. At the very least, this scheme was worth testing. To begin with, Maxim gave himself a day off from all his training. In the afternoon, Oxana got him out to an art museum. In the evening Maxim asked her to the movies. Oxana said yes; Maxim was proud and happy. It was a good day; Maxim once again realized that everything Boris had said had solid ground. Maxim tuned into a lucky wave, and there you go – a really great day.

He didn't have any lucid dreams that night, but he decided not to pay it any attention or start speculating on his feelings. The next day, he followed through his regular schedule, starting with the morning practice at the sports hall and ending with a two hour evening meditation on the dry chestnut. Now Maxim remembered that Rada too recommended him not to be too eager to enter the world of dreams, he shouldn't strain himself, but just go and take what he needs. The scheme was a complete match to what Boris had told him to do: weak intention – strong action – strong result.

The following night didn't bring any luck either, but the night after that stuck to his memory with a whole cascade of short, but very bright dreams. In one of them Maxim even saw Oxana – he tried talking to her, but immediately 'fell out' of the dream.

In the morning he visited Oxana in her studio and asked

whether she'd seen him.

'No,' the young women answered with a smile. 'It was probably a sprite. But through him you could actually find me.'

'I know,' Maxim nodded. 'Rada explained it to me.'

'All the better. Would you like me to find you today?'

'Of course. Will you be able to, though?'

'We'll see...' the young woman replied evasively and turned back to the easel.

Maxim smiled. Only a month ago Oxana would have treated his doubts in her talents with disdain; now, however, she had become much more restrained. And Maxim knew why – Iris has started teaching her the art of stalking. As far as Maxim knew, all lectures were held at the Glade and he really regretted that he couldn't attend these meetings.'

'I'll be waiting,' he said. 'Okay, I won't bother you anymore.'

He went to bed at one am. Before that, he was busy sorting out the details of the network structure of the world. Maxim lay in bed for a long time, thinking about the upcoming return to Rostov then he tried to enter a dream. However, he didn't manage to maintain his attention upon entering the dream, and very soon he was deep asleep. He dreamt of the Black Sea. Maxim watched the water sparkling in the sun and was happy that he once again managed to come out here. He felt like swimming, so he looked around, searching for a changing booth – he had to change into swimwear. And suddenly someone grabbed him by the arm.

'Oxana!' He was very happy to see her. 'I didn't even know you were here. Is Boris here too?'

'It's a dream, Maxim.' Oxana firmly squeezed his hands and stared into his eyes. 'Just a dream. Remember, I promised I'd find you in a dream.'

Oxana's gaze summoned a very strange feeling, for a second Maxim even felt fear. And at the same moment his consciousness started to prevail.

'Hi again!' Oxana said merrily. 'Weird that people cannot have lucid dreams. It's so easy!'

'Not for everyone,' Maxim answered. 'I'm just having problems so far.'

'Don't worry!' the young woman smiled. Maxim noticed how beautiful she was. 'If you want, I can show you a really lovely spot. Come on!' Oxana didn't wait for him to answer and dragged him after her.

The sea and the sandy beach became blurry and disappeared, only to be replaced with magnificent mountain scenery a few moments later. Maxim carefully looked around.

They were standing on the edge of a steep; Oxana was still firmly squeezing his hand. Maxim already knew that it helps him maintain his awareness. Below stretched a mountain valley overgrown with woods. It all looked amazingly picturesque. Only now did Maxim realize that he'd seen this place on one of Oxana's paintings. And behind them, literally five steps away, towered a medieval castle, it was almost as if it was growing out of the mountain slope. And what's more, there were roses growing everywhere – red, pink, large and small ones. The castle was literally drowning in roses; between them remained only narrow paths faceted with pebbles.

'This is the Castle of Roses,' Oxana said. 'I'm here almost every night. It's beautiful, isn't it?'

'It is,' Maxim agreed, examining the castle. 'Who built it?'

'Maxim, we're in a dream. And no one builds anything here. At the very least, nothing is built here the way it is in our world. This castle is Rada's creation. You can find the original in Georgia. Rada really liked it, and so she recreated it in a dream. Of course, she made a couple of changes to fit her taste.'

'Does that do any good?'

'It provides you with experience. If you want, you could even live in a world like that – that is, of course, if you get it into shape.'

'But you said yourself that it is just a dream?'

'It is a dream,' Oxana agreed. 'And Rada is a witch. The best of all the witches I know. And there is nothing impossible for a witch. Remember, people say that our world was created by God. Sometimes I think that God is an excellent dreamer.' Oxana laughed, her laughter sounded surprisingly loud. 'Dreamers can create their own worlds – remember, you've read about it in Castaneda's books. Now you see one of such worlds. Its design is not complete yet, but it's only a matter of time.'

'But it is not real?'

'You are just used to seeing your world as real,' Oxana retorted. 'You master only your world, while Rada is no longer limited by it. Someday even I will learn all of these tricks. Would you like to fly around?'

'Here?' Maxim looked down with fear.

'Where else? You'll see how awesome it is!' The young woman didn't wait for a confirmation and decisively pulled him along.

A chill of fear slipped through his heart. Having pushed away from the steep, Maxim slid down, a couple of seconds later his fear was replaced with delight – that's how great it was. Maxim started laughing and his eyes met Oxana's. He felt truly happy.

The rest of the dream got more or less wiped out of his memory. Maxim remembered them flying over the valley, touching the tree tops. Then they spun with their hands interlocked, looking into each other's eyes. Then everything disappeared – that happened when he hugged Oxana and made an attempt to kiss her.

In the end of September Maxim felt he was ready to go back to Rostov. Boris did not object.

'These months were not in vain for you,' he said. 'You've become much stronger. Of course, you've still got a long way to go to become a magician, but you are no longer your average man. Your image of the world has changed, even if only a little. And later you'll start getting your own group together, just like we've discussed.'

They spoke about putting together a group about a week ago. Everything started with Maxim's question – wasn't it boring for Boris and the other members of his group to spend time explaining things to Oxana and him? Because whichever way you look at it, their knowledge level was simply incomparable.

'Your mistake is that you keep assessing people's relationships from a moral point of view,' Boris answered. 'There's no doubt that moral is important, but in the case of magicians it is not a defining variable. For example, you could decide that I, by teaching you, am displaying some sort of generosity or God knows what else. But, in fact, it is much simpler than that and determined by the laws of the real world. Namely – to obtain new knowledge, I have to share old knowledge. It's not a whim, but an objective necessity. In order to get something; you need to give something away. That's how you shape the chain of knowledge transfer, and in due time you too will be explaining all of this to someone else – in order to develop yourself. So, in this particular case no one owes anyone anything. I do you a favor by telling you something. You do me a favor by accepting my knowledge. Thus, everyone is happy.'

There was something unpleasant about this explanation. Maxim involuntarily frowned. Boris smiled; apparently he had noticed Maxim's feelings.

'And again it's your moral talking,' he said. 'Don't frown. If nothing else, I really do enjoy talking to you – if that makes you feel better. Now, for the first time, you have touched yet another border of magic. Feelings and calculations drive people; the actions of magicians are dictated by the Spirit. Thus, an ordinary person will never guess what motives lay behind a magician's doing.' Boris went quiet for a few seconds. 'Again, your question also has a flipside: if, say, I could consider spending time with you was boring, then how do you enjoy feeling like a student all the time? Feeling like someone who can never keep up, who will always be behind, despite his sincere desire to advance? Hence the necessity of creating groups of people with about the same level of knowledge. That's why, even if I really wanted to, I couldn't take you into my group; that wouldn't be right. At the same time, I can help you organize a group of people who are at the same level of knowledge as you are. So far, there's just two of you – you and Oxana. You'll be the core of a future group. You'll find a few more people, and it's all systems go, into the bright Nagual future.' Boris grinned. 'You'll do your own research and have your own circle of friends. Well, and we won't retreat into the shadows, of course. The chain of knowledge transfer will remain nonetheless. That's how it has to be. That's how it is going to be.'

Now, recalling the details of that conversation, Maxim once again realized that Boris was right. True, it's nice when someone is sharing their knowledge with you, but at some point you have to get on your own feet. That's why leaving for Rostov made Maxim feel happy and he couldn't wait until the day when he'd be on his way. He'll see Rostov again. He'll once again walk the familiar streets. That was great.

'There's something else I wanted to ask you about the group.' Maxim glanced at Boris. 'According to Castaneda, there should be at least eight people in a group. Why don't you stick to that rule?'

'Rules exist for us to break them,' Boris replied. 'Seriously speaking, though, there is not one single solution. Say, there are five of us – Roman, Rada, Iris, Danila and I. That is, there are five of us now.' Boris sighed, obviously remembering Dana. 'Even though Denis is with us, he is not part of the group, he is not a searcher. He's got other interests, other responsibilities. If we wanted to, we could introduce an additional three people into the group, but that can't be done by force; everything must happen naturally. In time, the right people will come – the group will grow. If not, then it will remain the same. What's important here is not so much the number of people in the group, but their compatibility, how comfortable they are working with each other.'

'But are there any real advantages in a group of eight people?'

'There are,' Boris nodded. 'First of all, a group of eight is very stable. Second of all, a group like that enters a new energy level. That is, two plus two in this case is no longer four, but much more than that. New structure – new possibilities. At the same time, we make the assumption that man is capable of achieving everything on his own. That's why, to us, such a group has never been and is not a goal in itself. We just like being together, that's all. And that is, probably, the correct answer.'

Happiness is always relative. You could have very much, but if someone has more… Being happy is impossible, when someone is ahead of you. That's exactly what caused the break up between the searchers and Yana some time ago. She always wanted to be first, and realizing that she would never catch up to Dana and Rada truly pestered her life. Sure, you could try outrunning those ahead of you. Or you could get rid of them. That's how Yana ended up in the Legion.

At first she was happy. Life was good; she had money now, quite good money, there was no longer the need to hide. She also got power, though not enough. Yana was in charge of a small group of Legionaries. Kramer became her direct supervisor – a rather mediocre individual in Yana's opinion. Yana never made plans with Kramer; she knew that Kramer was but a step in her career. And when Kramer was no more, Yana even felt relief. Sly did a really good job: at least now she didn't have to do it herself.

Her new position brought her lots of advantages. Firstly, she got a raise; it was now quite an impressive amount of money. Secondly, having nevertheless managed to wring the right to manage the analytical department and the fifth department of the security service from Dags, Yana got lots of new opportunities. Not to mention that she was now the one receiving all the information. Twenty elite fighters and eight experienced criminal investigators were now under Yana's command.

First thing Yana did, once in her new position, was to fire several people – she got rid of all that riff raff she told Dags about. Yana was even surprised – how could they ever hire all of these people, on what grounds? Or did Kramer assume that idiots are easier to manage? Now that she's here, everything will be different.

Her activity didn't pass unnoticed; people were somewhat afraid of her now. They even started to treat her with pronounced respect. From being Yana she somehow immediately turned into Yana Igorevna. She had reinforced the reputation of a tough bitch, though that didn't bother Yana one bit. She liked that image – it went well with her nature.

But the moment that Yana had been waiting for the most was getting access to the Legion archive. It was what she had been dreaming of all her life, for the sake of the archive she risked arguing with Dags. As a result she came out victorious – having received the key to the desired e-net, Yana hoped to familiarize herself with the most secret magic mysteries.

Alas, she was in for a disappointment. True, there were plenty of very valuable books and documents in the archive. Back in the old days, she would have been delighted for sure. Now everything was different, Yana knew that most of that garbage was not worth a dime. And the things she was actually interested in were not here. Where was the famous Ecuador library of Erich von Däniken? People say that CIA agents stole it from him. But then it should have been there, in the archive, at least in its encrypted form. It wasn't there. Where was the original version of Necronomicon? Where were all these rarities, just thinking of which makes a magician's heart skip a beat? There was nothing in the archive that could be of any real interest to her or develop her magic skills.

Of course, she didn't fail to vent her indignation to Dags.

'Your archive is not worth a nickel!' Yana ended her angry

speech during another meeting with Dags. 'It's either one of two things: either you are fooling me, handing me this pile of garbage on purpose, or someone is fooling you. It's not the archive I need.'

Dags was silent for a while, thoughtfully examining the young woman. Then he reluctantly opened his lips.

'Let's take this one step at a time,' he started. 'First of all, you have to get rid of the filthy habit of raising your voice in my presence. It entertained me at first, now it's irritating. There won't be a second warning – just keep that in mind. Do you understand me?'

Yana was about to object, but stopped short, having stumbled upon Dag's cold gaze. Perhaps she went too far after all.

'Yes, Sovereign. I understand.'

'That's good.' The corners of Dag's lips twitched in a grin. 'Now, about the archive. The archive is real; most mortals would have been thrilled to get an opportunity to work with it. At the same time, you do not have access to the most important files. I can tell you that not even I have that kind of access. Only the executive management of the Legion can access these documents. I'll never end up there – only because I had the misfortune to get born in the Soviet Union. Anyone born in the former USSR and modern Russia are not trusted in the Legion. More specifically, they'll never be completely trusted. You won't end up in the executive management of the Legion either – only because you are a woman. And there has never been a woman among the Hierarchs. I've accepted my place; I suggest you do the same. Learn to be pleased with what you've got. Otherwise, you might lose all you have. Got it?'

'Yes, Sovereign.' Saying these words wasn't easy for Yana. But she knew very well when she could press on, and when it was better to keep your mouth shut.

'Wonderful. Then you may leave.'

'Yes, Sovereign. Forgive me, if I was too harsh with you.' Yana got up from the armchair and exited Dags's office. As usual, having closed the door behind her, she went for her cigarettes.

'No one dares to stand in my way,' she said, lighting up. 'Not even you.'

Chapter Three

Solitary Sailing

Rostov greeted Maxim with summer-like warm weather. Maxim stepped down on the platform and sighed with relief – he was home.

He put the suitcase down, took a piece of chewing gum out of his pocket and sent a stick of gum into his mouth. Then he grabbed the suitcase and confidently headed for the hotel.

Maxim made this small break on purpose – it marked the beginning of a new chain of events. Now, already out of habit, Maxim noticed little things that were pleasant to the eye while walking to the hotel. Doing this drew him into the flow of success.

He stayed at the hotel for two days. It was strange for Maxim to settle in a good room and pay quite a lot of money for it, but he had to get used to it. He was a businessman, and a businessman cannot rest in cheap rooms of third-class hotels. It was not a whim, but a feature of the flows. If you save on little things once, twice, three times – you'll end up in a situation where you will have to keep on saving all the time. True, a real magician couldn't care less about little things like that. But Maxim knew that he still had a long way to go before he would become a magician. And thus, he must take into account the attributes of the flow.

The two days spent at the hotel left him with plenty of pleasant impressions. Friendly staff, excellent interior – all of these things tuned him into a good vibe. He even had to decline certain services. In the evening of his first day in the hotel room, there was a phone call – a soft female voice inquired whether he was bored all by himself and whether he'd like to spend the time in the company of a lovely girl. Maxim politely declined. Having put the receiver down, he even laughed – that's the flow for you.

He rented a flat in the Kamenki area. It was a rather modest flat, with a phone line, that filled the bill in terms of taste and affordability. Maybe in the past Maxim would have allowed himself some rest before getting down to business. Now he understood that a break could throw him out of the flow. Strike while the iron is hot – the old proverb acquired a completely different meaning.

He started by getting a computer – a very basic one, without any excess gadgets – an ordinary good quality working machine. Then it got really busy; Maxim discovered that working as a businessman involved a lot of running around. Setting up his own firm was surprisingly quick; it took a little more than two weeks, during which he almost didn't have any spare time. He really did have his hands full – he had to learn about the market he was going to work in, which he so far did not know anything about. He also had to meet up with potential employees. Still, things were gradually improving and Maxim was happy to realize that he was actually getting somewhere. True, not everything went as planned – the flow wasn't a magic wand, granting any of your wishes. But on the whole, everything was going well; already by mid-October Maxim's new firm received its first orders. Maxim would never have managed on his own, but now experienced programmers were part of his staff. By the end of October the first payments started coming into the firm's account, which made Maxim indescribably happy.

That is how his business career started. In the beginning, Maxim was the one in control; in December he appointed a manager by promoting one of the employees. The guy was honest and had a good understanding of management. Having given it some thought, Maxim decided that he'll probably not be able to find a better candidate, and he was right. In January Maxim handed everything over, into the hands of the manager.

Back in November Maxim changed his flat to a small private house, not far from the zoo. There were two reasons for that:

firstly, Maxim had bought a car, a used Lada. There was a garage in his new house, and he no longer had to keep the car in a parking space or leave it parked on the street. Secondly, Maxim arranged a payment plan with the owner – this made him feel like the rightful owner of the house, allowing him to make any adjustments he wanted. By then, Maxim already had some spare time on his hands, and he could finally busy himself with the plants – something he'd been dreaming about for a long time. And needless to say, he was happy.

And if business was going surprisingly well, then when it came to magic Maxim had nothing to brag about at first. Still, he didn't ever consider giving up. He no longer set problems; he didn't drive himself into a corner, preferring to calmly and methodically make sense of the magical world instead. And it bore its fruit: throughout the autumn Maxim managed to have three or four lucid dreams a week. It could be considered an obvious success. The best thing was that more and more often Maxim managed to enter a lucid dream right when falling asleep. And in the beginning of December he ended up at the Glade.

It all started with an ordinary dream. In that dream Maxim was walking down the Voroshilovsky Prospekt, when he suddenly saw Boris. He was happy to see him – and at the same moment he entered a lucid dream.

It really was Boris; he was looking at Maxim and smiling.

'Hello,' he said and shook Maxim's hand. 'I've heard about your progress.'

'What progress?' Maxim inquired. 'And who did you hear it from?'

'From Rada. She says your business is picking up. You see, it wasn't that difficult after all.'

'And how did Rada find out? Was she spying on me?'

'Don't offend Rada,' Boris grinned. 'Of course, spying on you is not a difficult thing for her to do, but she will never want to. And as for your progress, you regularly keep her updated.'

'I don't remember,' Maxim began, and stopped short. He just remembered that sometimes in the mornings he had a strange feeling – as if something important had happened, but he had forgot what exactly. On a couple of such occasions, he, for some reason, remembered Rada.

'Almost every week you meet up with Rada at the Castle of Roses,' Boris said. 'But these meetings happen on the left side of your consciousness.'

'But why can't we just meet up this way?' Maxim didn't understand. 'Why make it so complicated?'

'Because such knowledge won't hold any power,' Boris explained. 'You will have to remember everything Rada is teaching you in your dreams. But you'll only be able to do that once you've learned how to shift the assemblage point. And now, let's go. They are waiting for us.'

The transfer happened very fast; the Voroshilovsky Prospekt was almost immediately replaced with familiar forest scenery.

Danila, Rada, Oxana and Iris were sitting on the benches and when Maxim and Boris arrived they started applauding.

'And here's our Rostov-man,' Iris said with a grin, when Maxim came up close. 'Sit down. I even prepared a seat for you.' Iris clapped on the bench next to her.

'I think I'll better sit here,' Maxim answered, taking a seat next to Oxana.

'He's still afraid of me,' Iris said; everyone laughed. 'Maybe I should pay you a visit? I was actually just about to go to Rostov for a couple of days.'

'Why? Unless it is a secret,' Oxana inquired.

'Oh, you know…' Iris waved her hand with a lazy motion. 'One of my friends is in trouble. Some folks rigged a car accident for her – an ordinary set up, and now they want money. I found out who these punks are, now I have to have a chat with them.'

'Won't that be dangerous?' Maxim inquired. He was well-acquainted with the temper of the Rostov gangs. 'I mean – will it work?'

'If I go with you, it will definitely work,' Iris assured him. 'You won't let me go off alone and meet them all by myself now, will you?'

'Fine, we'll go together,' Maxim agreed. 'Just warn me beforehand. I will have to make the last arrangements and write a will.'

'That's better already,' Iris grinned. 'You're growing little by little.'

Further discussion didn't have anything to do with Maxim, so he mostly listened. First, they talked about the dramatically increased activity on the part of the Legionaries; it was obviously Yana's doing. Then the conversation turned to the Keeper School – they had found a new place for the school, a former boarding school. One half of the building was taken up by a drug clinic, set up by Roman. In the second half of the building was the school. Under the cover of the clinic they could continue teaching without having to worry about attracting anyone's attention.

Then they spoke of much more interesting things. Danila told them about his latest discoveries – namely, about the certain properties of time corridors. Maxim was hearing about time corridors for the first time, so he didn't understand much and decided to ask Boris or Rada about it whenever he would get the chance. Then Iris told them about certain features of the Net. She managed to find out that the cause-effect field of the event matrix had yet another level of order. This meant that not only did the chains of events have the direct cause-effect link, when one event dragged along the other, but they could also interact on the level of a network resonance. This was most evident in paired events – for example, in airplane crashes. If an airplane crashed somewhere, then it was very likely that in the next couple of days there would be another crash. There was also a less obvious connection level – for example, a forest fire happened somewhere in Siberia, as a result of which a powerful tornado wrecked a house in Arizona. A farmer yelled at his wife in Australia and that's why you fell and broke your leg. Iris said that not all events are connected this way, but at certain moments a resonance occurs, as a result of which one event provokes the appearance of another event – an event that is seemingly unrelated. Iris added that she still had to sort out the details of this scheme.

Maxim listened until he felt that he was losing consciousness. He didn't want to take French leave and 'fall out' of the Glade, so he hurriedly got up from the bench.

'I'm sorry. I have to go' he said, already having a hard time maintaining his concentration. 'See you later!'

'So we have a deal!' Iris had time to shout; Maxim heard laughter and opened his eyes.

It was dark. Without getting up from the bed, Maxim reached out and felt the digital alarm clock on the edge of the table. He pushed the light-button and looked at the clock dial – it was three-thirty in the morning. He put the alarm clock back in its place, sighed with satisfaction and smiled – he had been at the Glade again.

Maxim didn't expect Iris to actually come to Rostov – he hoped it was a joke. And that is why he was genuinely surprised when three days later Iris showed up on the threshold of his house. As usual, she was amazingly elegantly dressed: soft boots, jeans, chamois fur coat with a hood and a small leather suitcase in her hand – brown, matching the color of the fur coat.

'Hi!' Iris said and smiled demonstratively. 'I'm here to visit you. Will you accompany me to the house or will you keep the lady waiting on the doorstep?'

'Hello, Iris,' Maxim answered. 'Come on in. Happy to see you.'

'Oh, really?' Iris grinned on her way to the hall.

'If you'll start pestering me, I'll get angry. And when I get angry it is not pretty. Give me the suitcase.' Maxim took the suitcase from the young woman's hands. 'Take your clothes off.'

'What, already?' Iris inquired. Maxim actually started in surprise, Iris laughed.

'You're the most mischievous witch I've ever seen,' Maxim uttered peevishly.

'Relax, boyo.' Having taken off her fur coat, Iris handed it to Maxim then quite elegantly took off her boots. 'Come on, give me the grand tour.'

Maxim put the fur coat on the hanger and accompanied the young woman to the house.

'Oh, that's quite a nice place you've got for yourself!' she said, having looked around the living room. 'How many rooms are there?'

'Three. And then there's the kitchen. The bedroom is over there, and through here is the conservatory.'

'Really?' Iris went into the conservatory. 'Yeah, it's great here!'

Maxim called this room the conservatory, even though it wasn't a proper one. A couple of rows of shelves made out of pine dressed boards, daylight lamps and special growing lamps, dozens of potted plants – that was pretty much the whole conservatory. In the Spring Maxim wanted to add a real conservatory to the house, made out of aluminum profile and double glazed glass. Then he'd get his own little home paradise.

'Awesome!' Iris said; there was genuine admiration in her voice. 'I like it. And what's this bush full of holes called?'

'It's a Swiss cheese plant,' Maxim said in an injured voice – how could she call this wonderful plant a bush, and full of holes at that? – 'And that's dracaena next to it.'

'You only keep exotic plants?' Iris inquired.

'What exotic plants? Over there is an ordinary geranium, foxtail fern, coleus. And how did you get here – through a portal?'

'That's right,' Iris answered. 'Eight hours in a train portal and I'm here.' She looked at Maxim and laughed. Maxim involuntarily smiled.

'I'll put one some tea,' he said. 'I've got some boiled potatoes and smoked mackerel. We'll have supper. Sorry, I don't like cooking for myself.'

'And I don't really fancy cooking for others.' Iris looked at Maxim again and smiled. 'Do you at least have a bathroom?'

'Only a shower room so far. There's a water heater – come on, I'll show you how it works.'

'Living in your house is dangerous. We won't get blown up by any chance? Otherwise it would be an incredibly absurd death – to go through things like fighting enemies, surviving the labyrinths of the unknown and then kick the bucket in the shower – either just because of the gas, or because it will explode.'

'It won't blow up,' Maxim said peevishly. 'Just don't turn up the water too much, and everything will be ok. Otherwise it will start boiling, and we will really get blown up.' He added the last words on purpose, to tick off Iris.

'Just as I thought,' Iris said contritely. 'Dying at the age of seventeen is tough.' She looked at Maxim with a smile, then she couldn't control herself and started laughing again. 'Okay, show me your stuff. I'm talking about the shower,' she said. 'Or you'll definitely think of something indecent.'

Maxim smiled. Despite all her meanness, spending time with her was interesting. You never knew what she'd do next.

Iris spent more than half an hour in the shower; Maxim heard her singing an aria in a clear voice. When the young woman finally came out, he had the supper ready.

'Too bad you didn't agree to take a shower with me,' Iris said, once in the kitchen. 'We would have made a wonderful duet.'

'Yeah, right,' Maxim said. 'And then Danila would come, and after that I'd sing falsetto all my life.'

Iris laughed; her eyes sparkled.

'I liked that,' she said. 'Very witty, and most importantly – spot on.'

They talked about all kinds of unimportant things at supper then Maxim asked, why Iris came to Rostov.

'I told you.' Iris reached for another piece of mackerel. 'I need to have heart-to-heart talk with a couple of morons. To be perfectly honest...' She lowered her voice in confidence. '...it's what I like best. After having sex, of course.' The young woman's eyes sparkled mockingly; Maxim never really understood whether she was joking or telling the truth. 'I hope you'll come with me tomorrow. Together we'll quickly make minced meat out of them.'

'All right,' Maxim agreed, having realized that he wouldn't get anything out of her now. 'We'll go.'

'I knew you'd say yes,' Iris answered and smiled demonstratively.

After supper Maxim wanted to ask Iris a couple of questions about magic, but Iris didn't even want to hear it.

'Can't you see – the lady is tired,' she said. 'So don't bug me with your nonsense. I saw you have a DVD player. Come on, we'll watch a movie. Do you have anything worthwhile?'

'Sorry, I don't keep porn,' Maxim answered. Iris smiled.

They watched *Waterworld*, starring Kevin Costner. Iris chose the movie, having searched through Maxim's collection of DVDs.

'Put this one on,' she said and handed Maxim the box with the film. 'At least, it's done beautifully. The rest is just rubbish.'

'And what's not rubbish?' Maxim inquired. 'What do you watch?'

'I like abstract films. Like *Interstate 60*, or something psychological, like *Basic Instinct*. I can watch a good comedy – say, *How to Steal a Million* – it's that movie where they stole a statuette. Another movie I like is *The Thomas Crown Affair*, and the one; what's its name?' Iris winced, remembering the name of the movie. 'Sean Connery and Catherine Zeta Jones play in that movie. It's the one where they were breaking into some computer in a tower.'

'I've seen it,' Maxim nodded. 'I can't remember the name either. So what, you like movies about con-artists?'

'You don't get it. It's not about the con; it's about beauty. I admire people who turn their profession into art. Okay, enough talking – put it on.'

Maxim put Iris to bed on the sofa in the living room. As usual, this was accompanied by a lot of suggestive jokes on her part. But Maxim simply didn't react to them – that was the only way of dealing with the insufferable witch. He wished her good night and went to bed.

He had a pretty good night's sleep, only once did he feel Iris's presence – she dragged him out into a lucid dream for a couple of seconds, looked at him and asked: 'Did you really think you could get rid of me that easily?' then she burst out laughing and disappeared.

To Maxim's surprise, in the morning, Iris actually did start getting ready for the meeting with the gang. Once he realized that he couldn't dissuade her from going or, even less so, let her go all by herself, Maxim also started to dress. However, he didn't feel particularly enthusiastic about it. On top of the closet in the living room was his Swiss army knife – Maxim tried to put it into his pocket, so that Iris wouldn't notice, but she did anyway.

'Hey, Rambo. No weapons!' Iris confidently went into his pocket and retrieved the folding knife. 'We're not some hired killers. Don't worry; everything's going to be tip-top. I promise you that as a witch. Just stay close, keep your hands in your pockets and make a square face.' Iris looked at Maxim and laughed.

As it turned out, the guys Iris was interested in worked in a booty shop. Maxim appreciated that: they organize a set up and make the poor driver pay through the nose. Then they fix their car – and they're ready for another run.

The shop was located in the Temernik area. Maxim really didn't care for any kind of confrontations, so he felt quite ill at ease. True, Denis did a good job teaching him, but this was a completely different situation. Getting into a fight with someone is one thing, but clashing with the local gang is something completely different all together. These guys don't like fooling around – a conflict with them could mean very serious trouble. So all he could do was hope that Iris knew what she was doing.

The gates of the booty shop were closed, yet the "open" sign dashed Maxim's last hopes. Once at the gates, Iris confidently opened the built-in door and entered; Maxim followed. He closed the door behind him and looked around.

It was a rather big room, filled with cars, machines, shelves with spare parts and tools. Just next to the gates was a silver Mercedes; a little further away, above a pit – a blue Volvo. There was someone working by that car; a bit to the side another two people were tinkering with an engine hanging on some chains. Then Maxim heard a burst of laughter – having looked closer, he saw another three people. Seated on a low bench, or rather, on a board put on a few bricks, they were smoking. By their appearance you could tell that they hardly had anything to do with the workmen from the shop.

'Those guys,' Iris said, nodding at the trio. 'The one in the middle and the guy on his right side. Come on…' She confidently headed for the gang. Maxim, with a silent cry of desperation, walked next to her.

'What a beauty!' one of the three said, when Maxim and Iris had come up close. 'And you're here to see us?'

'To see you, Misha honey,' Iris nodded. 'And Lyosha.' She looked at the plump big fellow in the centre. In Maxim's opinion, fighting this thug was pointless – this one could only be shot. 'I have come on a little business.'

'We're always happy to do a service to such an attractive lady,' Misha smirked. 'So, what's the problem?'

'Two weeks ago you knocked my friend's car. Her name is Anya Andreeva. You took her registration and driver's license. We need to settle accounts.'

'Oh, so you've brought the money?' Misha perked up. He put

out his cigarette on the floor and got up in an imposing manner. 'You should have said so from the start. Three thousand bucks – you know that, right?'

'Fine,' Iris smiled. 'Let's say three. All in all – you owe me three thousand bucks and the car documents. And keep in mind that I don't like waiting too long.'

Misha froze for a second, then laughed. His friends burst out laughing too; the bull slowly got up. He looked pretty impressive.

'Hey, girlfriend?' Misha asked. 'Are you nuts?'

'Watch your language,' Maxim advised him, demonstratively putting his hand into his pocket. 'She clearly said – hand over the money and the car documents. And don't make us wait.'

Maxim was bluffing, hoping that Iris knew what she was doing. He could, say, take down Misha, and the third guy, who just got up from the bench. But taking care of that heavy...

'I'll make a monkey out of you!' the bull said threateningly and moved towards Maxim.

'And you'd do that with your legs broken?' Iris inquired. The heavy twitched, then suddenly screamed and fell down to the ground.

'Oh, f...' he moaned, his face distorted with pain. 'You little bitch!'

'I guess I'll have to shorten your tongue too.' Iris looked at the thug with a somber grin. He twitched again and wheezed. And in his eyes Maxim could swear he saw a flash of horror.

'So, what about the money?' Iris turned to Misha, who was clearly lost, and gave him a pretty smile.

'She fucked up my car!' Misha suddenly flew off the handle. 'Who are you to threaten me?'

'I? Threaten?' Iris put on a surprised face. 'I'm actually your guardian angel. Because only I can rid you of your tooth ache. So get a move on and fetch the money and the papers.'

'What?' Misha asked again and suddenly froze. His face assumed a strange expression, as if he was listening to something.

Then he quietly moaned and squeezed his cheek-bones with his hands, pain surfaced in his eyes.

'It will only get worse,' Iris told him. 'And not a single dentist will be able to help you – only me. And what's up with you?' Iris looked at the last guy of the trio; he recoiled with fear.

'Listen, I have nothing to do with this.' He put up his hands in reconciliation. 'I was just having a smoke with them, that's all.'

'All the better. But still, go and help Misha find the money and the documents – alright?'

'All right. I'll help... Misha, where are the papers?'

'In the store room...' Misha moaned, tears were running from his eyes. 'I'll bring them...'

'And don't forget about the money,' Iris reminded.

Misha left, with his companion supporting him by the arm, they went up a metal ladder. Maxim discerned a door upstairs. The bull was still wheezing on the floor; drops of sweat had emerged on his red face.

'Another one's coming,' Maxim warned Iris, having noticed one of the shop personnel, a guy about thirty years of age, approaching. He held a crowbar in his hand and looked very menacing. The man glanced at the thug lying stretched out on the floor.

'What's this?' the man asked coldly, then he suddenly jumped up to Maxim and raised the crowbar.

That didn't pose any danger; after Denis' classes such attacks were childish antics to Maxim. Having dodged under the blow and simultaneously taken a step forward and to the left, he let the crowbar pass above his head, then hewed the enemy with a kick of his leg on the back of the knees and cut the guy down with a punch in the throat. He didn't hit hard, controlling his movements on purpose – he didn't want to cripple the man. The crowbar fell to the concrete floor with a clank and Maxim's opponent fell flat next to it. He slowly turned on his stomach, gave out a moan and started coughing.

'Not too bad,' Iris commented with a smile. 'I didn't stop you on purpose.'

'Yeah, I got that,' Maxim replied. 'Damn it, two more…'

Two more men were coming at them. One of them was squeezing a large piece of chain in his hands; the other one had armed himself with a cut pipe.

'They're like children,' Iris grinned. 'Stretch out your hand in their direction. As if you are aiming a gun at them. Go on.'

That was silly, but Maxim didn't dare to disobey Iris. He threw up his arm – both mechanics froze. The pipe made a clinking sound when it hit the ground; a second later it was joined by the chain.

'No problem, man,' one of the mechanics babbled. 'Don't shoot, we're leaving already.'

'Lower your arm,' Iris ordered quietly. Both mechanics moved back and hid behind one of the cars. Then they slipped along the wall and jumped out onto the street.

'And how did that happen?' Maxim inquired.

'They saw a gun in your hand,' Iris answered. 'That's called an "induced hallucination". And here's our Misha.'

Misha was already downstairs; he was still accompanied by his friend. Tears were streaming down Misha's cheeks.

'Here,' he babbled. 'Documents and… money. It's two thousand seven hundred here. That's all I've got on me.'

'Okay, let's say two thousand seven hundred,' Iris big-heartedly agreed, having taken the money and the car papers. She looked at the documents and nodded with satisfaction. 'Wonderful, Misha honey. Very well, I forgive you. There's no more pain. But know this – if I find out that you're crashing cars again, I'll get you from whatever rock you'll be hiding under. Give that guy a glass of vodka.' Iris glanced at the lying bull. 'He'll sleep it off and everything will be just fine. But we have to go. Bye-bye, boys.' Iris demonstratively waved her little hand and headed for the exit. Maxim followed, happy that everything ended so well.

'Well, how did you like it?' Iris asked, once they were back on the street.

'Awesome,' Maxim admitted. 'What's with the big guy's legs?'

'Oh, nothing,' Iris smiled. 'Just your basic suggestion. Well, maybe not that basic. I could have put on a whole show – with snakes, crocodiles and all kinds of creatures. But then people would talk, and I don't need that.'

'And people won't talk after this?'

'They will, but they won't have any problem finding an explanation. They'll say that they ran up against a hypnotist, have a drink – and then forget about it. By the way, you were pretty good back there.'

'I'm doing my best,' Maxim answered. Iris laughed.

Iris left in the evening; Maxim followed her all the way to the train station. Once he got home, he sighed – it was probably the first time he regretted that Iris wasn't nearby. True, you could always expect some trick from her. But being with her was exciting, and that made up for all of her flaws with a vengeance.

Again, ordinary days dragged on. Maxim continued practicing dream mapping and meditation, he spent at least two hours working out. Boris was the one who advised him to continue doing sports, having said that a magician must not only have a strong spirit, but also a healthy body. A healthy body is a healthy life force. And without a healthy life force you shouldn't even think about a normal dreaming practice.

As it turned out, Boris was right. Maxim noticed an obvious link between his physical condition and the frequency of lucid dreams. The better and more energetic he felt, the more often he had lucid dreams. And the other way around; he only had to neglect his workout a little, and it immediately had an effect on the quality and the quantity of his lucid dreams.

Winter passed this way, during which Maxim had seen Boris

and Rada in his lucid dreams only a couple of times. Although, that was true only for the lucid dreams he remembered. Maxim was convinced that there was a whole layer of lucid dream memories that he simply couldn't access yet. He woke up several times with the feeling that something important had happened that night. But what it was exactly, he couldn't remember, even if he really wanted to.

From time to time Maxim sent Boris messages by e-mail and received answers to his questions, yet he didn't dare bother him too often. He simply knew that Boris wasn't too fond of such correspondence; his answers were always very brief. Just like most searchers, Boris preferred action before words.

'If you want to talk about something, come to the Glade,' Boris told him once in a lucid dream. 'The Glade's energy will help you maintain your consciousness long enough, and we'll be able to have a normal conversation.'

'And how do I get to the Glade?' Maxim inquired.

'Why don't you experiment,' Boris smiled. 'You know that ready-made solutions aren't good enough. Make it a part of your research.'

It was sensible advice, so Maxim tried to figure everything out by himself to the best of his ability. So far, his main obstacle was the short duration of lucid dreams – usually, Maxim was thrown out of the lucid dream before he had a chance to investigate. Nevertheless, gradually, he got some experience of lucid dream travelling. Maxim learned how to use the wind and the walls to travel from one place to another. To fly with the wind, it was enough to have the intention – Maxim would jump up, with a destination in mind, and immediately out of nowhere a wind picked him up and carried him to his goal. If during the journey Maxim didn't get thrown out of the dream, he sometimes reached his goal. He heard about travelling with the help of the wind, but moving in space using walls was his own invention. The method turned out to be very simple: having spotted a house wall – of any house, you had to move through it, *knowing* that behind that wall is a place where you want to go. The wall in this case worked like a transit, and moving through it happened almost instantaneously. Though, Maxim still couldn't get to the Glade – he thought he had found it a couple of times, but each time he discovered that it was only an illusion. His Glade was always different, not like the real one. And the most important thing – he was always there alone.

In the beginning of March he received the long-awaited news of Oxana's arrival – the young Keeper had finally moved to Rostov. Maxim was secretly hoping that Oxana would spend some time at his place, and it grieved him to learn that a flat had already been bought for her. Two days before Oxana's arrival Maxim had a rather delicate conversation with Boris.

As usual, it all started with Boris dragging Maxim into a lucid dream. This time they did not end up at the Glade, but on a bank of a wide, deep river. On a low ledge was a piece of an old darkened board. After an exchange of salutations, Boris suggested they take a seat.

'Where are we?' Maxim asked.

'In one of the worlds,' Boris answered. 'And this world is quite real. As Castaneda would have put it; it possesses energy.'

'It's just like our world?'

'No, but it is very much like it. I want to tell you a story…' Boris fell silent for a brief moment. 'Remember, when in Sukhumi, you asked me where I got all these scars. I laughed it off back then, having said that I fell into a tiger's paws. Now I'd like to tell how it really happened…' Boris fell quiet again. 'Have you ever heard about the flyers[4]?' he asked after a long pause.

'Yes. Castaneda mentions them. He says the flyers are a sort of predatory form of life that feed on our energy. Something like that.'

'If the flyers only fed on our energy, it would have been half the trouble. The problem is that they are the true masters of our life.

We are the puppets, they are the puppet masters. At any moment, they could do anything they want with you, because they are the ones that control reality. Don Juan said that even our mind is imposed on us by the flyers. I see it differently – in my opinion, the flyers have simply modified our mind, having installed patches, special correctional plug-ins. Basically, they've turned us into zombies, energy milking cows. The flyers take most of our energy – what lucid dreams, what penetrations into the unknown could you speak of in that case? The flyers leave us only enough energy necessary to keep us from a premature death. Ordinary people don't have a clue, and they attribute their feeling unwell, their spiritual bankruptcy to anything else but the flyers. Recall that in order to improve the quality of your lucid dreams, you have to do sports, you have to meditate, you gather and save energy by any means possible. This helps you reach lucid dreams, you think you're getting better and better at having lucid dreams. And then – bam, and nothing again, the lucid dreams have disappeared. Why? Because the flyers have gnawed round you again, you are left with no energy, and you have to accumulate it again.'

'I've read about the flyers, but I didn't think it was that serious,' Maxim said. 'Can we get rid of them?'

'It's not that simple. You see, there is a myriad of flyers out there. You get rid of one, another one or even several of them immediately take his place. They are what they call demons in Christianity. There is the devil too – a creature of a higher level. Basically, it is the king of the flyers, the lord of darkness. So, the task is not to keep eliminating the flyers, but to become inaccessible to them – outgrow the level where they can feed on your energy. You may very well warm yourself by a cozy little fire, but if it blazes with unbearable heat, it's better to run away. Especially, if there is plenty of other nice and warm fires nearby. It's an analogy, but it gives you the rough idea. To become inaccessible to the flyers, we need to get rid of the alien insertions embedded in our consciousness. Most flyer patches are aimed at limiting our awareness. For instance, one such insertion is a ban on awareness in a dream. The same patch operates IRL, that's evident when we are caught up in the ordinary pointless bustle. In fact, we too are acting according to some program, just like in a dream. Having awoken in a dream, we find ourselves in a lucid dream. Having awoken IRL, we start realizing what lies at the core of the processes that happen around us. However, such initiative doesn't pass unnoticed by the flyers. They need obedience. As a result the flyers start pressing down on you. They set up a train of problems, from very small to really serious ones. They literally hit you on the head, forcing you into obedience. That is no longer just a natural reaction of the real world to your attempt to change something, we spoke about it once, it's already much worse. The level of impact changes, they literally start bumping you off. And they go for the most vulnerable points...'

Boris fell quiet. 'I had a fiancée once,' he continued after a very long pause. 'We were planning on getting married; I was ready to throw the whole Universe at her feet. Back then I was at war with the flyers. I was trying to find ways of fighting them. Quite often they'd give me a thrashing, but I just didn't pay it any attention – I thought I could hold out. I didn't give a damn about myself or the flyers – I just didn't recognize their power over me. And then the flyers stabbed me in the back. Olga and I were coming back from a picnic, and the flyers set up a car accident. Olga died at the scene; I spent almost six months in the hospital – I had numerous fractures, a brain concussion and plenty of other injuries.'

'But why do you think that the flyers did that?' Maxim asked. 'Anyone could get into a car accident.'

'The flyers did it. At first it was only a suspicion. Then my suspicions were confirmed by my dream teacher – an old witch, who lives in a small log hut. Someday you'll definitely meet her. And she was the one to tell me what's what. There were several occasions after that where I learned that she was telling the truth. The problem is that the flyers are actually rather stupid creatures.

Not even stupid – they just have different reference points, a different scale of values. They took my fiancée; they took everything I had. They thought that would make me obey them. They are unable to understand one simple thing – a person who's lost everything has nothing more to fear. The flyers tried pressuring me again; I kept getting into dangerous situations. I only laughed in response. Three years ago, in the mountains of the Caucasus, I had the last confrontation with the flyers – rather, with their master. He has an amazing intellect; the human mind doesn't stand a chance in comparison. He could kill me, but he couldn't subjugate me. I put him in an awkward situation – having killed me, he would only have proven his defeat: his inability to handle me. He raged a little.' Boris barely noticeably smiled, 'then left me forever in peace. Since then I'm free, but I got this freedom at too high of a price.' Boris sighed, then looked at Maxim. 'And this is the reason why I just told you my story: I know you like Oxana. Don't deny it.' Boris stopped Maxim who was ready to object. 'There's nothing special about that. But the problem is that the flyers may notice your interest in her. Think about what consequences that can have for Oxana. Don't repeat my mistakes.'

'And what should I do?' Maxim asked quietly. 'I can't get her out of my mind.'

'I don't ask you to. No one has the right to forbid you to love; just be careful in expressing your emotions – don't scream about your love to the whole world. Let it be your – or your and Oxana's – little secret. Keep it, cherish it. The flyers notice only intense emotions. Don't speculate with your feelings; don't show them off. Let the flyers think that Oxana is indifferent to you, or that it's a fling of yours, nothing more. Then you'll be ok. I'm not the only one who paid for not knowing these rules. That's all I wanted to say.' Boris clapped Maxim on the shoulder. 'See you later.'

A moment later Maxim was left alone, then the river scenery became blurry, faded and disappeared.'

To Yana, the first couple of months on her new job flew by almost unnoticed. Reorganizing the structures under her command, getting things rolling – all of that definitely had to yield some result. Yana didn't doubt that very soon she would be able to justify Dags' trust. She had been fortunate in some respects – to be more specific, she had managed to place one large magic school under the Legion's command. There were smaller victories too, but in counteracting the searchers Yana still hadn't gotten anywhere. To Yana's great disappointment, the searchers, having sensed ever increasing pressure, simply left the Net. Yana suspected that closed Internet forums and real meetings still occurred. But information about these events didn't get out on the Net; there was not a single lead that could bring her to her goal. The searchers simply disappeared, went underground. That worried her. Not without reason did Yana assume that the searchers were planning something major, and that's why they were hiding.

They needed information like air. Yana's people were checking everyone who could have anything to do with the searchers. They put up trap-questions on Internet forums: questions that only searchers could answer. Several major discussions of searcher techniques were organized on purpose – in hope that the searchers or their followers would crack and leave the shadows. Some people actually did crack, but it was all rather small fry. A thorough check showed that none of these people had a real connection to the dream searchers. It became evident that leaving the Net was a well thought out decision on the searchers' part. Upon leaving, they covered all of their tracks. Even the so-called "searcheros" were now out of work; Yana got the impression that the searchers had renounced any further collaboration with these groups as with people that had not justified their hopes. There was another version too, that searchers used these groups as a cover up, working in parallel with real groups. There were many theories; they all underwent serious consideration, in hope of finding some kind of key. But time was creeping on, and in early spring Yana was forced to admit that she had lost this phase of the war.

On the surface, Dags was pretty calm about her failures, besides Yana was doing a good job handling all the other branches of her activity. She was doing such a good job that on International Women's Day, Dags congratulated Yana on her achievements in person.

'In half a year you've done what Kramer couldn't do in five.' Dags got out from the table and approached Yana. 'It is now a fact that ninety percent of the religious and occult life in the country is under our total control. I'd like to compliment you on your progress.'

'Thank you, Sovereign.' Yana slightly bowed her head then smiled. 'I'll tell you a secret – right now I'm preparing another huge project. You know that we haven't really been able to get along with the Orthodox Church. It's not a secret that the patriarch is living his last years. We will try to make one of our own the next patriarch.'

'That's a very good idea.' Dags rubbed his chin, closely looking at Yana. 'A very good idea indeed. You've already found the right man for the job?'

'Yes, Sovereign, I have,' Yana smiled. 'But allow me not to name him just yet. I don't want to jinx it.'

'Very well,' Dags agreed. 'But I ask you to keep me posted on this project.' Without waiting for Yana to answer, Dags returned to his table and retrieved a small flat box, covered in dark leather. Smiling for some unknown reason, Dags got up to Yana again. 'This is for you,' he said and handed the little box to the young woman. 'It's a gift on International Women's Day.'

'Thank you, Sovereign.' Yana anxiously took the gift. She carefully opened the clasp then slowly lifted the lid. 'Oh!' Yana drawled in surprise. 'How lovely.'

Lying cozily on red velvet was a black gun. Next to it, in the specially made depressions laid a long black silencer and two sets of bullets.

'"Walter PPK",' Dags said, looking at Yana with a smile. 'James Bond's gun. Assembled by hand; made by special order. I hand you this gift on behalf of the Supreme Hierarch. He's impressed with your work.'

Yana closed the box and glanced at Dags. 'Thank you,' she said. 'Tell the Supreme Hierarch I'm deeply grateful.'

'If the opportunity arises, I certainly will,' Dags smiled. 'You may leave now. And I really hope that next time you'll bring me good news about the searchers.'

'I'll try, Sovereign.' Yana said quietly. She turned around and exited the office, carefully closing the door behind her.

In the hall, a few meters away, a couple of people were awaiting audience with the Sovereign. With Yana's appearance two of them – those she didn't see on the way to the Sovereign, respectfully got up from the sofa and greeted her. Yana replied with a smile, but there was a gnawing in her heart. What do you know – Dags gave her a gun! Turns out he is an even bigger idiot than she thought. Just like his Hierarch.

Oxana arrived in the beginning of April. Maxim was truly happy she came; however, with Boris's advice in mind, he tried to control his emotions.

Oxana's apartment was on the Sholokhov Prospekt, right across the stadium. Maxim joked that Oxana could now watch soccer games right off her balcony. He gladly helped the young woman bring in the furniture and introduced her to the city. Oxana liked Rostov, but she liked the warm weather even more. When Oxana was leaving Klyonovsk, there was still snow on the streets.

It was a good time. Maxim tried to be very proper with Oxana; the young woman clearly appreciated that. Maxim saw that she was happy to see him every time and that filled his heart with joy.

The summer was ahead; Maxim thought about how much joy it can bring him and his imagination painted truly amazing images. Oxana was in every one of them.

Unfortunately, dreams do not come true – Maxim realized the truth of these words already around mid-May. It all started with Boris once again dragging him into a lucid dream. Maxim saw the already-familiar lake.

'We need to chat,' Boris said in confidence. 'Let's sit…'

They sat down. Boris was quiet for a couple of minutes, thinking about something. Maxim patiently waited. He expected Boris to start talking about Oxana again, but this time they spoke about something completely different. Boris looked at Maxim and said, 'You're doing well. At the very least, you've learned how to have lucid dreams and you've managed to set up a good business. Oxana told me that you've already built a conservatory.' Boris smiled. 'That's all wonderful; you've done a great job. At the same time, this is exactly the moment when you are standing at a dangerous crossroads. Your life is now going well; everything is fine – you've got money, a favorite hobby. Finally, you've got a woman you love. You're on the top of the mountain, and from that mountain top there is only one way to go – down. You could fall down from it, or you could get down nice and easy, so that you could climb another top later. It's all words, but you get the picture.'

Maxim felt ill at ease. It seemed to him that Boris wasn't telling the whole story.

'I have to give up my business?' he asked.

'No.' Boris shook his head with a smile. 'Nothing will happen to your business. You just need to understand that your present calm and sense of peace is just an illusion. – something that could fade like smoke. You could wait for it to happen or you could go through this stage in a controlled fashion. Change the situation you are in, without waiting for it to change on its own.'

'I don't understand,' Maxim said quietly. 'Explain. Why

should anything happen?'

'Because those are the rules of the real world. Remember the model of the DNA of the Tonal – we've already talked about that all events are joined into chains; one sphere of perception will definitely give place to another. Definitely – you understand? I too went through this stage and I understand your feelings well. Everything is fine with you at the moment, and in order for you not to ruin everything, you need to consciously get yourself out of this situation. Your problem is that you still treat the world around you like reality, and that's wrong.'

'Well, and how else should I treat it?' Maxim looked closely at his companion. 'I understand that we are now in a dream, but you cannot call our real world an illusion after all. And everything that happens to us happens for real.'

'I didn't express myself right. True, that world is not an illusion in its usual sense. What's illusory is its static nature and stability. Everything is moving. Everything is changing. You could understand that and see the change of situations to be much like a change of stage scenery in a theatre. Or you could live in a situation, be drawn into it. Having lost a detached perspective on the situation, you become its hostage. Remember computer games and their heroes – how free are they in their actions? They are string puppets; their actions are determined by an appropriate program. I'm trying to teach you not to be one of those puppets.'

'But we still live in a real world, and while we are alive we won't be able to avoid interacting with it,' Maxim objected.

'No, we won't,' Boris agreed. 'But magicians replace their being involved in a situation with controlled foolishness. Say, I'm a businessman, and you are a businessman. But what's the difference? You really see yourself as a businessman, while I only play the part of one. In this sense the world really is an illusion – these are the spheres of perception; they change in order. And what happens to us is determined by the program of the current sphere. Look around – there's a river, a forest. But it's only one sphere of perception. The same goes for the real world – when walking in the city, you need to understand that everything around you is just a set of decorations, a design of the present sphere of perception. By taking the world around you at face value, you risk ending up back at square one.'

'But being back at square one will also be just an illusion?'

'That's right,' Boris agreed then softly laughed. 'You are good at getting the point. Being left empty handed will indeed be just an illusion – in the sense that it will just be another sphere of perception. But you shouldn't carry this scheme to absurdity – we're talking about principles, about the way reality works. And any of these illusions could potentially kill you.'

'I see where you're going,' Maxim agreed. 'You should treat the world as the interchanging spheres of perception?'

'Yes, and not only that. You need to get rid of attachment to specific spheres of perception. As you recall, I've already mentioned that the real world is always counteracting our desires, hopes, expectations. And if you, for example, are too attached to your car, then the chances of your car getting smashed up in a vehicle accident are significantly higher. But if you treat it with care, but without particular awe, nothing will ever happen to it. The same goes for the spheres of perception – a magician understands that there are many spheres, and he simply chooses the ones he likes.'

'And I did choose a sphere I like,' Maxim said. 'Isn't that so?'

Boris smiled. 'Well, you see, what we're talking about here is one of the Abstract Cores. Therefore, I am forced to keep beating around the bush, trying to get you to understand it through words. You really did choose a sphere of perception that you like. But that's the choice of a person, and not a magician. You don't have the pause, the gap between perceiving a situation and accepting a situation, which every magician has. You react directly, spontaneously; you are inside your situation. But we'll change that.' Boris looked at Maxim and smiled. 'What are your thoughts on travelling?'

'Where exactly?'

'First to Ulan-Ude; one of my friends lives there. I'm sure you'll be interested to meet him. And then there's this other place.' Boris grinned. 'Let it be a surprise.'

'Actually, I wanted to build a conservatory,' Maxim uttered, feeling all of his plans go to ruin. 'A real one, just next to the house. Will it be a long trip?'

'It might be,' Boris agreed; the corners of his lips twitched in a grin. 'Therefore, it'd be better if you'll make all the necessary arrangements for your business in advance – just in case of a longer absence. And I think Oxana will be happy to look after your plants.'

'All right,' Maxim nodded. He had already realized that he wouldn't be able to get out of this one. 'And when are we going?'

'I think I'll give you a couple of days to get ready.' Boris's eyes glistened mockingly. 'You might have to take a nature walk, so buy a backpack, a sleeping bag, a kettle and so on – basically everything, except food. And don't be shy; buy everything you need. This walk could turn out to be quite long. You won't have to carry anything on your back, so bring along everything you need.'

'Do I need a tent?'

'It will come in handy,' Boris agreed. 'Not a big one, just for yourself. On Wednesday morning, sometime around noon, come to Oxana's place with all your stuff, of course.'

'To Oxana's?' Maxim was surprised.

'That's right. You'll get all the details on the spot. See you then.' Boris smiled and faded.

When Maxim woke up in the morning he spent a long time recalling the details of his meeting with Boris. He still hadn't learned to treat dream meetings like something real, and that's why he felt a bit silly. It would be funny if he packed his backpack, got to Oxana's and it turned out that the whole thing was just a dream.

Nevertheless, Maxim started getting ready for the trip, methodically carrying out all of Boris' instructions. He told the manager about his departure and made the last arrangements. He spent two days running around different shops, getting together everything necessary, and then spent a whole evening packing his backpack, trying to squeeze in a whole pile of the things he bought. The following morning, Maxim wrote down on a piece of paper detailed instructions on how to look after the plants. He looked at the conservatory and sighed – there was still so much work to be done there.

On Wednesday, about half past eleven, he got off the tram and went up to Oxana's house, bending underneath the weight of his backpack. That's her doorway – Maxim entered the code, went in and headed for the elevator. Finally...

Oxana lived on the eighth floor. Maxim got out of the elevator, dragged his backpack to the door and pressed the call button.

The door opened almost immediately and Maxim saw the smiling Oxana.

'Come on in, Maxim. Boris is already waiting.'

Boris was indeed already there.

'And here is our traveler.' He greeted Maxim with a smile, who had by now entered the living room. 'Are you all set?'

'Yes.' Maxim collapsed in an armchair and sighed with relief. 'It's just that I think I've got too much stuff. I'll go through it now and leave some of it here.'

'Don't worry,' Boris calmed him down. 'I've told you, you won't have to lug the backpack.'

'I still haven't asked you, where are we going – the central station or the airport?'

'We'll see,' Boris answered evasively. Then he shouted, 'Oxana, how's the lunch going?'

'Just a couple of more minutes!' Oxana's voice came from the kitchen.

'Actually, I just had lunch,' Maxim said.

'That's ok, you'll have another snack. Oxana made vareniks[5].'

Maxim decided not to object, and the vareniks turned out to be quite delicious.

After lunch Boris ordered him to get dressed. Maxim handed Oxana his house keys.

'I wrote a note about how to take care of the plants,' he said. 'In one of the table drawers you'll find the letter of attorney for the car – it's on you; the keys are there too. Use it.'

'And what if I smash the car?' Oxana squinted her left eye mockingly.

'That's okay,' Maxim smiled. 'We'll buy a new one.'

'Hey, are you coming?' Boris called from the hall.

'Yup!'

While Boris was waiting for the elevator, Maxim was saying goodbye to Oxana. He suspected that the trip could drag on for a couple of months. Having mustered his courage, he pecked Oxana on the lips. The young woman did not recoil, and that was inspiring.

'Bye!' Pleased, Maxim grabbed the backpack and dragged it into the elevator. Before the elevator doors closed completely, he waved to Oxana once more.

The elevator started crawling down; for a minute Maxim felt tears in his eyes. He turned away and started blinking rapidly, not wanting Boris to notice his display of emotions.

The elevator stopped, Maxim got ready to exit. But for some reason, Boris pushed the third floor button; the elevator started crawling back up.

'Where are we going?' Maxim was confused.

'You'll see,' Boris smiled mysteriously.

The first thing that struck Maxim when they got out of the elevator was the color of the walls. It was different from the design on Oxana's floor. And the apartments were arranged differently too.

'This way.' Boris got up to one of the doors and pushed the call button.

'Who lives here?' Maxim inquired, sensing that something strange was happening.

'My friend, I already told you about him.'

Maxim didn't have time to ask another question. The door opened and a solid stocky man, about forty-five years of age, appeared on the doorstep. He was quite a colorful individual, with a swarthy face, dark mischievous eyes and a little moustache. His clean-shaven head shone in the light of the corridor lamp.

'Hi, Igor. It's us. Meet Maxim.'

'Hi, little brother.' The master of the house hugged Boris, then looked at Maxim and stretched out his hand. 'Hello. Boris' friends are my friends.'

'Nice to meet you, sir,' Maxim replied. The host's handshake turned out to be pretty firm.

'Let's skip the formalities,' the man offered. 'We're all our own here. Come on in.'

Maxim put the backpack in the hall, took off his shoes and his jacket, then followed Boris and the master of the house. Now Maxim understood why they bought an apartment for Oxana in this building – turns out that one of their own was already living here.

'Take a seat, Maxim; no sense in standing when you can sit,' Igor suggested. He spoke with an apparent accent. He didn't look like an Uzbek or a Kazakh; Maxim concluded that he was either a Yakut or a Buryat. Probably the latter – you could tell by the features of his face.

'Thank you.' Maxim sat down in an armchair, feeling rather uncomfortable.

'Well, I brought him here for you to take care of.' Boris nodded at Maxim. 'Will you take him on?'

'Why not?' Igor shrugged his shoulders. 'I've actually got some spare time right now.' He softly laughed, Boris smiled too.

'Just don't poison him with your toadstools.'

'I won't,' the master of the house promised.

'When are we going?' Maxim asked.

'Friday morning,' Igor answered. 'We'll go through your stuff, see if we need anything else and buy the rest tomorrow. There won't be any shops where we're going.'

'That's fine,' Maxim shrugged. Then he glanced at Boris. 'I'll just run over to Oxana's. I forgot to tell her about the fertilizers.'

Boris closely examined Maxim, then smiled and shrugged his shoulders. 'Go, if you want to.'

'And don't forget to say "hi" from me,' Igor asked. He and Boris looked at each other and burst out laughing.

Maxim didn't see what was so funny, so he just tactfully smiled. He got up from the armchair, went into the hall and put on his shoes and jacket. Once on the stair landing, he carefully closed the door behind him and headed for the elevator.

The elevator was still there – the doors opened. Maxim entered the elevator cabin and pushed the eighth floor button. The elevator twitched and started drifting up.

Finally, the doors opened. Maxim took a step forward – and halted. At first he thought he got the wrong floor – it was a strange stair landing. He looked at the elevator buttons – eighth floor. Only everything was different here.

The skin on his back prickled; Maxim held the doors of the elevator that had started to close. Something was terribly wrong.

Once back inside the elevator, he pushed the button of the first floor. He waited for the elevator to descend then headed for the entrance doors; his gaze caught more and more details that didn't match. It was a completely different entrance – Maxim didn't have any more doubts about that. He pushed the entrance door – it was without a combination lock – and went outside.

What Maxim had been suspecting all along was confirmed once and for all. The Sholokhov Prospekt disappeared; instead Maxim saw a completely unfamiliar street. Feeling a sickening shiver in his knees, he got down from the porch. He spotted a young chap walking down the street and stopped him.

'I'm sorry,' he said in a hoarse voice. 'What town is this?'

The young fellow looked at Maxim in surprise. 'Ulan-Ude,' he answered and hurriedly moved on.

'Thanks,' Maxim mumbled in response.

When he got back up to Igor's flat, the first thing he heard was a loud burst of laughter.

'Igor was telling me a joke,' Boris explained, having glanced at Maxim who had entered the living room. 'I'll tell you later.' He laughed again.

'Well, how's Oxana doing?' Igor inquired with a smile.

'This is really Ulan-Ude?' Maxim asked.

'That's right,' Igor confirmed. 'Why? Is something the matter?' His eyes glistened mockingly.

Maxim sat down in an armchair and looked at Boris.

'I didn't even notice the moment of transfer,' he quietly said. 'And I didn't know that you could take someone along through a portal.'

'It's the elevator,' Boris answered. 'Elevators are mostly of one type, the small difference remains often indiscernible to the human eye. You get into an elevator in Rostov, and get out of an elevator in Ulan-Ude. It's all very simple.'

'And practical,' Igor added. 'I actually don't know how to do that.'

'We've all got our talents,' Boris noted tactfully.

'That's right. Well, should we take fifty grams each – for new friends? I see Maxim could clearly use a drink.'

'Only if it's fifty grams,' Boris agreed. 'And no toadstools.'

The last few weeks turned out to be very troublesome for Yana. She had to travel a lot, at some point she was even catnapping. Her new position gave her plenty of opportunities, but it also robbed her of a lot of energy. Still, Yana didn't complain. She needed to prove her worth on the new post, make a good showing before the Hierarchs. True, women had never before become Sovereigns. But there is a first time for everything.

It was a Wednesday evening; Yana just got back home. She went up to the second floor of her estate, opened the water tap in the bathroom then spent a long time examining herself in the mirror, sadly thinking that youth was gradually leaving her. True, magic helps her stay in shape. But how long would that last?

She climbed into the bathtub and spent a long time lying in the hot water, thinking about her life. Did she get what she wanted? Not really. Did she have a chance? Yes. And that was worth living for.

She entered the living room, combing her hair and thinking that she definitely had to find someone – there were too many lonely nights in her life now. And suddenly she screamed and halted – someone was sitting in the armchair.

It was Kim. At the sight of Yana, he got up; in his arms the young woman discerned a piece of strong black cord.

'Kim?!' A shadow of surprise and fear slipped through Yana's voice. 'How did you get here?'

'Didn't expect to see me here?' he sullenly inquired, slowly binding the ends of the cord around his hands. 'You're such a bitch.'

Kim was one of the people Yana dismissed, once appointed Curator. She just felt that they had different paths, that you could not entrust any serious matters to riffraff like that. Kim wanted to meet up with her a couple of times; he even tried to book an appointment. And every time he was rejected. And now he came by himself.

'What do you want here?' Yana asked sternly. 'Get out of my house!'

'And I trusted you,' Kim said and slowly moved towards Yana. 'What an idiot I've been.'

'Don't be silly!' Yana slowly backed away. 'Kim, don't! What are you doing?!'

'Why don't you guess three times,' Kim answered with a gloomy grin. Then he added in confidence, 'You know, I've never killed a woman before. But I'll kill you.'

His eyes were cold and austere. There was no way Yana could take on Kim – having realized that, she threw the hair brush at him and took to her heels. Kim darted after her.

'You can't get away from me!' he exhaled, climbing upstairs in big jumps after her. He tried to grab Yana by her foot, but missed it by a split second. Yana ran up to the second floor and dexterously slipped into her office. A massive door made of red wood shut before Kim's very nose. A moment later there was a click of a lock turning.

'You still won't get away!' Kim yelled and kicked the door. To his surprise, it held the blow. He was forced to kick it harder; the door opened with a crash. And at the same moment Kim saw the barrel of a gun aimed at him.

'Get this!' Yana said and pulled the trigger.

The bullet hit Kim right in the chest. He swayed then, as if in disbelief of what had just happened, he touched the wound. He looked at his fingers covered in blood, then switched his gaze back at Yana.

'You bitch,' he mumbled, swayed and fell down to the ground.

For some time, Yana remained standing, continuing to aim at the prostrate Kim. Then she warily got up to him and gave him a poke with her foot. He was dead.

Having moved aside from Kim, Yana sat down on the edge of the table, she was shaking. Never before had death crept up to her this close. She glanced at the gun in her hand – turns out, this gift wasn't that silly after all.

For some time she sat there, coming to her senses, then she reached for the phone. Without letting go off the gun, she dialed.

'It's Yana,' she said, coldly looking at the dead Kim. 'There's some garbage that needs cleaning up. Send a car.'

Igor turned out to be an excellent storyteller. As far as Maxim could tell, his host had spent a long time working as a geologist. Even quite simple stories became incredibly funny when Igor was the one to tell them. And it is possible that alcohol had something to do with it – they didn't stop at fifty grams. In the evening, which considering the time difference came very quickly, Maxim already felt quite comfortable in Igor's company. Even his journey through the portal no longer caused fear or aversion in him – so, there was a portal, so what? They are magicians to do stuff like that.

It was past one am when Igor suggested they go to bed. Maxim didn't want to sleep just yet, but he had to concur. Boris, however, said that his mission was now completed, and he was going home. He glanced at his wrist watch and added, 'I've still got some things to take care of.'

'Don't make excuses,' Igor said. 'And don't worry about Max; everything will be ok.'

'I hope so,' Boris grinned. 'Bye, Maxim. Be seeing you.'

'I'll see him off.' Maxim followed Boris to the hallway. 'Am I going to be here a long time?' he asked quietly, knowing that the master of the house didn't hear.

'Here? No.' Boris answered. 'But you won't go home for a while. Just accept the fact that your journey will take a little longer. Igor will explain all the details.'

'I'll explain everything to him,' Igor added. Apparently he had come up and heard the last phrase. 'What are you guys talking about?'

'About his trip. I said you'll tell him everything.'

'Of course,' the master of the house agreed.

Maxim and Igor followed Boris to the elevator. There were a few last handshakes, and the doors of the elevator shut. You could hear it go down.

For some time Igor listened to the noise of the lift then glanced at Maxim. 'It's funny to think that he's no longer in the elevator – right?' he quietly asked then smiled. 'Let's go to bed, Maxim. We'll have way too much to do tomorrow.'

Indeed, it turned out to be quite a busy day. In the morning Igor made Maxim shake all of the things out of his backpack, and then carefully looked them over. He rejected a part of them as unnecessary or useless; some things he found to be quite useable. Then they went shopping – Maxim's wardrobe was replenished with a green weatherproof jacket, waders and lots of warm things: a cap, sweaters, warm tights and woolen socks. All of that made Maxim a bit dejected – by the looks of it; he really wouldn't go home before long. Although very soon he accepted his fate and preferred to enjoy the show. New people, a new region, new adventures – wasn't that great?

In the evening Igor folded out a map on the table and showed him where they'd be going.

'Look,' he said, having called Maxim to the map. 'This is the first part of our journey: first, we go by plane to Bagdarin, right here…' Igor moved his thick finger along the map. 'Then about four hours on a cross-country vehicle along this little river to a little village; it's not on the map. I've got a house there.' Igor looked at Maxim and smiled. 'That's where I spend the summer. And during winter I stay in the flat.'

'And what about the second part of the journey?' Maxim inquired.

'You'll find out about that later,' Igor answered evasively.

Maxim didn't argue. During the evening he made several attempts to find out something about his host – particularly, what his connection to the dream searchers was, but each time Igor tactfully refrained from answering. Finally, having lost his patience, Maxim asked him straight out – was he or was he not a magician?

'I am,' Igor agreed. 'In some sense.' He smiled again. 'But this place doesn't favor talking about magic. Boris can speak about magic anywhere, he's not like me. I can't do that. And this apartment – is the apartment of an ordinary person, not a magician. It's not the place where I live.'

Insisting was pointless, Maxim realized that. So that whole evening they spent talking about everything else, but not about the real deal.

Friday morning they woke up early. Maxim already knew that someone was going to pick them up and drive them to the airport. Everything was ready to go for the trip, Maxim's things, packed in his backpack and a large bag, stood in the hallway.

Igor's friend rang the bell about eight o'clock. It was a meager elderly man. In Maxim's opinion, there's no way that guy could be a magician. And it was true.

Outside, waiting for them was a green little "UAZ" with a red cross on its side. Apparently, the car belonged to some hospital. Maxim dragged his things and Igor's bag into the cabin and shut the door. Igor settled in the front seat, next to the driver.

Maxim was silent all the way to the airport; Igor on the other hand had a lively conversation with the driver. At first Maxim listened to what they were saying then his thoughts drifted away.

At the airport, having said goodbye to his friend, Igor confidently dragged Maxim along. Obviously, it wasn't his first time here; you could tell by the way he acted. Not even an hour and a half had passed and Maxim was already getting onboard the plane, an Antonov AN-24[6]. Maxim had never before flown a plane like that, so he took in every detail of what was happening with interest.

The flight took even less time than what they had to spend at the airport. When the airplane suddenly dove and initiated landing, Maxim's heart skipped a beat. But everything turned out just fine – a couple of minutes went by, and the plane touched the landing runway.

After arrival they had to wait once more. Igor went somewhere and Maxim spent more than an hour of tedious waiting a hundred meters away from the landing field. Finally, Igor turned up.

'Follow me, amigo,' he said with a smile. 'We're in luck. We'll get there today. Come on.'

The trip took about twenty minutes. The two men stopped by a squat house. Igor put the bags by the fence and sighed with satisfaction. 'It's here. We'll have to wait a little.'

'And who are we waiting for?' Maxim inquired, lowering his backpack.

'Goldsmiths will be going home now; they promised to give us a ride. It's on their way.'

Maxim already knew that people in this region were mostly into gold mining. Igor had spent several years working here, so he knew a lot of people and had plenty of friends. Now it came in quite handy.

They waited for more than half an hour. Then there was some kind of noise, Igor smiled with satisfaction. 'It's coming.'

The noise gradually turned into a real rattle, then out of the turning appeared a heavy creeper tractor. It stopped nearby, covering Maxim with clouds of smoke; the right door opened slightly.

'Get in!'

It took them a couple of seconds to throw in their things into the car body. Igor was the first one to get inside the cabin, seating himself next to the driver. Maxim settled next to him and shut the door. The tractor revved up, twitched and started crawling forwards.

It was a strange journey. The iron mastodon – an artillery tractor, as Igor explained it – confidently crawled along the worn down roads, wobbling on pits and bumps. Some parts of the road reminded of sea waves. The tractor nodded, descending into another pit, then its engine revved up and it confidently made its way out of the pit. Immediately another pit followed, then another and another. A part of the road followed the channel of a stream – with its caterpillar tracks rumbling on the stony bottom, the tractor quickly crawled forward, creating fountains of spraying water. Maxim held on tight to the handle – on a road like that, breaking your head on the door was pretty easy.

When four hours later the tractor crawled out to some kind of settlement and stopped, Maxim sighed with relief – finally!

'That's us,' Igor said; his eyes were glistening.

Maxim got out of the tractor and with great difficulty got up to the back of the car to hand Igor the packing. Having jumped off the tractor, he stepped aside. Igor waved to the driver – he could go now. The tractor turned around and quickly crawled away.

'Well, we're here,' Igor said with a smile. 'Let's go.'

After a four hour long rumbling of the engine, the silence reigning was just overwhelming. Maxim was slowly coming around. The silence in this place couldn't even be stirred by the bark of some hairy mongrel and the screams of the children rushing towards them. Evidently, when someone came to visit it was always a big event.

A little boy ran up to Igor and said something to him in an unknown language – probably Buryat language. Igor replied. The boy ran off hand over fist.

'Come on, Maxim. My house is over there.'

The village was made out of about fifty log houses. Igor's house was located on the offside, just next to the woods. There was a rusty bolt instead of a lock, and having taken it out, Igor opened the door wide, looked at Maxim and said, 'Come on in.'

Inside the house it was quiet and dark. Once inside, Maxim looked around with hesitation, then took off his backpack and put it against the wall.

'You don't lock the doors around here?' he asked.

'Some people do, when they leave for the city.' Igor shrugged his shoulders. 'I don't. No one would dare get into a shaman's house.'

For the first time during these days Igor called himself a shaman. Still, his words did not surprise Maxim.

'Take off your jacket, Maxim. We're going to have supper now.'

'About half an hour went by. A kerosene lamp was burning; firewood was crackling in the furnace. It was warm and cozy. Maxim ate pasta a la sailor[7] and pondered on how quickly things can change. Only a couple of days ago he was thinking about conservatory design. And now he was in some trans-Baikal back of beyond and didn't have a clue about what's going to happen to him next.

Igor had time to change. He didn't array himself in a shaman outfit; instead he just changed his civilian city clothes into more simple ones. Now he was dressed in pants of a strange color – perhaps they were green once – a simple shirt and a thin green jacket. At the same time Maxim noticed that Igor himself had changed quite a bit. He was speaking much slower now; there was much more power in his gaze, in his movements.

Igor didn't speak during supper. Maxim was silent too. They started talking only when the plates had been put aside.

'I guess, you'd like to know why you're here,' Igor said, having settled comfortably in his chair and genially looking at Maxim. 'It's all very simple: Boris has asked me to tell you about the world of shamans. He said it'd be good for you to look at the world differently. I agree. But first, I'd like to ask you a question. What do you know about shamans, in very general terms?'

'I only know about them in very general terms,' Maxim smiled. 'Tambourine, ritual dancing. Communicating with good and bad spirits. Something like that.'

'Just as I thought,' Igor nodded. 'You see, there are almost no real shamans left. There are copies, fakes. They jump around, beat the tambourine; some of them can even get into a trance. But that's not the real thing. Many modern day shamans, Maxim, practice shamanism only for the money. It's a show, a set up, there's no real power behind it. Long time ago, when I was still a young lad, I tried to learn from one such fake-shaman. Maybe I too would be jumping around with a tambourine now, but I met another man. He was the one to make me who I am. He told me that times are changing, that more and more often people watch a practicing shaman like they would watch a circus. The knowledge is gone, there's only the external shape devoid of power. In some places you can still find real shamans, but their time is over for good. This man showed me that you can be a shaman without the tambourine and the shaman clothing. And shamanism is not just about communicating with the spirits, but about something much greater. It is about communicating with nature, communicating with the world. You…' Igor pressed his palms to his chest. '…and the world…' He motioned his arms around himself, his face was very serious. 'Do you remember; what's the most important thing in Christianity? Love. My world – the world of a shaman – is also based on love. You need to love this world, Maxim – every grass straw, every bird, every animal, every person. Love, beauty, harmony is the basis of all. You're probably quite familiar with Carlos Castaneda's teachings and you've read that magicians are very cold. "I'm cold like the arctic wind," his teacher Don Juan used to say. Many magicians take it as a guide for action – they get rid of the influence of the world; they become cold and hard-hearted. That's not the way to do it, Maxim. Love is the main creative force in the universe. It's big trouble if a man doesn't understand that. When people get rid of human foolishness, they often get rid of love too. They lose the foundation of life, the foundation of harmony. In the end many of them get sick and die – because life without love is destructive. We are the children of this Earth, and we must love it. It's not even that we must love it – not loving it is not an option. Everything is connected, Maxim – the murmur of a brook and the rustle of the wind, the mouse that ran past you and the eagle that flew by you. These are parts of a whole, and we are part of a whole. Become aware that you are part of this world, Maxim. Love it – sincerely and truly, and it will do the same. It will protect you from harm; it will help you, shelter you in an hour of need. Your life will be brimful with light and joy. Castaneda speaks of warrior magicians – I don't really like that term, I don't understand it. Who do you wage war against? Why? I've been told that a magician fights himself, strives to rid himself of all human foolishness. But that's not right either – you don't have to fight yourself, you need to love yourself. After all, you too are a part of this world. No violence, only love and harmony. You face the world, and the world turns to face you. Do you understand me?'

'I do,' Maxim answered diplomatically, having suppressed an involuntarily desire to grin. Igor spoke of all these things way too seriously. And what new did he say, really? Nothing. Love, beauty… People have been talking about these things before him and they will talk about it after he's gone.

'You don't feel it,' Igor shook his head. 'I've talked a lot to Boris about it, and he understood me. As did Iris and Roman. They are different now, not like before. And you'll be different. Not straight away, but you will. Here: you call yourselves dream searchers. But a searcher is a person that breaks things; am I right?'

'In some sense,' Maxim agreed. 'Although I'd say we're just trying to make sense of it all, trying to find out how it all works.'

'You can understand in different ways,' Igor didn't agree. 'You could take a shotgun and kill a wee bird. You could pluck it and take a look at what's inside. Or you could sit and enjoy the bird's singing. Do you feel the difference? There should be no violence. Boris said that you are lazy people, free-riders and instead of finding the key, you prefer fitting a lock-pick. But if the door is locked, there is probably a reason to it. Parents would also hide matches and gunpowder from a kid. But once he gets older, his father will give him the shotgun. There's time for everything,

Maxim. If there is love and harmony in your heart, the doors will open on their own. Do you understand, Maxim? The doors will open on their own; you won't have to break them open. Use the soft touch on the world; love the world. Take a look at yourself – you are so young, but your soul is already so callous. And don't argue!' Igor stopped Maxim who was about to object. 'I know what I'm saying. I see it, you know. It's like you're in a shell. You are always expecting the world to play a trick on you. You're always on your guard; you forgot how to see the beauty of the world. There are sparks in you, I see them, but there are very few of them. You're not glowing – you are dark. You have withdrawn into yourself. Remember your childhood, remember yourself as a child. Remember, how you enjoyed this world. You were connected to this world with a thousand strings. But then you got older, you started to have concerns. And the tiny strings were torn, there were fewer and fewer of them. Now you are fenced off from this world with a thick shell – there is the world, and then there's you. That's not right, Maxim. You are a part of the world. That's how it has to be. Not you and the wind – but you with the wind. Not you and the sun – but you with the sun. Not you and the river – but you with the river. You see? When you have the opportunity, discuss it with Rada – she's got light in her soul, she understands me better than anyone else.'

Igor was smiling; his eyes were glistening in the light of the kerosene lamp.

Maxim became thoughtful. First doubts appeared in his heart. Perhaps, there was something to what Igor was saying.

'I'll think about it,' Maxim quietly answered. 'You're probably right.'

'I am right,' Igor agreed with a smile. 'You'll see – once you understand your connection to the world, once you become a part of it, the world will change. Now animals run away from you – later they'll serve you. You walk in the woods, and the woods are talking to you – through the soft movement of little twigs, the gusts of wind, the cries of birds. If there's a bad person somewhere, the forest will definitely tell you about it. If there's trouble, you'll know about it right away. You and the world will be together.'

'And what do you think about hunting?' Maxim inquired. 'You've got shells on your windowsill – so you have a shotgun too?'

'I do,' Igor agreed. 'Only, hunting too can be different. It's one thing when you kill animals for yourself – after all, you have to eat as well, otherwise you'll die. And it's a different thing when you do it for fun. You may take as much as you actually need, not more. Again, you cannot kill just any animal. Some animals you can kill very few of – the musk deer, for one. If you see one – let it go, let it run. Don't shoot. The world will reward you three times later.'

'I understand,' Maxim nodded. 'That's pretty much what I thought.' He was silent for a moment. 'I've been meaning to ask you – where else are we going?'

'You're going,' Igor smiled. 'You'll boat. Look…' He quickly put away the left over plates and dishes, wiped off the crumbs with a cloth, went out to the other room and then returned with a map folded four times. He spread it out on the table; Maxim noticed that the map was laminated. Then, upon closer examination, he realized that it had simply been carefully taped over. 'Look, Maxim…' Igor peered at the map. 'One centimeter is two kilometers. It's a good map. We're here…' His fat finger touched the map. 'Right here, you see? And here's the river; it's about a hundred meters away from here. I'll give you an inflatable boat; it's in the shed. You'll go down the river to this place…' Igor's finger slowly moved down the map. 'It's marked here with a dot, you see? You can't miss it – there's an old shed on the river bank. Behind it, about five hundred meters from it will be a channel. Here it is. There you'll get out and drag the boat long the channel. That's about two kilometers. Watch your step, there are deep places there. And here…' Igor touched the map again, 'you'll see a little house. That's where you'll stay. It's about eighty kilometers from here. Five-seven days, and you're there.'

'Does anyone live there?' Maxim inquired.

'No,' Igor smiled. 'Only you and the world. They'll pick you up in the spring. You'll have time to become friends with the world.'

Maxim's worst fears were confirmed. Spending a year alone in a god forsaken hut… Nothing like that had ever even occurred to him.

'And what do I stoke with in the winter?' he asked. 'Is there a saw or an axe?'

'I'll explain everything, Maxim,' Igor smiled again. 'We've got the whole evening ahead of us.'

Maxim expected Igor to have an ordinary inflatable boat that he bought in a shop – but he was wrong. The boat was a rather large one, made out of black rubber – must be army stuff. When Igor retrieved it from the shed, unfolded and inflated it with a foot pump, Maxim thought it to be just huge.

'It's a good boat, Maxim,' Igor reassured him. 'Safe. Boris has gone on it, Roman too. Rada didn't – she's a woman, they flew her down there by the helicopter.' Igor smiled. 'I'm sure you'll like it. Just be careful. Watch out for the rocks – there will be rapids in a few places. You'll see it, where the breakers are white. Well, and I've pretty much covered the rest.'

The preparations didn't take long. In the company of the kids and the local gawkers Maxim and Igor moved the boat down to the river and put it in the water. They loaded Maxim's things and some supplies into the boat. As Igor explained it, most supplies were brought by helicopter a month ago, when they were taking back the former habitant, a guy from the Moscow group.

Finally everything was ready to go. More than anything, Maxim feared the first few minutes of boating – he had never gone by boat before, and here, before the eyes of the gawkers he was afraid of slipping up. Igor already explained to him in general terms how to operate the boat, but theory is one thing and practice is something completely different.

The boat quietly wobbled by the lopsided footbridge. Having said goodbye to Igor, Maxim untied the rope and carefully got into the boat. He sat down on the seat, grabbed the oars and carefully turned the boat around with its nose facing the current. He glanced at Igor and waved.

The little river was quite narrow. Every now and then Maxim had to help out with the oars. One turn, another – the little village disappeared behind the forest wall. Maxim looked around and was surprised to feel joy. The river, the boat, the forgotten hut somewhere ahead – wasn't that wonderful?

It took about an hour for him to get used to the boat. He felt something wasn't quite right. Having docked to the bank, Maxim dragged the boat halfway on to the bank and rearranged the weight so that it'd make a support for his back. Then he sailed on, tried the adjustments and was left extremely pleased with himself.

Now he was sailing, as if sitting in an armchair, occasionally using the oars and enjoying the amenities of nature untouched by man. The sun was shining bright. He was even forced to take off his weatherproof jacket. The current wasn't strong, only a few kilometers an hour. Having appreciated the speed of the current and the remaining hours of daylight, Maxim arrived at the conclusion that he could be at his destination the day after tomorrow.

He spent the first night on a sandy spit. Already in the evening Maxim brought firewood and made a fire. Having cooked a very simple supper in a kettle – porridge from a bag – he ate, after that he spent a long time sitting by the fire, looking at the darkening sky and the river slowly carrying its waters. It seemed strange that there wasn't a single person nearby for miles; that Maxim was on his own. Civilization was left somewhere far away. It was only him and the world now.

Following Igor's advice, he slept on the bottom of the boat turned upside down. You got a sort of hammock, quite comfortable in use. Above, Maxim stretched out the tent – it couldn't fit the entire boat, but it still secured something that resembled comfort.

He slept quite uneasily. At first Maxim had a hard time falling asleep then he kept waking up. The forest lived its own night life – Maxim imagined someone walking the bank; he heard the cries of some bird. A hunter's knife hanged on Maxim's belt and there was an axe wrapped in a bag by his feet. Although not too impressive, those were still weapons.

Maxim woke up when it was already daylight outside. He glanced at the watch – past seven am; time to get up.

It was quite chilly; a cold draught was coming from the river. He was forced to put on some warm clothes. Maxim made a fire, had a quick breakfast, then loaded the boat again and set it afloat.

That day he sailed for nine hours. According to Maxim's calculations, he had to cover about thirty kilometers; however the calculated mileage did not match the map. Only now did Maxim realize that the actual distance was much greater than the calculated one – the river winded unscrupulously. When he saw one of the channels marked on the map, there was – according to the map – only twenty two kilometers from the point of departure to the channel.

Still, Maxim was left satisfied. He was in no rush, so he simply enjoyed the beauty of these parts. Every now and then, he'd come across a few rapids and carefully chose the deepest places. Occasionally, when the boat was carried along the foamy breakers, he screamed with delight – that's how amazing it was.

'In the open spaces of the big blue ocean! I'm the steersman! I'm the captain!' Maxim was singing a song from a cartoon about baron Munchausen. 'Oh-oh-oh!'

Only now, alone in a remote taiga, did Maxim suddenly realize that he had never shouted at the top of his voice in his life. There was always something in the way – people, circumstances. Now, nothing was in his way, and Maxim gladly yelled at the top of his lungs, enjoying his freedom.

He liked this journey; he liked being one on one with nature. Having woken up one morning, Maxim saw bear prints nearby the boat – the master of the taiga threaded so softly that Maxim didn't even wake up. Another time he saw a pod of ducks; the birds almost didn't get startled by the boat and calmly swam ahead of it. Then, when the boat caught up with them, they all dove at once. Maxim tried to make out where they'd show up, but he saw only two of them – they surfaced by the bank.

'Don't be afraid, ducks,' Maxim told them. 'I won't touch you.'

The water in the river was exceptionally pure – to have a drink you only had to bend down. Primeval nature untouched by man amazed with its beauty. Maxim's heart was filled with a sense of peace – it was his world, his country.

Maxim got to the right channel only by the sixth day. The channel turned out to be quite shallow; there were rocks jutting out everywhere. A little earlier he noticed the debris of a shed that had grown black with time, so he knew that he was on the right way. Once out on the bank, he rolled out the top of his swamp boots and had some rest. Then, having caught on to the rope, he dragged the boat up along the current.

It turned out to be the hardest part of the way. The boat kept getting stuck; he had to stop and drag it first by one side, then by the other, pulling it over the rocks. Igor's warning about the deep places was confirmed – having taken a step forward from yet another rock, Maxim fell through up to his waist into the water. He cursed and got out onto a shallower place. Then things became easier; Maxim was no longer afraid of getting wet and simply plodded on, dragging the boat behind him.

More than anything he was afraid that he wouldn't find the cabin, or it would be burnt, blasted. That's why, when on his left he saw a board covered roof, Maxim sighed with relief.

The house was intact. Having gotten out onto the bank, Maxim first of all took off his boots and poured the water out of them. He thought about it, pulled the backpack out of the boat and changed into dry clothes and put on his sneakers. And only then did he walk up to the house.

It was an ordinary log cabin, a rather old one; in several places the roof was already green with patches of moss. There was no lock; the iron ears were tied together with a piece of wire. Having undone it, Maxim opened the door and cautiously stepped inside.

Almost one third of the room was taken up by a big plank bed – for five people, not less. Closer to the wall, was a rolled up mattress. There was a table by the window, a pair of benches and small metallic stove, and on the walls – shelves with pots and plates. In the right far corner – a big box, made out of thick blocks.

The box was locked; however, a key hanged on a nail in the wall just next to it. Maxim opened the lock and lifted the lid up.

The box contained groceries – flour, cereals, noodles, canned goods. The reserve was more than impressive. Maxim remembered Igor's instructions and took out some of the products from the box, then reached the back wall. Having caught the lower back board with a knife, he tore it off. The board revealed a niche. There was a long package wrapped in sacking. Maxim retrieved it, untied the laces and unwrapped the sacking.

Just as Igor promised, there was a shotgun in the package – a sixteen caliber single-barrel gun. Maxim rummaged in the niche and found a cartridge belt with shells, a few cans with gunpowder, little pouches with small shots and case-shots, and a box with primers.

Maxim checked the gun, then broke it in two and put a shell in the chamber. Having closed the shotgun, he sighed – now he felt a bit safer.

He hung the shotgun on the wall. Maxim looked around his new lodging once more and went outside to unload the boat.

The strangest thing for Maxim became the feeling of freedom that came down on him – the lack of necessity of doing anything at all, of caring about anything. True, there were things to do here as well, but it was a whole different matter. Before, Maxim was always burdened by the weight of things he had to do – first it was studying, then working. It's one thing or the other, an endless line of concerns and problems; all of that required attention, took power and time. Concerns didn't go away even after Maxim joined the searchers – it was rather the other way around, he got even more of them. The loss of the ordinary way of life, the danger of getting into the Legionaries' clutches, organizing your business... Then he was building the conservatory, plus the constant practicing magic – mapping, meditation, stopping of the inner dialogue, everyday physical exercise. He couldn't wave it all away just like that, he couldn't throw it out of his life.

And now he discovered that the former bustle was gone. Or rather – he ran away from it. Even if only for the time being, but he did run away. For the first time Maxim got the opportunity to be in charge of his time, choosing what to do and what not to do. And if he did decide to do anything, then how and when was also up to him. This river, this forest, this forgotten forest hut belonged to an entirely different world. The silence surrounding Maxim was so profound that it wasn't even disturbed by the rare cries of the birds or the purl of the river. The first few days this silence was simply overwhelming. Being used to the constant noise of the city Maxim experienced a real sensory hunger. He even sang songs, screamed, even though all his efforts couldn't ever stir the calm that reigned over this world.

During the first week Maxim examined the closest surroundings of his new property. He didn't go far, afraid to get lost. He always took the shotgun with him – just in case.

About three kilometers away from the hut Maxim discovered another river, it wasn't very wide, but deep. In one place by a high cliff was a large pool. When Maxim saw the pool, it immediately occurred to him that it would be a good place for fishing, and in the same instant he realized that someone had already taken a fancy to this place before him. At first he became alerted and only later did he realize that the people, who used to fish here, were the former inhabitants of the hut.

Indeed, fishing turned out to be excellent. In the shed, next to the hut Maxim found two old bamboo fishing rods, fishing line and fish hooks he had brought with him. He didn't manage to dig up any worms, so he had to use batter for bait. At first it didn't bite at all, Maxim only caught a couple of tetras. Then, he got an idea – he cut one tetra in little pieces and tried to use them as bait. And immediately everything changed – within literally one minute Maxim pulled out an excellent umber. He unfolded its dorsal fin and studied it with admiration – that's how beautiful that little fish was.

Since then Maxim went fishing every day. It helped him save groceries, and besides, fishing was exciting. The calm surrounding also gradually entered his consciousness. Maxim more and more often remembered his talk with Igor about becoming one with nature and realized how right Igor was. Here, in the remote taiga land, Maxim was part of the nature surrounding him. Rather, he tried to be a part of it, he strived towards it. By looking at the river, at the flaming sunset, at the eagles soaring majestically in the skies, Maxim learned to love this world anew, learned to see its beauty. Igor's words about the shell that he lived in no longer seemed to be a metaphor.

The first few weeks Maxim just rested; rested from everything, even from magic. Here, in this world of calm, everything was different. If Maxim had serious difficulties in trying to make sense of the subtleties of the magical structures, then here knowledge came on its own. It just appeared in his consciousness, putting everything in its place. The same thing happened with "practicing magic" – Maxim suddenly realized that there was no point in forcing himself with a strict schedule; there isn't any point forcing himself to do things. If you don't want to meditate – don't; give yourself a breather. If you're tired of everyday workouts – take a break. Wait for the body to ask for exercise. Periods of rest are just as important as periods of activity.

Realizing this simple truth brought Maxim plenty of pleasant moments. The routine disappeared, collapsed; Maxim did whatever he wanted and whenever he wanted. He could spend several days in a row sawing firewood with an old chain-saw, or he could just lie on the grass, looking at the bottomless pale blue sky. At times he wanted to run, and he ran with great pleasure along the river, jumping on rocks and dodging between trees. Then came the time when Maxim returned to meditation – not because he had to, but simply because he wanted to. He meditated on the water, the forest and the slopes of the hills. He meditated on the rocks. Maxim was literally being imbued with silence and calm. Sometimes he had to consciously restore the inner dialogue – the silence that had taken place in his head was just frightening; sometimes he even felt nauseous, dizzy. But soon he got used to this inner silence and started enjoying it. Silence didn't mean that his thoughts became completely shut off – rather, not thinking was more pleasant than thinking. Maxim was already familiar with this feeling thanks to the chains of the Patience of Medici. But now silence came on its own.

More than two months passed before Maxim felt bored. He had long ago explored the length and breadth of all the surroundings, the prepared firewood no longer fit under the awning. The fishing gradually lost its charm, having become a simple way of obtaining food. Maxim even got scared; having sensed that the magic of this place was slowly disappearing. More and more often thoughts of home slipped in his consciousness. And there was fear too – Maxim realized more and more sharply that he'd have to live in this hut for a very long time. It was the end of July – so, he's got the whole of August ahead of him, the whole autumn and the whole winter and almost the whole spring – about nine months – it was a very long time.

Maxim chased away these thoughts anyway he could. He came up with new things to do – fixed the hut, made an original musical instrument out of empty bottles and cans. Then he applied himself to physical training – he exercised until he was covered in sweat and completely exhausted. Everyday jogging in the forest became just as necessary to him as food or air. He didn't forget about magic practices either, but there was still no peace in his heart. More and more often Maxim thought about whether he had made the right choice, having joined his life with the searchers, or whether it was the biggest mistake of his life. Thanks to them he had lost the accustomed way of life. Thanks to them he was now sitting in this squalid forest hut. True, the world of the searchers is full of secrets; they are interesting people. But is it worth it? Wouldn't it be better to just live a quiet life – just like everyone else?

That was one side of the coin. However, next to it always appeared the other. Maxim thought about how much he'd learned lately, he thought about the dream world. Finally, he thought about Oxana. If it wasn't for the searchers, he never would have met her.

More than anything Maxim was surprised by how easy his opinion changed. Only a minute ago he could feel happy about what had happened to him. And then anguish would be gnawing at him again. He wanted to get into that boat and sail away. A hundred and twenty kilometers down the river, then leave the boat, about thirty kilometers by foot – and he'd see people. Then it would all end. A couple of minutes went by, and Maxim once again got horrified with his thoughts – how could that even enter his mind?

Such a mess in his head resulted in a surprising outcome. Maxim stopped trusting himself. He had been fully convinced that our desires, thoughts, emotions are solely determined by the position of the assemblage point. If it shifts, the consciousness changes as well. And that means, so does our view of things. The best way of thinking is not to think at all, that's what Castaneda's teacher used to say. Now Maxim perforce had to agree.

The whole end of August and the first half of September it was pouring rain, then in the morning it started to frost. Winter was approaching. Maxim could feel it and he was involuntarily dreading it. Yes, he should be set for firewood, but the colds here aren't a joking matter either.

In the beginning of October the earth was covered with snow; Maxim almost didn't leave the house any more. He realized that the warmth would only come about five months from now, not sooner, but this time it didn't make him feel any particular way. Gradually and very slowly, calm was settling his heart. It wasn't a result of some logical reasoning; this calm was simply there. Maxim even thought that he started to catch a difference between the different types of calm. That's how, when he only just got here, he was amazed by the quiet that governed this world. It had literally engulfed him, imposed its silence on him. But that was the silence of the place. Present silence was different, it belonged to… other dimensions? Maxim couldn't answer that question, but he sensed that this silence was different. There was nothing that could break it – not the crackling of logs in the furnace, not the moan of the wind behind the frosty patterned glass. This silence simply came – and stayed.

Maxim celebrated New Year's a whole four times; first, by his local time then, by Novosibirsk time. He knew that at these minutes glasses were being raised in Klyonovsk. The third time he celebrated New Year's by Moscow time, together with the people living in Rostov. Finally, the fourth time he celebrated by Kiev time. He regretted deeply that he couldn't call his parents, that he didn't even come up with the idea of writing them a letter and leaving it with Oxana – she could have put it in the mailbox before New Year's. Alas, clever thoughts always come too late.

The advent of the New Year Maxim celebrated with wine

made out of great bilberries – he made it himself, picking berries just for this occasion. He was even a little proud of this wine, regretting that he didn't have anyone to offer the wine to.

He nevertheless did congratulate his parents, having found them in a lucid dream. It wasn't easy, but Maxim managed. He didn't know whether they would remember this meeting, but that wasn't that important. He didn't look for anyone else, remembering Boris telling him not to. Now this ban no longer seemed foolish or cruel – Maxim sensed how much he got out of these months of solitude. He became a different person; his view on many things had changed completely. Calm reigned strongly in his heart and he felt that he was much closer to the world around him now. That shell, which Igor spoke of, if it didn't fall apart completely, had definitely become very thin.

In the beginning of February Maxim stopped meditating. That happened after a very memorable event. It was late evening and Maxim meditated on a piece of sugar that he put on an upright shell from the shotgun. Everything was going very well. But then something happened, something that made Maxim really scared – he suddenly sensed that there was somebody outside the hut. It was a sensation of a body – Maxim jumped up, pulled the shotgun off the wall. Then he froze, listening closely to what was going on outside.

That it was not a person, Maxim realized right away. Walking around the cabin was something really huge, its movement echoed in Maxim with a painful itch in his stomach.

Suddenly the creature stopped in front of the front door, then it tried to enter. Only now did it dawn on Maxim that the door was locked only by an ordinary door hook.

If it wasn't for the hook, the door would already open. The unknown guest pulled once, twice, then pressed against the door, the door started to crack. Maxim threw up the shotgun; he knew that the hook wouldn't take another charge like that.

Fortunately for Maxim, the creature didn't make another

attempt to get inside through the door. Maxim felt the creature come up to the window; it made him shiver. His hands were slightly shaking, it continued to itch in his stomach – it seemed his stomach echoed every movement of the unknown guest.

At some point Maxim realized that the creature had pressed against the window and was now looking at him, but he couldn't see anything himself – it was pitch-black outside. Then the creature moved away from the window and slowly circled the hut a couple of times. Standing in the middle of the room, Maxim slowly turned, following the stranger's movement with the barrel of the gun. Then something changed – suddenly debris came falling from the ceiling. Maxim felt the creature jump up on the roof. Again there was cracking; the boards of the ceiling shook. The furnace started giving off smoke – it seemed someone had covered the chimney. Then a mysterious weight pressed upon the whole house – even the logs gave off a cracking sound, as if being squeezed by the tentacles of an invisible octopus. And suddenly, everything went away – the cracking stopped, the furnace stopped smoking. The itch in Maxim's stomach was gone too.

His legs shaking, Maxim heavily lowered himself on the bench. He was shivering all over. Having put the shotgun on his knees, Maxim ran his shaking hand along the blued surface of the barrel.

Maxim didn't get any sleep that night; he expected the beast to come back any moment. But it didn't. He dared outside only after the break of dawn.

First thing that struck him was the absence of any kind of tracks. The day before there was a snowfall, the night guest had to leave some tracks. But there were none. The snow on the roof was untouched as well. That explained a lot.

To all appearances, Maxim was visited by a so-called ally – one of the creatures of the magical world. There were clear indications of that – the itch in his stomach, the fact that there were no tracks. Having thought about it, Maxim decided to stop meditating for a while; he attributed the appearance of the ally to his meditation practice. Meditation makes your inner dialogue stop, it shifts your assemblage point. And that, in turn, allows you to perceive the world around you in a new range. And that's where allies dwell. Maxim didn't feel like meeting the ally just yet. True, they say that with time allies become magicians' assistants. But better to leave that for now.

Once Maxim spoke to Rada about safety precautions, which a magician must observe. According to Rada, thoughtless behavior on a magician's part could lead to very serious trouble, to the point of death. Therefore, a magician must be aware of his actions. And if some of his manipulations caused the assemblage point to shift with consequent unpleasant effects, then the best thing to do in a situation like that was to bring the assemblage point back into its original position as soon as possible. You could do that by temporarily becoming the most ordinary person. Namely, you had to forget all about practicing magic and focus on very normal things. You could go to the movies, visit museums and theatres, you could read books – obviously, the books should have nothing to do with magic. You could work, do sports, go to parties. According to Rada, practicing magic often leads to a person's energy cocoon getting damaged, and these damages could only heal when having the assemblage point in its usual position.

Maxim didn't have any books, so he dedicated himself entirely to the household. He cleaned up the hut and took an interest in cooking. He started singing songs at the top of his voice. That helped, the ally – if it really was an ally – didn't show.

Spring made its presence known with the strongest blizzard. The wind was howling outside; there was such a draught that the hut kept shuddering now and then. The blizzard didn't make Maxim anxious; he perceived it with the same calm that had been reigning in his heart for several months now. He even liked the noise of the snowstorm – he welcomed any distraction.

The last winter days brought another kind of entertainment. It all started with Maxim's attempt to get rid of the automatism of his movements. Maxim read somewhere that we perform most of our habitual actions with a minimum level of awareness. It was advised that magicians got rid of this automatism, bringing out all of their actions into the sphere of awareness. Having thought about it, Maxim decided that it's a worthy substitute for meditation.

The most difficult part was remembering about his wish to get rid of the automatism. At first Maxim remembered about it only a couple of times a day, then it happened more and more often. Gradually he became enthralled with the new activity, it was not only exciting, but it also helped him kill time.

By the results of the first few days of practicing, Maxim arrived at the conclusion that you had to perform all of your actions very thoroughly and with great interest. That helped you focus your attention on them, and the most amazing discovery to Maxim was that this practice stopped the inner dialogue just as well as meditating. If attention was glued to what he was doing at the moment, there was simply no room for thoughts.

Maxim truly enjoyed following his own actions. Here he is pouring tea in a big aluminum mug – first the tea, then the hot water. Now he takes the spoon – the hand slowly reaches for the spoon, attention is completely focused on the action. He grabs the spoon, scoops some sugar, pours the sugar into the mug, and now another spoonful... Now he has to stir thoroughly. You could stir clockwise, and – anticlockwise. The important thing was to have your attention completely glued to the process.

Gradually, Maxim realized that he was enjoying this practice. The most interesting thing was that it helped him get completely absorbed by the present moment, to be here and now – and not let his mind wander.

Weeks passed. Maxim continued to master the subtleties of the technique he used, by this time he had learned to almost always be in the present moment. What's more, he absolutely didn't want to return to his former state. He simply liked the new way of perception. Maxim felt a strange feeling of being. He felt power within, confidence; his body got filled with unusual weight. Or maybe not weight – Maxim couldn't yet find the right word to describe his new condition. It was a strange harmony with the world around him; he felt that he was intertwined with this moment, with this space. His movements gained smoothness; all these things reminded him of active meditation. And perhaps that is what it was; Maxim didn't really feel like classifying the new state he was in.

His new state continued to bring him new discoveries. First of all, to his surprise, Maxim discovered that while being in this state he could practically instantly read information off the objects around him. He just looked at something, and then there was a strange tickling feeling in the back of his head. A moment later knowledge came to him. This trick didn't always work well, but when it did Maxim was overjoyed. The most surprising discovery was that objects kept information about their former owners. Maxim knew for sure that Rada touched the gun only once or twice. But Roman had been walking around with it quite a lot. Just like another person – Maxim didn't know his name, but he sensed that it was a guy about twenty-five years old. And he was sure that once he sees him he'll know who he is.

Rada didn't like the aluminum mug either; the young woman preferred to use a small ceramic cup with a broken handle. Boris was the one to break it, having dropped the cup. Maxim actually smiled when he realized that. He really did know that: things kept the memory of their owners. This mostly resembled a smell, but a smell filled with specific information. Difficulties arose only when trying to put this knowledge into words.

Maxim didn't know how reliable this information was. Or did he? The usual human stereotypes came into play here. The mind opposed this as hard as it could, trying to prove the groundlessness of all of these concoctions. Maxim was ready to agree with its arguments. At the same time there was another part of his "I". And that part watched the mind's attempts to maintain its power with a grin. That part didn't have to prove anything; it simply knew what was what...

The state of being seemed very prospective to Maxim, he felt its huge potential. Sometimes he thought that any moment now he'd fuse into one, the real world and the world of dreams – that's how illusive the line between them was. Still, Maxim restrained himself, remembering the visit of the ally. Besides, he preferred to proceed slowly. Something told him that during these months he'd done more than what was expected of him.

However, not everything went as smoothly. Once he started working on his state of being Maxim noticed to his surprise that he no longer had lucid dreams. They disappeared all together, all attempts to bring them back proved fruitless. Having thought about it, Maxim decided that it had something to do with his new practice. It required heightened attention in real life, and there was simply no attention left for lucid dreaming. Maxim was put before a choice – to continue his research in real life or to abandon it and get back to lucid dreaming. However, working on the state of being seemed so very promising that Maxim, having thought about it, decided to sacrifice his lucid dreams for now. He just knew that he could get back to them anytime he wanted.

In April it got quite warm. The spring brooks purled, Maxim spent increasingly more time outside, breathing fresh air. He knew that he'd be home within a month's time, yet the upcoming return no longer stirred any particular emotions. If necessary, Maxim could stay here one more year. Basically, it didn't matter to him, to return back home or to stay here, both options promised a lot of pleasant things. At home waited Oxana, the plants. Having stayed here another year, he'd get the opportunity of conducting magical research in peace. That's why Maxim waited for May to arrive with a calm heart.

Closer to May, the lucid dreams returned. Maxim didn't do

anything special; he didn't even stop his practice of being in the present moment. And there was no real practice to speak of anymore, the new way of awareness became ordinary and habitual to Maxim, having replaced the old one. Now Maxim didn't understand how he could live before, being torn apart by hundreds of stupid thoughts. Well, perhaps not stupid – but still there was no use in them, now Maxim was sure of that. Slowly, step by step, he entered a new way of cognition, where the habit of thinking proved unnecessary. The knowledge of how and what to do simply appeared in his consciousness. The most difficult thing was not to resist it, not to oppose it. Very often the habit of thinking prevailed, Maxim did what he thought was right, and not what the knowledge out of nowhere told him. And the result was always poor; Maxim then understood that it would have been better to follow the command of his intuition.

Soon it got really warm outside, Maxim spent more and more time walking around the forest, trying to feel like a part of the world around him. At some moments he could almost feel the strings connecting him to the world with his body; it was a very strange and pleasant sensation. The feeling of harmony, unity with the world amazed him. Maxim noticed that even animals and birds were much less afraid of him. Nevertheless, even in this case his mind handed him a convenient explanation – perhaps, they just got used to him.

In the beginning of May Maxim met Boris in one of his lucid dreams. Rather, Boris found him.

'Ah, there you are!' Boris said, having suddenly appeared nearby. In this dream Maxim was walking down a street of an unknown city.

'Hi!' Maxim glanced at Boris with a smile. 'Happy to see you.'

'Ditto. Well, you're not too bored with your taiga odyssey yet, are you?'

'Not really,' Maxim shrugged. 'I even like it. There's time to think about things.'

'You're growing!' Boris praised him. 'But too much of a good thing is good for nothing. A chopper will come for you on Sunday. Get your things together; don't forget to bring the boat. And clean up the hut; a new guest should arrive in a couple of weeks.'

'Mind telling me who it is? Unless it is a secret,' Maxim inquired.

'Kostya. It wouldn't hurt him to spend a year out there.'

Maxim smiled. He liked Kostya.

'All right, I'll get everything ready,' he said. 'But there aren't many groceries left.'

'They'll bring more groceries by helicopter,' Boris calmed him. 'You'll lug everything across to the hut, and try not to linger – the pilot's also got things to do, he won't wait too long.'

Boris's eyes were shining. Maxim never understood, whether he was joking or telling the truth.

'There's only going to be the pilot?' he inquired.

'Yes. His name's Sergey, he flies a "Mi-2" – a cute little chopper. He'll drop you off at Bagdarin, and Igor will meet you there. Got it? Don't forget, on Sunday. He'll come sometime around noon; therefore get everything ready so you won't have to rush about later. Better if you drag over all of your stuff close to the landing spot.'

'I got it, Boris. Thanks.'

'Then until Sunday.' Boris squeezed Maxim's hand. 'I'll see you in Ulan-Ude. Bye!'

'See you later, Boris!'

Boris disappeared. Maxim was left alone. He made a couple of steps – and woke up.

Friday morning he started getting ready for departure. He cleaned up inside the hut, put some things into the backpack – he decided to leave most of the things here. He went fishing for the last time, sadly realizing that he'll never be back here again. Or will he? After all, no one could stop him from coming here again someday – on his own, when there's no one here.

The last preparations for departure Maxim decided to leave for Sunday morning – he knew that he'll be able to finish packing by noon and drag everything out on the spot a hundred meters away from the hut. Obviously, that's where the helicopter will land.

Saturday morning Maxim dragged the boat outside and rolled it out – he wanted to inspect it, and see if it was still ok after spending the winter. Having made sure that everything was in order, he rolled it back together and tied it up with a piece of rope. It occurred to him that it would be nice to put the boat in a bag, when far away he heard a low rumble. He listened closer – just as he thought, a chopper. They must have come for him earlier!

Maxim cursed, grabbed the boat and dragged it towards the landing spot then he ran to get his backpack. Having pulled it outside, he saw the approaching helicopter.

It was a Mi-8, Maxim halted in confusion, put the backpack down on the ground. Boris promised a Mi-2. Maybe, this one is not for him?

The helicopter started slowing down, clearly getting ready to land. Maxim watched it carefully – and suddenly he felt fear. Or perhaps it wasn't fear – Maxim didn't know how to describe this feeling. It was that same silent knowledge, lately Maxim had already learned to trust it. And now he suddenly realized very clearly – there are enemies onboard that helicopter.

The enemy helicopter was already making a landing approach; things were clearly taking a turn for the worse. Maxim glanced at the house door, not knowing what to do. The rifle had already been packed and hidden – he could get it out in time, but then he'd definitely not be able to get out of the house. He could just run away – but what if his gut feeling was wrong?

It wasn't. The chopper hovered in the air above the landing spot then it carefully touched the ground. The door slid open, and one after the other, well-built guys in camouflage started jumping out of the cabin. They had guns in their hands – having realized that, Maxim turned around and broke into a run.

Chapter Four

The Hunt for the Searcher

Dags thought last year had been unsuccessful. So far the present year hadn't been great either – alarming information arrived almost every day, Dags frowned, while carefully reading the reports. And it wasn't the economy that worried him, not Russia's timid attempts to restore its former positions. Something else troubled him – people were changing. Young people have again started to value education; that sole fact made Dags furious. You'd think that you've given everything to these morons – drink your beer, chew hamburgers. Have fun to the hoarse cries of the voiceless pop stars. Shoot up, if you want to – what else does a slave need to be happy?

They've let it get out of hand. You couldn't tell just yet, but Dags had a good sense of the situation and knew that it would only get worse.

There were plenty of problems on the magical front too. The searchers were still not making their presence known in any way and Dags wasn't happy about this. If the enemy is keeping a low profile, then he is up to something. Yana had done good on her new job, but she couldn't handle them either.

The searchers themselves were obviously not sleeping. The materials that got into their hands because of Kramer's negligence did their part – the Legion suffered quite a number of serious misfortunes. Take, for instance, the incident with that little unremarkable defense factory – if the Legion had gotten its hands on it and ruined it, the whole of Russia's army aviation would have been left without engines. And it almost worked! But information about this operation got into the hands of special agencies, and everything went down the drain. And that's just one example, while there are tens of them. Remembering the recent failures, Dags truly regretted Kramer's death. Alas, Sly robbed him of the opportunity of personally strangling the scoundrel.

Dags was just reading a report on the situation in the oil department, when his secretary announced that Yana was here to see him.

'Let her in,' Dags commanded solemnly. He sighed and hid the papers in the folder. Perhaps, this time it'll be good news?

'Good day, Sovereign!' Yana greeted him, having entered the office.

'Hello,' Dags said. 'What have you got?'

Yana frowned a little; she didn't like the Sovereign's unfriendly tone. Nevertheless, she tried to hide her displeasure.

'I think, we've got a chance of capturing one of the searchers,' she said, approaching Dags.

'Really?' The Sovereign glanced at the young women with a gloomy grin. 'Well, tell me.'

'May I take a seat?' Yana inquired.

'You may. Sit down and get on with it.'

Yana's eyes glistened unkindly. Still, even this time she composed herself.

'The searchers have a couple of places,' Yana began, 'where they leave the new guys for about a year. I've heard about two such places – a cave at Altai and a hut somewhere in Transbaikalia. The searcher spends a year there alone then comes back. The last few years I've been trying to locate these places. I can't tell you anything about the cave just yet. But I think I've found the hut.'

'You think, or you found it?'

'Perhaps, it is the place we're looking for,' Yana said with emphasis. 'I knew that every spring a helicopter flies over to the hut. We started gathering information on all aviation companies, on the pilots working in that region. And finally, we've managed to learn a few things.' Yana smiled. 'I've got all the information now. I know the name of the pilot. I know where he'll go. I know when he'll go. Nine out of ten that the helicopter will go to pick up a searcher. Now we only have to decide what to do with this information.'

Dags became thoughtful. He sat with his eyes slightly closed for a couple of minutes then he looked at Yana.

'You've got a plan?' he quietly asked.

'Of course. There are two options: we could just go there and catch the searcher. Or we could let him go back. We'll start shadowing him – perhaps then he'll lead us to a bigger fish. It's your choice.'

'Why don't you put it in simpler words – you want to lay the responsibility on me,' Dags muttered.

Yana smiled.

'I just want to know your opinion, Sovereign. If we were to talk about me, I'd prefer the first option.'

'Why?' Dags inquired.

'It's safer. Remember how many times we've shadowed the searchers, and how many times they have managed to get away from us. They always notice when someone is watching them.'

Dags became thoughtful again, softly drumming his fingers against the table. 'Very well,' he said after a long pause. 'Act. You know what, no…' Dags scratched his neck. 'I think I'll go with you; I too need to get my mind off things. I hope, you won't mind?'

'Of course not, Sovereign,' Yana answered. 'It would be an honor for me.'

'That's settled then.' Dags's lips bent in a grin. 'When would you like to go?'

'Tomorrow, Sovereign,' Yana answered.

They noticed his flight almost immediately. There was shouting, and then instantly followed the bursts of machine-gun fire. Bullets rustled above Maxim's head, he automatically bent down. Then he realized – they are just trying to scare him, they need him alive. He turned around for a second – and in that moment he saw the sniper.

It was an experienced man. Having run off to the side of the chopper, he got up on one knee, leaned towards the sight; the barrel of his rifle was slowly moving, feeling the target.

The remaining twenty meters to the forest Maxim ran like a drunken sprinter, chaotically jumping from one side to another. Meanwhile, the sniper had time to make three shots: the first bullet slipped next to Maxim's hip, the second scratched his knee – Maxim gave out a cry, but didn't stop. The third bullet went through his trouser-leg and sent little grains of rock flying out of a boulder in front of him. And here's the saving forest – desperately dodging between trees, Maxim felt the sniper's thorny gaze with the back of his head. Just a little more, behind these bushes… That's it, he's gone…

The sniper didn't shoot anymore, having lost the target. However, Maxim knew very well that this was just the beginning. He looked at his wounded right leg; a bloody stain had already spread on his pants. But there was almost no pain, just as there was no time to examine the wound. Again, the rumble of the helicopter was heard, Maxim looked around and broke into a run.

The helicopter caught up to him almost at once; the gunmen in the chopper immediately opened fire from the open door. They were shooting right in front of him – the bullets pierced the ground, knocking chips out of tree trunks. Maxim dashed to the left, trying to hide behind the bushes. He looked around – behind him, in the gaps between the trees; he could already make out the flashing silhouettes of his pursuers.

If it wasn't for the helicopter, Maxim would have disappeared long ago. But the damn vehicle, milling the air with its blades with a crashing sound, relentlessly hovered above his head, not leaving him any chance of rescue. The sparse deciduous forest didn't let him hide – no matter where Maxim ran, everywhere he was accompanied by a din that pressed him into the ground.

He didn't have any chance of escape. The actions of his pursuers were clearly being coordinated from the chopper; Maxim realized that he was being pressed to the river. That's where he had been fishing. Swollen from the freshet, the river posed an insuperable hindrance; the people sitting in the chopper knew that very well. And so did Maxim – he looked up at the helicopter and once again took to the left, hoping to jump out of the trap. And immediately bullets ploughed up the earth in front of him, Maxim involuntarily slowed down. Then, having made up his mind, he desperately threw himself under the fatal rain falling from the sky.

They wanted to get him alive no matter what. The submachine gunner immediately seized fire, Maxim, feeling hopeful, darted forward. He had to make it…

He really could sneak off. Apparently, the people inside the chopper realized that too. Having turned around, the rotary-winged piece of machinery outstripped Maxim and remained hanging above the trees a couple of hundred meters ahead. Maxim took a closer look and slowed down. They've outplayed him…

Two gunmen were quickly descending from the helicopter, cutting off the only escape route. He wouldn't be able to slip past them – having realized that Maxim started running towards the river. There was simply no other way.

He jumped out to the exact spot where he used to fish. The muddy river, carrying garbage and snags, instilled him with horror; it took him one look to understand that there was no way he could get across. Maxim halted, not knowing what to do. The chopper was hovering in the air at some distance away from him; the sniper in the doorway had Maxim on target.

The end was near. Maxim looked at the chopper, at the water rushing by his feet. He looked around; his gaze caught the glance of the fighters hurrying towards him. He turned around and stepped into the water...

He went under at once. The icy water burned his body; the rapid flow picked him up and carried him on, threatening to crash him on the rocks at any moment. He surfaced for a second, gasped for air. Like in a dream, Maxim saw the motionless chopper hanging in the air, the perplexed face of the fighter that had just run out on the river bank. And then he went back under.

Maxim didn't think about that he'd manage to get away. He was thrown from one side to another; it was shaky, just like driving on pot-holes. A couple of times he painfully touched upon underwater rocks. With great difficulty Maxim made it up to the surface – and at once he disappeared in the deep, dragged away by some snag. He tried to push it away – it didn't work. Feeling that he was losing control, he darted to the surface with all his might. He felt his shirt tear – and there it was - the saving gulp of air.

Breathing heavily, Maxim looked around, trying to locate the helicopter. There it was – turning around above the forest, its hated green belly just nearby. There was nothing else to do but to go back to hiding under water...

Having surfaced once again, Maxim didn't see the helicopter. For some time he drifted, then he made an attempt to get out on the bank. He just knew that he wouldn't last long this way.

The first attempt of getting out failed. His frozen hands slipped on rocks, Maxim got turned round and carried onwards by the river. He had more luck the second time: ahead was a tiny creek that had formed nearby a huge boulder. The water by the boulder boiled and foamed – Maxim dashed to the creek and prepared himself for the inevitable impact with the rocks. A blow, another – and there he was, arduously getting out on the bank...

It was very cold. Water was squelching in his sneakers; something was making a noise close by. It wasn't the sound of the river – it was something else. The chopper... Escape, hide – Maxim started running, slightly limping on his right leg and fell into some bushes. The rotary-winged vehicle slowly went above the riverbed. Deafened by the strained roar, Maxim pressed himself against the ground. The din went away, it almost faded all together. Then it came back. The helicopter returned, made a circle and checked the riverbed one more time. "Just don't let them see me…"

The helicopter noise faded again. Maxim lay there, pressing himself to the ground, and it occurred to him that they'll find him here anyway. They'll comb through the whole bank, but they'll find him. He shouldn't have gotten out here; he should have gone to the other side. But it just happened. Thank god he made it out at all.

He listened. It seemed quiet, although in the distance he could still hear the helicopter's din. He sat up, rolled up the right trouser leg and examined his knee – it wasn't serious, the bullet tore off a piece of skin. Bruises and scratches didn't count. And now he had to get going – he scrambled up and ran into the depth of the woods.

Running made him a little warmer. Maxim didn't know how much distance he had covered – a kilometer or less. He stopped and collapsed on the ground. For some time he lay, heavily breathing and looking into the amazingly blue sky, framed by the larch tops. Having caught his breath, he sat up and untied his sneakers. He poured out the remaining water then squeezed out his socks. He put the sneakers back on – that's it, they won't squelch now. He glanced at the watch – hey, it's still working. Waterproof – the capitalists didn't fool him.

The chopper was still circling somewhere nearby, but that didn't scare Maxim anymore – they had lost him. He now had to get as far away as possible from this place.

He allowed himself another break only an hour later. Having rested for fifteen minutes, he started out again, orienting by the sun. If his calculations were right, he soon should come out to the river – the very same one he rafted down last year.

And that's exactly what happened: by noon Maxim had caught the glimmer of water ahead. He got up closer – just as he thought, it was the river. It too was flooded, but it was that river. If you go upstream, you'd come out to the rapid leading to the hut. And if you go downstream...

Maxim became thoughtful – he just didn't know where to go. Either eighty kilometers up the river, to the village where Igor lives, or a hundred and twenty kilometers down the river, and then about another thirty kilometers through the forest. He could get something to raft on, if he went downstream. If he chose to go up, he would have to go by foot. And you don't really know at once, what's better.

The answer came on its own: he just had to get away from the dangerous place and wait for a little while, then find Boris in a dream and tell him everything. And Boris would definitely be able to find a way of getting him out of there.

Maxim decided to go downstream: that route appeared to be the safest one. Surely no one would look for him there. He walked for more than an hour and a half, until he stumbled across a couple of fallen trees blocking the way. They made out a natural hiding place. It occurred to Maxim that no one would see him there, not even from a helicopter. His thrashed body craved rest, and Maxim couldn't deny it...

Several hours he slept, having made himself comfortable on putrid grass and twigs. He didn't think he'd be able to fall asleep, and only once he opened his eyes, he realized that it was already four in the afternoon. He listened – silence, there was only the soft splashing of the river.

He was thirsty. Having gotten down to the river, Maxim scooped some water and slaked his thirst. The fact that the water was dirty didn't bother him. He got back to the fallen trees, thinking that it wouldn't be a bad idea to use branches to make a shelter. He halted, considering the best way of going about the construction; he thoughtfully scratched the back of his head. Or perhaps it wasn't worth wasting time on this nonsense?

He didn't have to build a shelter. He heard the soft crunch of a twig behind his back, Maxim turned around with a jerk. Just in time to make out a rifle butt flash before his eyes.

He woke up because of someone talking. He opened his eyes a little, and immediately grimaced from the pain in his mouth – his jaw must be broken. Or not... He felt his teeth with his tongue, moved his jaw. It hurt, but everything was intact by the looks of it.

He slightly turned his head, moved his gaze onto the man speaking. And started, having recognized the familiar sniper. About thirty years old, thin and wiry, dressed in an army camouflage outfit; the man was sitting on a log, talking to someone on the portable radio transmitter. In his left hand was a sniper rifle – a very serious opponent.

Only now did Maxim realize that his hands were fixed behind his back. He moved a little and his eyes met the eyes of the sniper.

The fighter had just finished talking. Having hidden the transmitter into the pocket of his coverall, he leisurely took out a pack of cigarettes and lit up. He silently offered a cigarette to Maxim, who shook his head in response. The sniper put the cigarettes back and fell deep in thought. He let out a small cloud of smoke then looked at Maxim.

'You make us run, mate,' he said, having grinned ironically. 'I should have shot you by the hut, there'd be less hassle.'

'So why didn't you?' Maxim inquired, making himself comfortable.

'That's what I am saying; I should have.' The fighter carelessly flicked the ash off the cigarette and went quiet for a moment. 'Get up. It's time to go. They're waiting for us.'

'And what if I won't?'

'What's the point?' the fighter noticed reasonably. 'If you want, I can call the chopper. They'll send down a couple of guys, and they'll deliver you anyway. So it's up to you.' The sniper demonstratively inhaled.

He was right. For some time Maxim sat there, thinking about what to do, then struggling, he got up to his feet. He unobtrusively glanced at the fighter, thinking that he still had a chance. If he'd get only a half a meter closer...

'Don't be a fool,' the sniper warned him. 'And keep in mind that there won't be a second warning. I'll shoot you in the knee, and let them deal with you. So you'd better start walking.'

'Where?' Maxim inquired.

'That way.' The fighter threw the cigarette butt to indicate the direction. 'Forward.'

Maxim could only obey. And that's how they walked – Maxim ahead, a couple of meters behind him – the sniper. Occasionally, the fighter told him which way to go; Maxim didn't realize right away that his escort was checking against the data of a pocket GPS-navigator. About an hour later they got to all the familiar places, during all this time he didn't get a single chance to escape.

And there was the hut; the helicopter had settled down nearby on the clearing. Right beside it were the gunmen with a couple of civilians, among them a tall young woman. Maxim looked closer – and started. It was Yana.

'That wasn't a nice thing to do, young man,' a tall meager man said, looking coldly at Maxim and standing next to Yana. Apparently, he was the one in charge here. 'You're wasting the time of serious people.'

Maxim was silent. And what could he say?

'What's your name?' Yana asked.

'Sergey,' Maxim said. 'Sergey Savchenko.'

'Where are your papers?'

'Don't have any,' Maxim shrugged. 'What idiot would bring his documents to the taiga?'

He was telling the simple truth; all his documents were at Igor's place. As Igor told him, he wouldn't need them in the taiga – there's just no one to show them to, but losing them or getting them wet was more than easy.

'We'll have time to talk,' the man slowly said. 'Let's go.' Having turned around, he leisurely headed for the helicopter.

Obviously that man was Dags – Maxim heard Yana call him Sovereign. That made matters even more complicated; it occurred to Maxim that this time he got himself into a real mess. It was somewhat of a comfort that they hadn't recognized him yet – probably because of the moustache and the beard. He wanted to shave today, but didn't have the time.

The packing took a couple of minutes. They dragged Maxim inside the helicopter, sat him down on a seat. Through the chopper window, he saw two fighters pour gasoline over the hut; one of them took out a lighter.

The fire leaped up, greedily licking the logs. Maxim turned away – it hurt him to watch.

The engine hammered, the blades of the propeller starter turning. One minute, another – the din of the engine got louder, the vehicle smoothly got off the ground and started to climb.

The trip took a couple of hours, and all of that time Maxim was being closely watched. They didn't even let him close his eyes – he only had to lower his lids, and immediately followed a shout or a push in the side. Maxim knew why they were being so careful; Dags and his people were afraid that he would disappear – open a portal or leave through a dream. If it hadn't been so serious, Maxim would have only laughed at them thinking that he was a mighty searcher.

Indeed, there was nothing funny about his situation. Maxim had a pretty good idea of how it could end. That's why he tried to open a portal during the whole trip. He knew that he needed it, he hoped it would open. He even tried talking to the Net, he asked it – come on, dear, help me out! Take me out of here!

Alas, the Net remained impervious to his pleas. All Maxim's attempts to open a portal were fruitless.

They landed at a big airport. Not even twenty minutes had

passed before Maxim was already sitting in a luxurious seat of a private jet. The airplane was headed for Moscow.

Apart from Maxim, Dags and Yana, there were two more guards in the cabin. The others either didn't come with them, or were seated in the other cabin – Maxim didn't know which. There was no thinking about an escape; especially here, six thousand meters above the ground.

Dags was sitting opposite to Maxim and was studying him closely. Maxim felt rather uneasy under the gaze of this man. Yana was quiet; from time to time she'd cast a glance at Maxim with a smile.

Finally Dags's lips moved.

'Is there anything you'd like to tell us?' he asked, intently looking at Maxim.

'You've been fooled, boss,' Maxim answered. 'There's no gold out there.'

'Gold?' Something twitched in Dags's face. 'What are you talking about?'

'What do you mean?' Maxim tried to express confusion.

'Repeat what you just said,' Dags demanded.

'I didn't say nothing.' Maxim lowered his head. 'And to tell the truth, boss, I don't know nothing. You've got the wrong guy.'

'Hey, just don't play stupid, ok?' Yana broke into the conversation. 'We know perfectly well who you are.'

'Really?' Maxim demonstratively smiled. 'Then why don't you tell me, don't be shy. And I'll listen.'

Dags glanced at one of the guards; the guard got up and punched Maxim in the gut with all his might. Maxim folded up, with difficulty gasping for air. Dags and Yana waited until he'd come around.

Finally he managed to get his breath, Maxim once again leaned back in his seat – as much as his arms chained behind his back allowed.

'Let's try this one more time,' Yana said with a smile. 'Let's start with the easy bit. What were you doing in that cabin?'

'Having a vacation,' Maxim answered and immediately folded up from another punch.

This time it took him noticeably longer to recover. Still, Maxim remained rather pleased with himself. It seemed he had managed to plant some doubt in their hearts.

'I'm waiting,' Yana reminded, staring straight at him. 'I'll repeat the question: what were you doing there?'

'Looking for gold,' Maxim said and burst into a cough. 'Only there ain't any gold back there.'

'And how long have you been there?' Yana asked.

He smelled a rat. Should he say that he only recently arrived? But the hut was lived-in, surely, they have realized that. His lie must be very calculating.

'Since last summer. I've been digging prospect-holes all summer long, all autumn. As the snow melted away, I set out again. Only there ain't nothing there. Empty.'

'Then why did you sit on an empty space?' Dags inquired. 'Isn't there some gold in the area?'

'I don't need *some*, now, do I?' Maxim grinned. 'I wanted a lot. Everyone says there's gold there. And so I looked.'

'What do you know about dream searchers?' Dags glued his gaze on Maxim's eyes.

'Who now?' Maxim asked. 'What are you talking about, boss? I ain't never had a computer. I know motorbikes, cars. But computers – that's not my thing.'

Dags pursed his lips with hostility.

'Your name and last name?' he asked. 'Quickly!'

'I've told you already,' Maxim replied. 'Savchenko Sergey Alexandrovich. I live with my aunt in Bagdarin. I've got my documents there.'

'Then why were you running away from us?' Dags inquired.

'How could I not run?' Maxim grinned. 'It's not the first day you're married, you must understand. First I thought you were cops, then mobsters. Now I'm not sure – either you are an FSS-man or from some other office. I'd feel better not to meet anyone at all.' Maxim demonstratively snorted.

'Very well,' Dags agreed. 'Let's assume you're telling the truth. Then tell us, why was there a chopper coming to get you tomorrow? The whole summer is ahead of you; you could dig away all you want.'

Maxim lowered his eyes, portraying momentary confusion. Then he looked up at Dags:

'What chopper, boss? What are you talking about?'

'Vanya.' Dags looked at the guard, who got up again.

This time they beat him harder and longer. Finally the guard took his place again, leaving Maxim squirming on the floor.

A couple of minutes went by. Having made sure that Maxim had come around, the guard came back up to him, grabbed him by the collar and hoisted him back into the seat.

'So, what's with the chopper?' Dags inquired again.

Maxim was silent. Despite the pain, he knew well that it was too early to give up.

'You should know better,' he hissed, wincing with pain in his side.

'I'm afraid you don't appreciate the whole seriousness of the situation.' Dags was looking closely at Maxim. 'I don't need you; you're a pawn in a big game. Tell me everything you know, and I'll save your life.'

'I've got nothing to tell you.' Maxim demonstratively turned away.

'When we'll be approaching Moscow,' Dags began, 'and get a bit lower, I'll tell the pilot to slow down. Then I'll open the door and throw you out of here. My desire to do so grows with every minute.'

'We don't need clams,' Yana put in. 'Either you tell us every-thing, or you'll have to learn to fly. Your life is in your hands.'

Maxim got sulky. He lowered his head and sat like that for a long time, then with a scared look he glanced up at Dags: 'I can't. They'll take my guts out otherwise.'

'You've got nothing to fear,' Dags assured him. 'You're completely safe here with us. More than that, if you won't disappoint me, I'm even prepared to find you a place in my team. It's big money and a great honor.'

'Fine,' Maxim slowly nodded. 'I'll tell you. The chopper was indeed coming for me. Rather, for the gold... I've got almost eleven kilos – sand, nuggets... It's a really great place; ain't nothing like it anywhere else. In town – in Ulan-Ude – I'll hand in the gold to a man. I don't know his last name, everyone calls him Vasily Sergeevich. He pays every time, never cheats. And in the beginning of June I'll come back. I wanted to go back – but there's nowhere I can go now. You've burned the house, haven't you.'

Disappointment flashed in Dags's eyes. He gloomily looked at Yana; she shrugged her shoulders and turned away.

'And where does your Vasily Sergeevich live?' Dags asked.

'Don't know the name of the street. I can only show you,' Maxim readily answered. 'It's where there's a head on a pedestal. From there – it's a couple of minutes walk.'

He first saw the huge Lenin head on a pedestal on a postcard in Igor's flat. Then, when they were shopping, he noticed the statue and couldn't resist the temptation to take a closer look. Now it was the first thing that popped into his head.

'There's a head?' Dags glanced at Yana.

'There is,' she nodded.

Dags went quiet for a few moments, thinking about something. Then he turned to the guard:

'Vanya, take him to the guys. Let him sit there for now.'

'Okay.' The guard took a step towards Maxim, but he already got up on his own.

While he was being taken through the cabin, Maxim was gloatingly smiling – so that the guard wouldn't notice. True, he didn't know yet how it would all end. But he'd managed to instill doubts in them, and that's already something.

They didn't take the handcuffs off. In the next cabin, three fighters were playing cards – they remained impassive to the appearance of the prisoner.

The escort pushed Maxim into one of the seats.

'Sit here,' the fighter said. 'Try anything, and you'll be sorry.'

Maxim only had to obey. Having made himself comfortable in the seat – as much as his chained arms allowed him to – he started watching the fighters play, thinking about how this flight would end for him.

When the prisoner had been taken away, Dags gave Yana a sullen look.

'What do you say?' he asked.

'Nothing.' Yana went into her bag for some cigarettes. 'Ok if I smoke?'

'Go ahead.'

Yana lighted up. She leaned back in the seat, smoked for a while, then her eyes met Dags's and she smiled guiltily.

'Looks like we took the wrong guy.' Yana reached for the crystal ashtray standing on a small table and flicked the ashes off the cigarette. 'He's got nothing to do with the searchers.'

'You were wrong,' Dags specified.

'Well, all right, I was wrong,' Yana agreed peacefully. 'It happens. What should we do with him?'

'He saw my face,' Dags uttered slowly. 'He heard people address me, here and in the helicopter. I don't need witnesses like that.'

'Young eagles learn to fly?'[8] Yana grinned.

'No,' Dags shook his head. 'First, we'll send him back to Ulan-Ude, let them find out what the deal with the gold is. We need to take such things under control.'

'Very well.' Yana shrugged her shoulders. 'So be it.'

The airplane landed at the Domodedovo Airport, Maxim

overheard the guards talking about it. He got ready for them to take him somewhere, but he was wrong. No one was in a particular hurry to get him out of the airplane – another half an hour went by, the guards started getting anxious.

'How much longer do we have to wait for that schmuck,' one of them said gloomily. 'It's already evening.'

He was hardly talking about Dags. Another forty minutes went by and Maxim finally saw the man they'd been waiting for for so long.

It was a stout man of about forty years of age. Balding, in a light leather jacket and a baseball cap; the guards were obviously relieved to see him.

'That's him?' the fat man asked, nodding at Maxim.

'Yes,' one of the guards replied. 'Well, we've done our part.'

'Of course, of course,' the fat man agreed. 'Move him to the first cabin.'

The last request was aimed at the people that came with him. There were three of them, all in civilian clothes. Maxim decided that these were his new guards, and he was right.

Once in the cabin they put him in the seat where Dags sat not long ago. The fat man seated himself in front of him.

'Take off his handcuffs,' he commanded. One of the guards immediately carried out his order.

'Thank you,' Maxim said, with pleasure stretching his arms that had fallen asleep by now.

'Oh, don't mention it,' the fat man bigheartedly waved it away. 'I see it's been a rough day for you. Would you care for some cognac?'

'I wouldn't say no to that,' Maxim nodded. 'Perhaps you've also got something to eat.'

'But of course. Misha, a little cognac, and make us a snack.'

The last words were aimed at the steward; Maxim already knew him from the first part of the trip.

'One minute,' the steward nodded and exited the cabin.

'Where are we going?' Maxim asked, feeling the engines of the airplane roar up.

'To Ulan-Ude,' the fat man smiled. 'But let's not talk business just now, we'll have time to do that later. By the way, I'm Alexandr Sergeevich. Just like the poet – Pushkin.' The fatso smiled again. Despite all his goodwill, Maxim sensed danger in this man. Something told him that he had to be very careful around the fatso.

'I'm Sergey,' Maxim introduced himself. 'Tell me, who were those people – the ones I arrived with?'

'People like people,' his companion smiled. 'Very powerful. If you help them, you won't be left unrewarded.'

'I hope so,' Maxim agreed.

Alexandr Sergeevich turned out to be quite a chatterbox, but he was far from stupid. Throughout the whole journey, he dragged Maxim into conversations discussing several topics; it took Maxim quite a long time to figure out that his companion was simply testing his level of intelligence. Everything was done very subtly and competently. Maxim had to control every word, every gesture. Perhaps, now for the first time he had real use of the skills he acquired back at the hut. The fat man kept pouring him cognac, Maxim couldn't decline. But he didn't feel drunk, his consciousness was very clear. When a couple of hours later the airplane touched the landing runway, Maxim silently congratulated himself – this round was also his.

It was long dark outside. From the airplane, Maxim was put in a microbus; the guards remembered to put the handcuffs back on, then followed a long journey. Maxim was watching the night city, thinking that he'd have to try to escape tonight. Already tomorrow they could unmask his lie – surely the Legionaries would like to find out where this mythical buyer lives, or they could head back to the hut for the just as mythical kilos of gold. Both options promised big trouble for Maxim.

The microbus drove into the front yard of a big estate. Maxim was taken out of the car and into the house, followed by two guards.

'You'll have to excuse us.' The fat man was justifying their actions. 'But such are the rules. We'll have some sleep, and in the early morning we'll cut to the chase.'

The guards knew what they were doing; Maxim realized with sadness that he had no chance of escape. And in the morning, he'd have even less.

He was taken inside a narrow corridor, at the end of which was a metallic door. One of the guards opened it. Handcuffs were taken off Maxim and he was pushed inside. The door rumbled again, the lock clattered and Maxim was finally left by himself. However, that didn't make him particularly happy.

He examined the room: concrete walls, concrete ceiling, wooden plank bed with a mattress, a small chair nearby, a sink with a tap and a toilet bowl. A dim light above the door, in the right top corner – the eye of a video camera. Turns out, they didn't leave him unsupervised here either.

He had to find Boris – having thought about it, Maxim opened the tap and was happy to slake his thirst. Then he lay down on the plank bed and tried to fall asleep.

After a day spent travelling Dags was catching up on his sleep with pleasure. He slept without dreams, without lucid dreams – he just wanted to get some rest. Having woken up in the morning, he stretched with satisfaction, glanced at the watch – eight am: time to get up.

He entered his office past ten in the morning. His secretary handed him a list of booked meetings for today. Dags looked over the list and made a wry face – mayors, governors and businessmen, and everyone wants something from him. True, most of these little people don't have a clue about who he really is. They just think him to be a very wealthy and powerful man – "a person close to the Emperor". To some degree it corresponded to reality, but only to some degree. In the past, he could visit the former president anytime; he could advise him without any doubt – what's more, he could tell him what to do and how to do it. The current president wasn't as easy. The current president was the FSS, and these guys don't like being ordered around and being pressured even less so. They can make just about anyone toe the line.

His only comfort was that the court really makes the king. And the Legion's got pretty firm positions in the court.

His first visitor was Volgin, also known as Polecat, the Legion representative in the Kaliningrad region – or, as Dags liked to say, in Konigsberg region.

Polecat's report noticeably lifted Dags's spirits. For the last few years the isolation of the enclave had significantly strengthened the Legionaries' efforts to impede communications between the Kaliningrad region and the rest of Russia had been entirely successful. Now Polecat suggested focusing all attention on Baltiisk, the base of the Russian Navy. Listening to Volgin's suggestions, Dags was nodding with satisfaction.

'Very well,' he said, thinking that Polecat had to be celebrated somehow. 'I'll think about this. Now another thing: as I recall, you've promised to open a region market for Polish goods?'

'That's more complicated,' Polecat made a wry face. 'We're trying to get along with the governor, but we've been unsuccessful so far. But I'll definitely solve this problem.'

'I hope so,' Dags sighed. 'Very well, Victor Nikolaevich, you're free to go.'

'Have a good day, Sovereign.' Polecat quickly gathered his papers from the table, respectfully bowed and slipped out the door.

Dags looked at the list of meeting. Who is next...?

Yana was next.

'Good day, Sovereign,' she quietly said. Having taken a seat in the armchair, she glanced at Dags; he could tell by looking at her face that something had happened.

'Well, what have you got?' Dags unwillingly opened his lips. 'Spit it out.'

'I've got two pieces of news, Sovereign. As usual, it's good news and bad news.'

'Start with the good news.'

'The good news is that...' Yana smiled, '...our golden boy turned out to be a dream searcher, and not some criminal half-wit.'

Dags twitched. 'Are you sure?'

'Now I am. And the bad news is that he escaped last night.'

Dags's face darkened. Turns out they had been deceived.

'How did it happen?'

'I can show you.' Yana retrieved a videotape from her bag and went up to the VCR. She put the videotape inside and looked up at Dags. 'Turn it on, please.'

Dags grabbed the remote and leaned back in the armchair. A prison cell appeared on the screen – having looked closer, Dags discerned a man sleeping on a plank bed. The man was sleeping with his back to the camera, yet Dags recognized him by his clothes. That's the guy who was telling them stories about gold digging yesterday.

'Now,' Yana said.

At first Dags thought that the guy simply stirred. A second later, he realized that wasn't the case. His clothes suddenly went soft; one of his shoes fell to the floor. Everything happened so quickly that Dags didn't even notice the moment of his disappearance. Just a second ago there was a man, and now he was no more – just his clothes lying on the plank bed.

Having rewound the tape a little, Dags watched the searcher's escape one more time. It was a searcher alright; there was no doubt about that now.

'That's that,' Yana said. 'I was right.'

'Then why didn't you have your way?' Dags growled out. The

feeling that some punk had fooled him was unbearable.

'I can't argue with the Sovereign,' Yana replied. Then she added: 'I'm joking. He was lying so well that I believed him. I decided that we really did have the wrong guy.'

'Did you find out who he is?' Dags nodded at the screen.

'Not yet. The guys lifted his fingerprints off the tap; they're checking them just now.'

'And what if we work on the helicopter pilot?' Dags suggested. 'There's nothing stopping us now.'

'There's no point,' Yana shook her head. 'He's just a carrier. He's been working there for fifteen years; they know him well. He doesn't say no to a little money on the side. But that's it.'

'But someone did make a deal with him.' Dags didn't agree. 'Let him name that person.'

'Sovereign, you know very well that it's futile. It's all so obvious that the searchers have no doubt taken care of their safety. Best case scenario, we find a middleman who doesn't know anything.'

'And what do you suggest?' Dags asked.

'Nothing. We'll keep on working. Sooner or later we'll get them again. I'll leave the tape with you.' Yana got up from the armchair. 'For your collection. May I leave?'

'Go,' Dags said tiredly. 'And tell them not to let anyone in for five minutes.'

'Certainly. Good bye, Sovereign.'

Yana exited. Dags was left alone. Having taken the remote, he watched the tape again. Then, irritated, he threw the remote on the table and ran his hand down his face. He leaned back in the armchair.

'Sometimes I really feel like killing someone,' Dags tiredly sighed and stretched his hand towards the visitor list. 'And who's the lucky one?'

He was dreaming – a strange dream. Maxim was in Rada's room, looking at the young woman with a smile. She was telling him something, while holding his hands, but Maxim couldn't hear her for some reason. The air in the room had a strange yellowish tint; it appeared to be sticky and syrupy. The air was absorbing Rada's words. Again, Rada said something to him, thoroughly pronouncing the words; Maxim took a closer look at her lips. His vision went blurry then it turned to normal again.

'... hold on to me and wake up...' He heard a fragment of a sentence. 'Look at me... Come on!'

Maxim smiled, thinking that it looked very much like a lucid dream. That was enough for his consciousness to prevail.

'Rada!' Maxim exhaled. 'You can't imagine how happy I am to see you!'

'Later!' Rada cut him off. 'Squeeze my hands. Harder!'

Only now did Maxim notice that Rada was holding his hands. Not obeying Rada was impossible; Maxim pressed his fingers together. Now he was also aware of the fact that he was in Rada's room; his gaze caught the familiar potted plants.

'Now wake up, maintaining the scene of the room!' Rada commanded, the tone of her voice did not allow for objections. 'Come on!'

Waking up wasn't that easy. For a few seconds Maxim experienced the feeling of horrifying helplessness. He felt he was balancing on the edge of a knife, on the sharp verge of something unknown. He squeezed his hands harder, saw Rada's eyes in front of him – and woke up.

There was a sad slow ringing in his ears. For a moment Maxim thought that he was just about to faint, but he did not fall, having caught on to Rada's arms.

'He's here!' Rada yelled; the door immediately opened. Maxim turned his head and saw Iris. Boris came in after her.

'Hi!' Maxim wanted to say, but his lips weren't listening to him.

'Faster!' Rada said. Maxim felt them pick him up and drag him somewhere. Ah, that's the bathroom. And a bathtub full of water.

The water turned out to be terribly cold. Maxim thought it unfair – yesterday he was swimming in ice cold water and now again. He tried to get out of the bathtub.

'Sit and don't you move!' Iris said sternly and dipped him with his head underwater.

'Don't drown him now,' Boris grinned; he was standing nearby. 'And you know what, get out of here. You shouldn't be staring at a naked man.'

'You mean the blue skeleton over there?' Iris specified. 'All right, I'll leave it in your care. And make sure it doesn't get flushed down the drain.'

Maxim was listening to Iris and smiling. She's mean, but kind.

He sat in the cold water not less than a quarter of an hour. Then Boris helped him get out of the tub. Maxim dried himself with a towel and dressed into the clothes they had prepared for him. They put a blanket over him and led him into the bedroom. His bedroom – Maxim sighed with relief once he saw the familiar bed. He already knew what exactly happened, but his thoughts still stirred very reluctantly. So Maxim just took what happened into consideration, knowing that he'd have time to think it all through.

'Get some sleep, warrior.' Boris clapped him on the shoulder and left the room.

Once awake, Maxim lay in bed for a while, thinking about how strange all of this was. He brought his arm up to his face, wanting to know the time – and realized that his arm watch was gone. The last year he only took it off two or three times. Where did he leave it now?

However, his watch was the last thing on his mind. Maxim sat up on the bed and there was a painful stitch in his side. He winched, rolled up the t-shirt – a huge bruise. That's right, that's his pal Vanya's efforts. His leg hurt too, to his surprise Maxim noticed that the wounded place – where the bullets sliced his leg

– was taped over with band-aid. He touched it with his finger – it felt soft to the touch. By the looks of it – it was a piece of bandage, impregnated with some kind of ointment.

He dressed with difficulty and then went to the bathroom to wash his face. He looked in the mirror – a face of a bearded savage with long tangled hair saluted him. He could use a shave, but he had no tools. Besides, first he'd have to do some serious work with the scissors.

Maxim decided to leave shaving and hairdressing for later. Having quickly washed his face, he went downstairs.

The first one to see him was Galina – in an apron, cheerful and flushed.

'Hello, Maxim dear!' she said. 'Go through to the kitchen, everyone is already there.'

'Good day, Galina. Thank you.'

Maxim's appearance in the kitchen – or rather in the dining room next to it – was greeted with a loud round of applause and laughter. Almost everyone was gathered here – on the left side, sitting with their backs to the windows, were Boris, Rada, Iris and Danila. Oxana, Denis, Roman and Igor had made themselves comfortable to the right of the table.

'Salute, Maxim!' Igor greeted him, flashing his dazzling white teeth. 'They say you've burned down my house?'

This statement was greeted with even more laughter.

'Hello, everyone!' Maxim raised his hands peacefully. 'And as for the cabin, I think it really is gone.'

'Yeah, that's for sure,' Iris grinned. 'You cannot be trusted with any property.'

'And you've gotten all hairy too,' Roman said, looking at Maxim with a grin. 'Put you in a cloak, and you'll look like a real monk.'

'I'll get a haircut after lunch,' Maxim answered. 'I just haven't had time yet.'

'Take a seat, Maxim.' Boris pointed at the honorary place at the centre of the table. 'Let's celebrate your return.'

'Thanks.' Maxim took a seat, then winced again from the pain in his side.

'How about some cognac?' Iris asked compassionately; everyone burst out laughing again. It occurred to Maxim that they knew everything already.

'Anything but cognac,' he said. 'I'd rather have some beer.'

Perhaps, only now was he able to glance at Oxana. His eyes met hers – the young woman lowered her gaze in embarrassment.

'No beer,' Roman replied. 'Only medovukha[9] – the drink of gods. Your cognac stands no chance.'

Only now did Maxim realize that the honey-colored liquid in two big plastic bottles was medovukha.

After the first toast – to his return – they demanded that Maxim tell them all about his adventures.

'I'll tell you,' Maxim nodded. 'But first, how did you find out about it?'

'Oh, it was very easy,' Boris replied. 'I took an hour's nap yesterday at noon, and decided to pay you a visit in the meantime, to see how you were getting ready for the departure. I just tuned into you, and immediately I was attacked by a guardian. Woke up, and realized that you were in trouble, called Rada. We couldn't reach you for five hours, every time there were these creatures next to you. Then they disappeared – you were on an airplane, and some guy was feeding you brand cognac. While you were in the air, we were almost always next to you – me or Rada. Well, and as soon as you wound up in the cell and fell asleep, we immediately dragged you out of there. By the way, you've gotten much stronger. A year ago, you wouldn't have made it through this trick.'

'By the way, what Legionaries were with you?' Iris inquired. 'Who did those guardians belong to?'

'You don't know that?' Maxim asked, already realizing that any moment now he'll become the author of a small sensation.

'Maxim, we couldn't see him.' Rada was looking at Maxim with a soft smile. 'The guardians were watching all approaches. We simply couldn't surface to have a look around and see what's what.'

'It was Dags,' Maxim said, and in the same instant silence fell over the table. 'And Yana was there too. They didn't recognize me.'

'Well, I'll be damned,' Danila muttered. 'And are you sure that it was Dags?'

'Absolutely sure,' Maxim answered, convinced. 'They called him Sovereign. You think that changes anything?'

'It changes everything,' Rada replied very quietly.

Chapter Five

The Return

Yana wasn't too worried about the searcher's escape. It wasn't her fault that he ran away, so there can't be any complaints from Dags. Further still, Yana hoped to turn the situation to her advantage. Surely now the searchers will find out who Dags is in real life, and that meant that they will definitely try to get to him. Yana had nothing against it. Sly had already helped her career growth once, let him do it again.

Information about the escaped searcher arrived the next day. Having read the expert's report, Yana only grinned – well, what do you know! Who would have thought that the searcher and that youngster on the bus are one and the same person? And it's only been some two years.

Yana sighed; sadness once again stirred in her heart. It seemed she had it all – money, power. But there was no joy in her heart. The joy was left there, in the early nineties. They were so very young back then, her, Dana and Rada – three inseparable girlfriends, three young rollicking witches. The whole world was ready to fall before their feet – and this is what came out of it. Why, how did it happen? Where did the joy, where did the happiness go? Because she was happy once, she was. Everything was different then – the sky was bluer, people were better – not like the morons that surrounded her now. Back then it seemed that only the best lay ahead of her.

And then everything turned upside down. And it didn't start with the Legion – no, it began much earlier. It started with the discovery that Rada and Dana turned out to be much more talented than her. Many of the things that came easily to them came with great difficulty to Yana. She was always behind, always playing the second fiddle. She wasn't the one explaining the way things were – people explained things to her. Did she envy? Yes. Envy gnawed on her heart. Yana sensed that she'd never catch up with her more talented girlfriends. Time passed and her envy gradually developed into hate. And when the searchers ran into the Legion, Yana already knew what to do.

She was very well received, and she didn't come empty handed – she gave the Legionaries everything she managed to learn during those years. She handed in everyone and everything, with names and addresses. And what did that moron Kramer do? He ruined it all like the dullard he was.

Now it was all in the past. There was no way back; Yana knew that very well. She tried not to think about the past, tried to forget, etch out the disturbing memories out of her head. She even burned all the photographs reminding her of that former life. She did all she could, but now and then, from the depths of her heart, burst through a longing for something that had been lost.

Maxim's reporting that he saw Dags caused a real commotion. Maxim experienced a restrained feeling of joy – perhaps, for the very first time he was at least of some use. When everyone calmed down a little, Maxim was asked about how he ended up with the Legionaries. And so he had to tell them, although Maxim decided to leave out several details that he thought to be irrelevant – things like when he was being shot at or like how he almost drowned in the river. The searchers listened carefully; Boris was the only one to give the occasional ghost of a smile.

Right after breakfast Maxim retired with Oxana to her studio. There was a reason for that – Oxana had to sketch Dags's portrait following Maxim's descriptions. Maxim was happy to have the opportunity to spend some time alone with Oxana.

Once in the studio, Maxim saw a copy of the famous portrait of Joconde, which was not finished yet. Hanging next to it were several reproductions of famous masterpieces.

'Wow!' he said, examining Oxana's work with interest. 'Looks like you're into copies now?'

'Oh, that?' Oxana glanced at the painting with a smile. 'It's nothing, a pot-boiler. I was asked to paint it for a private collection. I couldn't refuse, besides it was kind of interesting for me too.'

'I see. I wanted to ask you – did you guys all gather here just because of me?' Maxim glanced at the young woman with curiosity.

'You think too highly of yourself,' Oxana replied mockingly, retrieving a sketchbook and pencils. 'Yesterday we were celebrating Rada's birthday, that's why we're all here. People just hadn't had time to leave yet.'

Maxim laughed. 'That really does explain everything,' he said. 'Because I was kind of surprised – why the honors? Oh yeah, I almost forgot – how are my plants?'

'Nothing happened to your plants. By the way, it's nice to see you. Sit down; let's sketch.'

Making Dags's portrait took more than an hour. Maxim was happy with the result; the portrait came out quite good.

'That's him,' Maxim said, having evaluated the sketch. 'Like a live one. Only the real one had colder eyes.'

'Don't be such a critic,' Oxana grumbled. 'Come on, we'll show the others.'

The searchers were waiting for them; everyone hushed when Maxim walked into the room.

'Here,' Maxim said, handing the portrait over to Boris. 'Oxana did a good job.'

Oxana, who came in after him, only shrugged her shoulders.

'I don't know him,' Boris said, having glanced at the portrait. Then he passed it along. 'Take a look.'

No one knew this man.

'The portrait looks like him?' Boris inquired when the drawing once again appeared in his hands.

'On the dot. The original's got a firmer and colder gaze. Even when he's smiling, his eyes still remain cold.'

'We need to scan this and send it to the St. Petersburg and Moscow folk,' Iris said. 'Perhaps they'll come up with something.'

'I'm on it.' Rada rose from the chair, took the portrait and exited the dining room.

Around noon people gradually started to depart. The first one to start packing was Igor, having previously mentioned that he'd got a train ticket, and that he had to be in Novosibirsk by evening. Shortly before his departure, he snatched a moment and beckoned Maxim over.

'Well, how was the wintering?' Igor asked with a grin on his face. 'Did you enjoy it?'

'Yes, I did,' Maxim answered. 'It did me good. A lot of good.'

'It shows,' Igor said, and there wasn't a shadow of mockery in his voice. 'Boris is right, you've become much stronger. Besides, you're much more open now; your shields have collapsed. And what's important for you now is not to create them again. The last events encouraged you to do that very thing. Don't withdraw into yourself; accept the world as it is. Don't react to people's attacks with bitterness. Just keep in mind that people will always be people, that they are not perfect. Forgive them their imperfections, don't take them seriously. You know what I mean?'

'I do,' Maxim nodded.

'That's good, Maxim. Don't let people shield the world's beauty from you, and everything will be fine. The world is always on the side of those who understand it.'

Igor left. Iris and Danila went home with him – up to Novosibirsk their journeys were the same. Roman volunteered to give them a lift to the bus stop. They didn't ask Maxim to come along, and Maxim was perfectly aware of the reason why. They just all thought that he'd go to Rostov with Oxana, and she was planning on staying a couple more days. Rada was teaching her some dream techniques. Besides, Maxim was still too weak to hit the road.

Denis also had things to do, so very soon Maxim was left with Boris, Rada and Oxana. Boris and Rada were sitting in the dining room, engaged in a discussion. Oxana went up to her studio – she had some work to do. After a momentary hesitation, Maxim, having made up his mind, followed Oxana upstairs.

'It's me,' he said, walking into Oxana's studio. 'I wanted to ask you something. Or rather, tell you something…' Maxim faltered, not knowing where to begin. Oxana glanced at him.

'What is it?' she asked with a smile.

'Marry me,' Maxim suggested. 'I really like you.'

'Are you serious?' Oxana stopped smiling, her cheeks blushed.

'Yes.'

Oxana lowered her gaze and turned to the painting standing on the easel. For some time she was silent, looking at the smiling Joconde then she glanced back at Maxim.

'Maxim, I like you – honest. But I haven't thought about marriage yet. It's all too sudden for me.'

'Well, think about it then,' Maxim suggested.

'No, Maxim.' Oxana shook her head. 'I'm not ready for that yet. I'm sorry, I've got to work. Don't be offended.'

'Fine. I'm not offended. Sorry to bother you.' Maxim left the studio and very carefully closed the door – he was afraid that he'd slam it with all his might, being so overcome with emotions. Having gone down the hall, he went outside to the balcony and stood there for a while, coming to his senses.

Calming down was difficult. He had never before told anyone he loved them. And he had never been rejected. In one instant, the world so bright and sunny turned into a dull and gloomy place. Who needs the world if there's no love in it?

He tried not to look at Oxana during lunch; she too averted her gaze. That probably didn't go unnoticed by the others, as after lunch Boris asked him to his room.

'Did you have an argument with Oxana?' Boris inquired,

looking at Maxim with a soft smile.

'A small one,' Maxim replied. He didn't want to talk about it. But Boris obviously had a different idea.

'Don't be angry with her,' he said. 'When it comes down to it, the greatest mystery of the world – is a woman's heart. You feel cheated – don't argue, I see it. But think about it, which is greater in you right now – your love for Oxana or the jealousy, resentment and annoyance that you feel because she said no?'

'You speak like a psychoanalyst.' Maxim involuntarily grinned, realizing that Boris knew everything already.

'I just know a few things about people. Now I see that you are upset, even though you try to hide your emotions. But try assessing the situation differently. Your expectations were not fulfilled – and why? Isn't that because you've been cherishing hopes, making plans? You forgot the most important thing – that a magician doesn't have a destiny of his own.'

'But even Castaneda said that magicians shape their destiny themselves?' Maxim disagreed.

'That is also true,' Boris nodded. 'But in this case we're dealing with one of the contradictions in magic. On the surface, one thing excludes the other, but a situation is easily resolved on a more abstract level. The main principle is this – the more you try to take upon yourself, the less is allowed, the less you're given. And the other way around; having rejected control, you get everything. See the point? Reject yourself – your identity, the constant attempts of your mind to put itself in the centre of the world. And then the world will automatically go towards you. Trying to organize your destiny, telling yourself "this will be this way, and that will be that way," you get the direct opposite effect. You already considered Oxana your property and the whole of last year you probably spent waiting to meet her again. Thinking about how well you guys will do – isn't that right?'

Maxim was silent. Indeed, that's how it was.

'The world opposes expectations, Maxim,' Boris continued.

'Trying to control the situation, you get the direct opposite effect. In the life of a magician that's even more pronounced – only because his connection to the world is especially solid. That's why a magician's mistakes have even worse consequences than the mistakes of an ordinary person. You could say that the system is much more sensitive when it comes to magicians. And the only way out – is the total rejection of control. Entrust your destiny to the Spirit, give yourself up. All of us usually have plans, hopes, aspirations – and that's our ruin. Remember, believers entrust their destiny to God. The magician does the same; the difference is only in the terminology. Give yourself up; imagine that you are dead, that your struggle with life has been hopelessly lost. You are defeated; all your dreams and aspiration will never come true. Tell yourself that you are completely bankrupt, and admit to it, come to terms with it. Having realized that everything is lost, you will get a new outlook on the world.'

'But a person cannot live without hope, without aspiration,' Maxim objected. 'If the soul is empty, then what's the point of such a life?'

'It's not empty.' Boris shook his head. 'It's free. Free from foolishness common to man, free from all of that garbage that from our very birth keeps accumulating in our heads. Think about how firmly programmed our behavior is; the path of practically any human being could be squeezed into a rather primitive scheme. Namely: you were born, you studied, worked, created a family, raised children, got old and died. That's the whole scheme for you. It could have small variations, but the idea is pretty much the same – we lead a fast life in pursuit of money, success, wellbeing. Some people understand that all of these things are illusory goals, and they look for new ones: children, family, love. But that too is but an attempt to justify your failure, an attempt to silence the longing in your heart – a longing for something that has been lost. Man clutches at any straw, only to justify his existence, to prove to himself that he didn't spend his life in vain.

Someone boasts with scientific discoveries, someone – with achievements in art and sports. Someone else is proud of his children. There are many straws, but they still remain straws. Magicians do it differently – instead of going through straw by straw, trying to find comfort, they simply chuck out the whole haycock. As a result the magician is left one on one with the universe. It's as if he's saying: "Here I am, Lord! Forever and ever I entrust my fate into Your hands." You see?'

'Not really,' Maxim admitted. 'How can you give up love? Because of the craving for the beautiful? I only just learned to sense the beauty of the world, and now you suggest I give it all up?'

'You don't understand.' Boris shook his head. 'It's not about giving up; it's about changing your attitude to all of these things. While you're holding on to something, you are not free. But if you renounce yourself, you'll be able to get everything you gave up. Do you understand? While you're fighting for something, while you're trying to get something, the world counteracts your strivings. But should you only give it all up; the world will meet you half way. The things that you've been fighting for so long and so hard will fall into your lap. Recall the scripture: "God opposes the proud but gives grace to the humble."[10] That's the same thing; the difference is only in the terminology used. Renounce yourself; give God, or the universal power that rules the world, the right to be in charge of your destiny, and you'll see how the world around you will start changing.'

'I always thought that God and magic were incompatible,' Maxim grinned. 'As far as I know, the church has at all times labeled magicians and wizards of all kinds as people who have sold their souls to the devil – isn't that right?'

'It's just that servants of the church know almost nothing about true magic. Similarly, many magicians – or those who consider themselves as such – know little about church. You cannot measure everyone by the same ruler – magicians vary, and religions differ. But any true system inevitably brings man to God. It's only a matter of who you consider God. To me God is the Spirit, the power ruling the universe. It's that elusive thing that is behind everything that happens in this world, that rushes this world to development. God – I will use this particular term – is the only true player; he is the one to decide how and what will come to pass. If a person understands that and entrusts his fate to God, God sends him to the happy paths of life. If, however, man resists, trying to do what his stupid selfness tells him to, then he will get the appropriate result. People are strange beings, Maxim. At first they do everything their way – the way they think is right. And then they damn God because nothing comes out of it.'

'Sounds reasonable,' Maxim smiled.

'Of course it does.' Boris smiled too. 'The problem is that the simplest truths are the ones that are most difficult to grasp. We can understand them with our mind, but they will only start working once they pass through your heart and become a part of you. Try to grasp everything we've talked about and you'll see how simple and wonderful your life will become. Give yourself into God's hands, feel His power behind your back. Stop planning your life, your actions, the way you are doing now. Leave that all up to God.'

'How's that?' Maxim didn't understand. 'I don't think God will do my job for me.'

'He won't,' Boris agreed. 'I'm talking about the right to choose. When you are the one making the choice, it is usually worse than the one that God was ready to offer you. And in order to see the right alternative, you just need to pay attention. Watch the events that happen around you; listen to your heart. No doubt, at first you'll make a lot of mistakes, but gradually you'll learn to perceive God's wishes. Then – and only then – will the world of magic really open to you.'

Maxim softly laughed.

'Why are you laughing?' Boris inquired with a smile.

'Oh… nothing.' Maxim waved it away.

Apparently, Boris decided that Maxim didn't understand him.

'Understand, Maxim,' Boris continued with a smile. 'Everything I tell you is absolutely real. You won't become a magician until you grasp all of these truths. It's difficult and painful, I understand. But there is no other way. In order for the magician to be born, the man must die, because a magician is a man wielding power. But think about it; can God entrust power to man who's as mad as a box of frogs? Who, having gotten hold of this power, immediately starts using it at his discretion? First he'll hound to death the neighbor he dislikes, then he'll think of something else. A magician like that is even more dangerous than a woman at the wheel. That's why everything is being written down in every detail up there, and skills come to a magician when he's ready.'

'Yes, I understand,' Maxim said thoughtfully. 'But as you said, I understand it with my mind. I need to think all of this through.'

'You do that,' Boris agreed. 'By the way, I'd really recommend you to talk to Rada about God – I'm sure her opinion on these matters will be of interest to you. As for Oxana, simply leave her to herself. Don't blame her; don't resent her. But don't avoid her on purpose either – know what I mean? Just be a friend to her. If she comes back to you – take it as a matter of course. If not – wish her happiness with her future partner. That would be the stand of a man.'

'I agree,' Maxim sighed. Then he smiled awkwardly. 'That's what I wanted to do.'

'Then we have an understanding,' Boris said and rose from the chair. 'And now, if you don't mind, I have to write a few letters.'

Maxim managed to have a chat with Rada the following evening. Having found out that Maxim wanted to talk to her, Rada invited him up to her room right after supper.

'So?' she asked, when Maxim had made himself comfortable in

the armchair. 'Anything wrong with your lucid dreaming?'

'No.' Maxim shook his head. 'I wanted to ask you something else. Yesterday, Boris and I had a little chat about God, about the mutual relationship between the magician and the universe. Today I've spent the whole day thinking about it, and I have some questions. Tell me; don't you think that we're going down the wrong path? Look what happens: our path in many ways is based on the tradition of Carlos Castaneda. But you can judge whether a tradition is good or not by its founders. As far as I know, Castaneda died not long ago. And he died of cancer – and they say that cancer is a product of disturbance of harmony in the relationship between a person and the universe. Again, most dreamers face illnesses of the body. And what else could that be than a product of disturbed harmony? Now let's take the searchers – it's not a secret that most of you have faced a hard response from the real world to your manipulations. That was manifested both as illnesses, and as a train of big and small trouble. On top of everything you've got the war with the Legion, a heap of other problems. So I am seriously beginning to experience doubts – perhaps the searcher approach is, when it comes to some things, wrong? And if the real world takes vengeance on the searchers, then it perceives them to be enemies? After all, the searchers even got the corresponding terminology – break in, enter…'

'I see what you mean,' Rada smiled. 'You've touched upon a very important topic. And you are absolutely right in that the relationship between a magician and the world must be harmonious. But what do we mean by harmony in this case?' Rada paused and looked closely at Maxim. 'First, I'd like to tell you a story. My parents didn't believe in God, but I still got baptized because my grandmother insisted. That didn't have any effect on me, and when I came to magic, there couldn't even be any talk of God. Back then I only started to have lucid dreams and almost immediately I ran into the vigorous attack of the inorganics. They were literally after me – I had only to fall asleep and at the same moment I'd be under attack. It was very scary. It got to the point where I was simply afraid of going to sleep. My mom even took me to the doctors; they gave me some kind of tranquilizers. The pills didn't do any good, I still couldn't sleep. We told my grandmother about it, and she grabbed my arm and dragged me to church. I was afraid of the church; its walls pressed down on me. My grandmother brought me before the icon of Virgin Mary, took out the prayer book and made me say the prayer a couple of times. I confused the words, made mistakes – but I kept on reading. Then we went back home and for the first time in weeks I fell asleep without anyone bothering me. After that I started going to church almost every day; the inorganics left me in peace altogether. I no longer feared the church, I felt joy; I was at peace. That's when it first occurred to me that people who believe in God are not that stupid after all; that their faith has some kind of a rational foundation. Gradually, I returned to lucid dreaming – at first I was afraid to have lucid dreams, but then I met mother Anastasia in a dream, she became my tutor. She was the one to actually bring me to God. She talked to me, told me how I should live in this world. At first I didn't trust her; I feared her so called prelest[11] – I was afraid that behind the image of mother Anastasia dwelled demonic powers. Then I believed her, since then I see her quite often.'

'And what does she tell you?' Maxim couldn't refrain from asking.

'A lot of things,' Rada smiled. 'We think ourselves to be free, but the only freedom for man, according to mother Anastasia, is the opportunity to choose between God and the devil. I'm very sad to say, but most magicians choose the devil. I am not saying that they do it advisedly – they are just mistaken. The greatest lie – is a lie spiced with truth. Where there is no God, His place is already taken by the devil. Man is seduced by promises of freedom, search for the unknown, but what does actually come out of it? Lives are destroyed, you lose God. And to lose God means to sell your soul to the devil. That's why I dare to claim that magic in its traditional sense – that is, without God – is a very bad thing. And I am happy that you've sensed that.'

'Fine, but why didn't you tell me about it earlier?'

'Well, first of all, everyone's got a free will and must choose his own path. Again, it's one thing, when you're led to God by the hand. And it's something else entirely, when you come to Him by the commands of your soul, when you feel that this is what you need. And as you know, experience is worth it. Second of all, there's another problem: a lot of people try to avoid everything that's got to do with God. Someone will call it social conditioning, costs of godless decades. Someone will say that it's the influence of demonic powers. You could explain it differently, but the fact remains, until now, believing in God was simply not in fashion; the mention of God pushed people away. That was especially true for young people. That's why I prefer talking just about the techniques of magic, leaving the rest to the person.'

'But isn't magic a heresy, even from the point of view of that very same orthodoxy?'

'It is,' Rada agreed. 'However, you first need to understand why you need magic, why you need magic skills. To get power, wealth? But what do power and money mean on the background of inevitable death? To maintain your consciousness after death? A worthy goal – in essence, the only goal that is worthwhile. Yet, the catch is that you cannot solve this problem by pressing forward. The same magic principle is at work here: the more you want something, the less are the chances of you getting it. And the other way around, by not wanting anything, you get a chance of getting everything. Correspondingly, being oriented at getting specific practical results inevitably leads a magician up a blind alley. That's why dream searchers change priorities – they are interested in knowledge as such, in the beauty of it. The same Boris, having unearthed something interesting, will jump with

joy, like a child. His soul is pure; the knowledge draws him, and
not the practical advantages it can give. And if it later turns out
that knowledge also gives some kind of skills, then all of these
skills become a sort of side effect, a consequence of going down
the right path. Appreciate it, Maxim: he, who chases skills, usually
never gets them. The searchers, on the other hand, simply study
the universe – without selfness, without thoughts about having.
And that goes for everything else – it's one of the main principles.
You've got to be pure – spiritually, morally. But what does this
purity mean? To be pure is not only about not doing evil deeds. It
means to experience any influences, without fixating on them. An
analogy – a lens and a laser beam passing through it; if the lens is
clean, it could pass even a very powerful beam without getting
damaged. But if it has even the tiniest little bubble, even a speck,
the lens will overheat and burst. Accordingly, a magician must be
absolutely pure – without stupid ideas, stupid selfness. He
shouldn't have anything that could lead to "overheating" and
destruction. A true magician is an element of a chain. If he is just
accumulating power and knowledge within himself, then a
similar overheating and destruction takes places. So that doesn't
happen, a magician must share his knowledge, transfer it to his
followers. He transferred some – he got some new knowledge. A
generous man will prosper – that's the law. It's the same with God:
a magician hands himself into the power of God, he admits to a
power of a higher hierarchy over him. Consequently, he also gets
the ability to command. While you are a medium, everything is
fine. Once you start withdrawing into yourself – you'll cork up
and burn down. That's why the path of knowledge is strewn with
the bones of those seeking. They forgot about God, having put
themselves on top of the pyramid, as a result they lost everything.
That's why I dare to claim that the only right way is walking with
God. Give up your selfness; give God your will and spirit. The
words of the prayer say exactly that: "Into Your hands I commend
my spirit; not my will be done, but Yours." God created this

world; He is the one that rushes it to develop. If you are with God, you are too a part of this work, you are actually making this world better. But there's a catch.' Rada looked into Maxim's eyes and smiled. 'Will the world meet you halfway in response?'

'It must,' Maxim shrugged. 'Otherwise, it doesn't make any sense.'

'Logic and magic are not really compatible,' Rada answered. 'Look what happens: you are kind of doing everything right, in the end you expect to get rewarded. And when you don't get what you expected, you feel cheated. That's the typical mind of a hired worker – having done something; he expects the lawful reward for his efforts. However, as applied to magic this mindset is completely inappropriate. Why? Because there are completely different laws and principles at work in magic and in religion too for that matter. And all those difficulties, illnesses and problems you mentioned in the beginning of our talk, are natural attributes of the right path – at least at some stage. It so happens that the right path is paved with thorns, and not with rose petals. In Christianity, they even say that if you have many problems and sorrows that means that God remembers you. But that is a shallow view of the problem. So let's try sorting it out.' Rada fell quiet, looking at Maxim with a faint smile. 'Let's depart from facts,' she suggested after a pause. 'So, a person starts studying magic, as a result, some time later, he suddenly faces a wall of problems. He sees with his own eyes that the world is up in arms against him, that things start going really bad. That causes surprise and indignation; the man doesn't understand. Where did it all come from? How did he provoke the wrath of heavens? By going somewhere he shouldn't have? Some people think that, and that's why they simply retreat. But if you'd leave emotions aside and look at the facts, then you could make a very important conclusion: the growth of our consciousness inevitably brings about a counteraction from certain powers. That is, while we remain like everyone else, everything is great. But should we only get out of the unanimous row of average men preoccupied with themselves, we immediately get hit on the head. And analyzing facts and circumstances allows us to make yet another important conclusion: fighting against us, is not the world but something else. And our relationship with nature, with the animal world has actually become very harmonious. Remember me talking to a sparrow in the park?'

'I do,' Maxim nodded. 'That was really amazing.'

Rada was speaking of something that happened a couple of weeks after Maxim first got to know her – that one time he, Rada and Oxana went to the park. They walked around and talked. At some point Rada stepped aside, stretched out her arm and at the same moment a sparrow landed on her palm. Rada carefully petted him, and the sparrow didn't make any attempt to fly away. It took wing only when Rada herself gently tossed him up in the air. To Oxana's question about how she did it, Rada gave but a mysterious smile. Then, when Oxana started insisting on an explanation, she explained that she is simply friends with this world. She doesn't disturb animals, they don't disturb her, and on the whole there is a complete mutual understanding reigning between them. Maxim accepted this explanation as granted; Oxana, however, declared that that sparrow simply knew Rada, that she had tamed it earlier. Rada didn't convince her otherwise.

'That sparrow was an excellent example of a harmonious relationship with the world,' Rada continued. 'It wasn't afraid of me, because it knew that I wouldn't harm it. It's like with Mowgli: "We be of one blood, you and I". The relationship of a magician with the world is so harmonious that the world doesn't perceive him as an enemy. Rather, the opposite, the world warns the magician in time of danger. Remember the Bible – before the Fall, the relationship between man and the world was very harmonious, but then everything collapsed. Magicians strive towards this harmony; they strive to return to the relationship that existed before the Fall. But let's ask ourselves a question: what is the Fall?

According to the Bible, Adam and Eve tasted an apple from the Tree of Knowledge. Consequently, they learned how to tell good from evil. I see in these lines a veiled description of the emergence of the flyers. It is said that ancient magicians picked up the flyers in their travels in the unknown by accident. They tried to cognize the unknown; as a result they accidentally picked up a bug. On the whole it's not that important where the flyers came from; what's more important is that being a predatory energy form of life, the flyers enslaved man, having established full control over him. Castaneda spoke of the flyers breeding people in human farms, like we're breeding chickens in hen-houses. Feeding on our energy, the flyers are not interested in the growth of our consciousness. Accordingly, they are actively counteracting any attempts of anyone freeing himself of their power. The devil of it is that the flyers have a good knowledge of the subtle mechanisms of the universe. With that knowledge, they are capable of controlling the chain of events, and hence the course of our life. The main part of the misfortunes a magician faces is explained by the counteraction of the flyers.'

'The main part – but not all of it?' Maxim inquired.

'Not all of it. Some part of it can be ascribed to the basic ignorance of the magicians themselves. It's just that the structure of the universe is a very complex one, and a magician must know that thoughtless actions may lead to very grievous consequences. That is, it's a question of observing the basic safety rules. It's all like in life – don't grab a bare wire, don't throw yourself under a car, don't play with fire. And if you were foolish enough to get under a car, then you can hardly blame anyone else. That's why the actions of a magician must be well considered; he must know exactly what it is he's doing. But the flyers still represent the main danger.'

'Boris said something about that the magicians' flyers and demons in Christianity are the same thing. Do you agree?'

'Yes. Demons are the lowest level of the flyers, but there is also the devil, a creature of a higher hierarchy. The devil usually appears where demons prove powerless. Although, in any case, it's just a way of saying – an attempt to describe something that's very hard, if not impossible, to describe adequately.'

'All right, perhaps you could tell me more about the flyers' influence on us? Where does it show – specifically, in practice?'

'It shows in everything,' Rada softly smiled. 'The thing is that man by his nature is a vessel. We have no ideas of our own; they come from without. And not just from without, but either from God, or from Satan. The human mind could be likened to a computer – a computer cannot think on its own, it works only with the data you put into it. And information can be divided into truthful, divine, and false, coming from Satan. The problem is that the human mind is damaged, so it cannot tell the lies from the truth. You could say that our computer is infected with viruses. As applied to our mind this results in control over it on the flyers' part. Our mind does not really belong to us – a computer infected with viruses cannot work properly. So our highest priority task is to get rid of these viruses, get rid of their influence on our mind.'

'Sounds rather controversial,' Maxim responded doubtingly. 'You can usually tell if there's a computer virus. And if my mind is infected with viruses, then I should be able to sense that – isn't that so?'

'You cannot feel it.' Rada shook her head. 'How can you analyze anything, if the analyzing apparatus is damaged? That's the whole point. God must reside in the heart of man, but the devil is the one to dwell there. So he simply doesn't give you an opportunity to see the way things really are.'

'Okay, but why can't God reside in the heart of man?' Maxim inquired. 'After all, initially God is stronger than the devil.'

'Because God is first of all about freedom – freedom to choose, freedom to love. In order for God to do anything for man, man must first turn to God. Again, God is Purity; he is the Truth. And while evil lives in our heart, God will never enter it.

Correspondingly, firstly we must clean all the dirt from our heart. God will help us do that, but it must be our initiative.'

'And what does that mean – specifically, in practice?'

'It means,' Rada answered, 'that we must ask God forgiveness. We must ask Him to forgive our sins, our ignorance, our foolishness. We must ask Him to bring us to reason, to teach us, to set us on the right path. If there's even a drop of sincerity in your soul, if you truly stand before God with a heart full of regret, He will definitely help you. Your mind will gradually become free of demons; it's like taking the curtains off – suddenly you see that the truth is not at all what you thought it to be just a moment ago. A spiritual vision opens in you; you clearly see all of the tricks demons do in their attempt to get you off the track. And you become horrified when you realize what swamp you have been living in. The flyers were ordering you about, like a slow-witted child, and you didn't notice. What you thought were your thoughts and ideas were theirs. And only once you have addressed God, once you have repented before Him and asked for His aid, you'll see the true picture. And that goes not only for magicians but for all people in general.'

'And you can achieve that just by praying?' Maxim asked. 'Surely there must be other ways?'

'You can always reach your goal by different means,' Rada smiled. 'The problem is that we are too weak to walk alone. If you try to get rid of the flyers without God's help, as most magicians do, you will no doubt end up in some trap. There's no doubt about that. Do you understand? Because the devil's mind is immeasurably more skilled than ours. That's why monks don't trust themselves, relying completely on God. And still, even they, having dedicated their life to God, now and then get into the traps set up by the devil. That is "spiritual delusion" that's well described in orthodoxy. The difficulty is that while the heart of a man is not completely clean, he can only see the crudest demonic devices. And in order not to get into more cunning traps, a monk must, firstly, completely entrust himself to God, and secondly, observe certain recommendations, the instructions of those who have already been through it. With time he acquires the ability to see even the most refined cunning of the demons. He obtains true spiritual vision; he obtains the ability to tell good from evil. On this particular stage, after getting rid of the demons' influence – and in another syntax, from alien inputs into our mind, implants – real skills come to the magician. You could say that these skills are gifted to man by God. God can do that now, because man is pure, because he's got the spiritual vision and will never use the gifted skills to do evil. Accordingly, your number one priority must always be spiritual perfectionism, and only then – everything else. And now compare this to the traditional approach of magicians – they immediately begin mastering specific magic skills, not paying a thought to whether they are allowed or not. Not being able to tell good from evil, they get directly into the arms of the devil. They think that they are taking the path of perfectionism, but in reality they are digging their own grave. And the worst thing is that any admonitions often prove useless. People just don't believe that anyone could be controlling them; they think it is all nonsense. Or am I wrong?' Rada glanced at Maxim and smiled.

'You're right,' Maxim admitted. 'All of this actually does seem somewhat unreal to me. I don't feel any alien control over me.'

'That's what I'm talking about. And your doubts are nothing else but a result of the activity of the implant imbedded in your consciousness. The flyers are afraid of man becoming aware of their presence, and they do everything in their power to stop him from actions that would mean harm to them. At the same time, they manipulate us so subtly that man simply doesn't notice the presence of an alien mind.'

'Ok, fine, but how do flyers show themselves on an ordinary everyday level? Could you give me a few very simple examples?'

'I could give you a million.' A grin flashed on Rada's lips. 'For example, you jogged your elbow against someone in a street crowd, that person snapped at you, called you a moron. In response you hit him in the face, and the whole thing took off. Both of you are seemingly acting on your own, but in reality there is an implant program working in each of you. The objective of an alien mind is to make you produce splashes of energy. All your reactions are preconditioned; you are both acting like string puppets in this situation. One of you snapped, the other could not stand the insult. As a result you're fighting, but the flyers are feasting, gulping down your energy. And that goes for everything, for every little thing – you think it's your desires, your thoughts, your motives, your emotions. While in reality all of it is the pranks of the flyers with the objective to milk you of a little more energy. That's why magicians strive toward an absence of desires, understanding that all of these desires are not our own. An ordinary person is like a string puppet, hanging on the strings of passions and desires. The magicians cut these strings one by one. As a result there comes a moment when the flyers lose the ability to control man, they simply have nothing to hook him onto. A magician like that is like water – no matter how much you grab it, it will still run through your fingers.'

'All right. That I understand. But what if I, for instance, just want to eat or drink? That too is an implant?'

'These are the needs of the body which could be subject to correction by the flyers,' Rada answered. 'Say, the need to eat turns into gluttony. Love degenerates into sex. Add tobacco, alcohol and drugs, and you'll see how good the flyers are at their job. We should applaud.'

Maxim involuntarily grinned.

'Tell me, do we have anything of our own?'

'Well, if we derive from the fact that man was created in the image of God, then we've got nothing of our own by definition. There's what God has given us, and the things imposed on us by the flyers. So our main task is to clear our consciousness of all alien things, of the things that are unnatural to us. Only then can we start talking about some sort of conscious personal growth.'

'I'm starting to get the general idea, although it is very strange, hearing that this very moment someone is controlling me.' Maxim glanced at Rada and smiled. 'Sounds like science fiction.'

'Do you trust me?' Rada asked pronouncedly.

'I do,' Maxim smiled. He already knew what Rada would say.

'Then just believe me and do as I say. I won't give you bad advice.'

'Good,' Maxim agreed. 'I'll take your word for it. The audience is over?'

'It's over,' Rada smiled. 'Go – and don't forget what I said.'

Maxim returned to Rostov at the beginning of the following week. He went back together with Oxana. Maxim apologized to her back in Klyonovsk, told her that he was wrong. He didn't feel particularly guilty, but he believed it was the best thing to do. It's not said for nothing that if a woman is wrong – apologize. And that's what Maxim did. On the surface everything went back to normal; they conducted themselves pronouncedly properly. Still, Maxim couldn't accept that Oxana didn't feel the same way. His mind accepted it, but his heart did not.

Maxim already knew from Oxana that his business was still prospering, over the last year the size of the staff had almost doubled. It turned out that Oxana had understated the progress of the business. Having familiarized himself with his firm's efforts, Maxim doubled the manager's salary – the guy deserved that. Neither did he leave unrewarded the average workers. The annual income came out quite impressive. Maxim transferred a part of it to one of the searchers' bank accounts. That made him rightfully proud – now he was not only taking, but also giving back. Still having quite a lot of money, Maxim started thinking about setting up another business. It would make him feel even more confident. He no longer wondered what he'd do – he would only work with plants. Now he had all the means to do that.

Unfortunately, he was forced to postpone the realization of these plans yet again. Maxim was already about to register his new business, when in another lucid dream he met Boris.

'Hi!' Boris greeted him. 'Well, have you been able to get some rest?'

'Hello, Boris. Yes, I've had a little breather. Want to send me some place again?'

Boris' laughter told Maxim that he wasn't far from the truth.

'Yes, I've got a suggestion.' Boris's eyes were shining; you could feel great power in the searcher's appearance. 'What do you think about a little martial arts practice?'

'You are asking me to beat up somebody?' Maxim inquired.

'No,' Boris smiled. 'I'd like to introduce you to the magic component of martial arts. Rather, I'm not the one who's going to do the introducing, but somebody else. He is our main expert in that area.'

'Let me guess – his name is Andrey, and he lives in St. Petersburg. Am I right?'

'Absolutely,' Boris agreed. 'Is it ok if we call him?'

It was a rhetorical question; Maxim didn't even have time to answer. He noticed some movement to his left and saw a man approach them.

He was twenty five years old at most. Tall, blond, dressed in worn jeans and a black shirt with rolled up sleeves. Showing from the narrow pocket on his left hip was the handle of a hunter's knife. Andrey's fingers were almost touching it.

'Wow!' Andrey greeted them. 'Hi, Boris. Hello, Maxim. I've heard about you.'

'Nice to meet you,' Maxim answered.

'You know, I'm thinking – maybe I should send him to you on probation,' Boris said. 'What do you think?'

'Well, if you can spare him.' Andrey looked at Boris and they both laughed. Their laughter, booming and loud, created a monstrous sound.

'A man's gotta do what a man's gotta do,' Boris said when they were done laughing. 'Basically, he's all yours. You can take him.'

'Right now?' Andrey inquired.

Maxim felt somewhat uneasy. 'Better if we do it in a couple of days,' he said. 'I still have a few things to sort out.'

'Then I'll be in touch,' Andrey agreed, then glanced at Boris. 'Don't forget to send me his e-mail. See you guys later!' Andrey glanced at Maxim, winked at him, then turned away, walked aside and vanished.

'All in all, you're in good hands.' Boris clapped Maxim on the shoulder. 'So get ready. Now I have to go.'

Boris disappeared. Maxim was left alone. He looked around, thinking about what to do then he remembered that he wanted to look for birds. In a lucid dream birds can show you places where our luminosity is hidden. In this dream Maxim was on one of the streets of Rostov. He looked up at the sky and saw birds. It was two pigeons; they were flying towards the Theatre square. Maxim pushed off and was up in the air, wanting to follow the pigeons, but he couldn't maintain his consciousness and woke up.

The train arrived in St. Petersburg early in the morning. It was agreed that Maxim would meet Andrey at ten o'clock, and so he went upstairs to the waiting room on the second floor and waited.

Andrey appeared fifteen minutes before the appointed time. He was dressed in jeans and a light jacket with a skinny backpack on his shoulder – at first Maxim didn't even recognize him; this person was punier and not as impressive as in the dream. His age was close to forty; in the lucid dream Andrey looked much younger. Nevertheless, it was him – to understand that you only had to look into his eyes.

'Hi!' Andrey shook Maxim's hand. 'How are you feeling?'

'Hello,' Maxim smiled. 'I'm loaded for bear.'

'Then follow me.'

Maxim thought they'd go to Andrey's place, but he was mistaken. First they took the metro to the Baltic train station; there Andrey bought two tickets for the el-train. Maxim refrained from asking questions. Andrey wasn't in a rush to start explaining. While they were waiting for the train, they talked about all kinds of everyday thing then they were riding the train. Finally, about one in the afternoon they got off on some small station.

'We're almost there,' Andrey reassured Maxim. 'Now we'll have to walk a little bit by foot, and we're there.'

Maxim couldn't really object, so he patiently followed Andrey. Having rounded the station from the right, they went deep into the forest. First they walked down a well-trodden road then they turned onto a forest path. At one place they made their way across a stream on the trunk of a fallen tree, and about an hour later they finally reached their destination.

'There you go; that's my estate,' Andrey said with a smile, when in the gleam between trees Maxim caught a glimpse of a construction of sorts.

'You live here?' Maxim inquired.

'No,' Andrey shook his head. 'This hut used to belong to my grandfather; he was a forest warden. Then they built the forest warden's house in a different place, about twenty kilometers from here and Grandpa bought this hut. In ninety-five he died, left the cabin to me. It's a good place – quiet, calm. Rarely does anyone come by here.'

The door was padlocked. Andrey fumbled somewhere above the door, fished out a key and opened the lock. He opened the door wide and glanced at Maxim with a smile:

'Come on in.'

An inner porch and a main room made out the house. Once in the room, Maxim discerned a couple of ordinary iron beds, a table by the window and a small metallic stove. The interior was supplemented by a couple of chairs and shelves, made out of wide shaved boards.

'Make yourself comfortable,' Andrey suggested. 'That's your bed. We'll get something to eat just now, and later we can have a chat.'

For lunch they had buckwheat with tinned stew. After a long train trip and a walk in the forest, Maxim was hungry, and so he didn't complain of poor appetite.

'I cook, you wash up,' Andrey said after supper. 'I think that's fair.'

It really was, so Maxim did the dishes and wiped off the table without further discussion.

'Now we can get down to business,' Andrey said with a smile when Maxim once again took his seat. 'As far as I know, you have already mastered the basics of combat technique. Those techniques are very useful, but they won't be of help to you in certain situations. I'll introduce you to the other view on martial arts. It is made out of two aspects: philosophy and applied technique. I'd prefer to start with philosophy, but it's better to show you something practical right away, so you'll get a rough idea of what we're dealing with here. Then you'll understand that my words are not fluff, and that there's actually something behind them. Let's go outside.'

Outside was quiet and very nice. The sun peered through the tree crowns; Maxim sighed with satisfaction. He liked it here.

Having entered a small shed to the left of the house, Andrey took a skein of strong white cord off a nail. He winded off a small piece – about a meter long – and tore it off without any visible effort, upon which he returned to Maxim.

'So, stunt number one.' Andrey smiled and looked at Maxim. 'Attack me. Don't be shy; you may hit me as hard as you can.'

Maxim had already seen Denis work the rope, twining it around the arms and neck of the opponent. Obviously, Andrey wanted to show him something similar. Therefore, the most important thing in this situation was not to let the opponent lash the rope around his arm or leg. Maxim took a step towards Andrey, made a few short false movements, then having snatched a moment, punched Andrey hard in the chin. Wanted to punch…

It was like a movie where some of the frames had been cut out. Maxim didn't even realize right away what happened; he felt a moment's shaking, a very unpleasant one, and immediately realized that he was standing on his knees. His arms were tied behind his back – Maxim tried moving them and became convinced that that really was the case. Next to him was a smiling Andrey.

'Well?' he asked, helping Maxim up.

'I don't get it,' Maxim honestly admitted. 'How did you do that?'

'Let's try it one more time,' Andrey suggested, having untied Maxim's hands. 'This time just stand still, that way it'll be easier for you to understand what's happening.' He placed himself a couple of feet away from Maxim. 'Get ready!'

Maxim got ready. Andrey was looking at him, smiling.

'I'm ready,' Maxim confirmed.

'Look at your hands,' Andrey suggested.

Maxim looked down at his hands and gave a start. One end of the rope was tied to his left wrist, the other to the right one. And yet Maxim could swear that Andrey didn't move an inch.

'How do you do that?' he quietly asked, dazedly examining the rope.

'That is the magic of combat,' Andrey answered. 'In this case I'm manipulating the perception of time. To you it remains the same, to me it practically freezes. Consequently, I can walk up to you and do whatever I want. By the way, it's a rather advanced level, and far from everyone is able to master this technique. Let's move on to something simpler.' Andrey untied the rope and carried it back to the shed. Then he returned, holding a piece of a crumpled water-pipe. 'Try bending it,' he suggested, handing the pipe to Maxim. 'With your hands.'

The pipe was about seventy centimeters. Maxim tried bending it and immediately gave up.

'I can't,' he said, returning the pipe to Andrey.

'There's nothing strange about that,' he replied. He examined the pipe closely and then calmly wound it around his arm as if it was a piece of ordinary rubber hose. Maxim could hear the twisted metal crack. Andrey smiled, coolly unwound the pipe and handed it back to Maxim.

'That's that,' he said.

Maxim cautiously took the warped pipe; it was considerably warm. He ran his hand across it, thinking what kind of power a man must possess to perform a stunt like that. He looked up at Andrey.

'The question remains,' he said. 'How did you do that?'

'Rather, it was my dream body that did that. In moments of need I can let it out. Not for long, of course, only for a couple of seconds. But that's enough to win even the heaviest fight.' Andrey smiled and started unbuttoning his shirt. 'Now yet another demonstration – last one.' He took off his shirt and threw it on the porch railing. 'And now hit me with this pipe – from the side, as if you were to cut me in half. Smash me up; swing that pipe. Hit me with all your heart – don't hold back. Come on, it'll be interesting.'

'I won't hurt you?' Maxim inquired, taking a more comfortable grip on the pipe.

'If anything happens, there's a shovel over there. You'll bury me.' Andrey grinned. 'I'm kidding. Hit away. Don't be shy!'

Maxim hit him – just as Andrey ordered him – with all his heart, with all his might. At the very least, a punch like that could break your ribs.

But that didn't happen – to Maxim's great surprise; the pipe in his hands met only a little resistance. It passed calmly through Andrey's body; Maxim could barely hold his balance.

'Damn it,' he muttered, with difficulty maintaining his balance. Bewildered, he looked at Andrey, who was softly smiling.

'The ability to let objects pass through you also comes from the lucid dreams,' he explained. 'You learn it when you go through walls in dreams. But there's no difference – whether you go through a wall, or something goes through you. Using this technique you can even let bullets pass through you. In ancient times, by the way, battle mages, who possessed this skill, horrified their enemies. No sword, no arrow could get them.' Maxim walked over to the porch and grabbed his shirt.

'Awesome!' Maxim admitted. What he just witnessed seemed to him like a miracle.

'Yes, it's amusing,' Andrey smiled, buttoning up. 'Let's sit.'

They sat down on a bench – an ordinary block supported by two billets of wood, installed by the house wall.

'Clearly, now you'd like to learn how to do this,' Andrey began, calmly looking at Maxim. 'As far as I know, until meeting the searchers, you hadn't done any martial arts. It was all different for me; I first got interested in martial arts and only later joined the searchers. What the outcome of merging the two systems was you've had an opportunity to see for yourself.' A shadow of a grin appeared on Andrey's face. 'So, when it comes to working with dreaming techniques, I don't have much to say – just learn how to pass through walls in your dreams. Go through them again and again, night after night. You must acquire a habit; you must get imbued with an appropriate feeling. Then one day you'll be able to use this habit in real life as well. To use the language that you're used to; for some time your ordinary cosmography charts will be replaced with magical ones. Then you'll be able to smash someone's head together with his helmet with a punch of your fist; you'll be able to tie his automatic into a knot around his neck. You could tear out his heart or liver – sorry for the details. Finally, you could go through a wall or let a round of bullets pass through you. Trust me, these are very unusual sensations. Your clothes get torn to pieces, but you remain alive.' Andrey sighed and fell quiet for a few moments.

'But that is only one part of the practice,' he continued. 'Remember, magicians are divided into dreamers and stalkers. Dreamers work mainly with dreams, stalkers with the real world. You'll work on your dreaming yourself; you don't need my help there. That's why we're going to talk about stalking now.' Andrey made another pause. 'Tell me, what's the most important thing in any martial art?'

'Psychology?' Maxim guessed, having already talked about these things with Denis.

'Rather, philosophy,' Andrey corrected him. 'Philosophy becomes the foundation upon which the entire structure of martial arts is built. Again, you know that there are many different types of martial arts. A man could pick any system of fighting, but on one condition – it must truly correspond to his demands. For example, you can do kendo – the art of the sword. An excellent system for perfecting your movement technique and strengthening the spirit, I know that Roman has taught you the basics. But what's the use of this system in a real fight? Only in movies do the protagonists carry around swords, in reality that's not possible. Again, in a fight with the Legion we're still the weak part and we cannot enter into an open conflict – they'll just spread us all over the concrete. Consequently, we've chosen the strategy of secret warfare, when the enemy doesn't know when and where we will strike. The best system of this class is ninjutsu – I think, you've heard about this art. We based the searcher school of fighting on ninjutsu. And we didn't as much adopt the technique, as the philosophy, the spirit of this art. The technique is transient, while the spirit is eternal. And here, in theory, I should warn you of one danger.' Andrey looked at Maxim and softly smiled. 'The thing is that the philosophy of ninjutsu cardinally changes a person's worldview. And it's of crucial importance to identify the line, beyond which you shouldn't go. You could say that ninjutsu is the dark side of the power. It draws you in – having sensed your powerfulness once, you might not want to go back. Why? If you feel like you're god, if you can be in charge of other people's lives, if you can decide yourself, who is to live, and who is to die? That's why you always must remember one simple thing – you're not a ninja, you're a searcher who masters the art of secret warfare. And this art is just an art, nothing more – one of the many sides of the world. When you need it, you enter the flow, turning into a demon, a deft and guileful assassin. You do your thing and exit the flow, turning back into yourself. The true art is in taking only what you need, and nothing more. Otherwise, the sensation of power could swallow you, and there'll be one maniac more on this earth.' Andrey glanced at Maxim and smiled.

'Yes, I understand,' Maxim replied.

'That's good. Let's assume that I've read you the safety instructions, and you've signed.' Another smile slipped across Andrey's lips. 'I think Boris has already told you that you're going to spend about three weeks in this place. Your most important objective is to feel the spirit of ninjutsu. I won't make you kill anyone, God forbid. Again, three weeks is way too little time to make a fighter out of you. But it will be a start; with time you'll master the entire set of techniques. Now we're just laying the foundation.'

'Who taught you ninjutsu?' Maxim asked.

'I didn't have a teacher as such.' Andrey shook his head. 'Of course, I've read books on ninjutsu; talked to a lot of wise people. I even learned things from some of them. But my main teacher was the spirit of this art. I just entered the flow of the tradition, tuned into it, and it took me down the right direction. The rest happened on its own. Florinda Donner, in her book, *The Witch's Dream*, has got it right – "Details tend to adjust themselves to serve the circumstances". And that's how it is. You just choose the direction of your movement; you enter the flow, and then it carries you on, shaping the circumstances of your life. You are about to see for yourself how well this method works.'

'I hope so,' Maxim grinned.

'Then let's not waste time and move on to your first

assignment,' Andrey suggested. 'About five kilometers from here – over there, right to the east – is a river. There are almost always fishermen there, and there are enough tourists too. Your task will be to sneak up to them unnoticed, to watch them for a while and then leave – again, unnoticed. Then one more time, this time with different people, and repeat that several times – the more, the better. Again, you shouldn't bump into anyone – if you see someone coming, hide – let that person pass you by. Your main task is to get a taste of this method. You must get a sense of satisfaction from the fact that you see someone but he doesn't see you. And while you're at it, don't feel like a scared rabbit, hiding from every little noise; on the contrary, you should feel like a predator, sneaking up to your victim. You are king and god, these people are entirely at your mercy, because you are the one to decide whether they should live or die. It's hard to explain, but if you catch this excitement, this feeling of power, things will get much easier for you later on.'

The remains of the evening they spent talking as well. They spoke of magic and of martial arts. When it got dark, Andrey lit a kerosene lamp. They went to bed early, about eleven o'clock – Maxim was tired from all the travelling and felt he needed to get a good night's sleep.

Andrey left in the morning, having said that he'll be back in exactly one week. Maxim was left alone. He took out a change of clothes from his backpack, got dressed and set out for the river.

Never before had Maxim had to watch someone. Even now he was rather exploring the surroundings, realizing that he could very well get lost here. In roughly an hour's time he came out to the river; it wasn't wide but pretty deep. He walked for a while along the riverbank, now and then noting the signs of human presence: fires, garbage, trampled down patches of grass by the water. Gradually it even started to annoy Maxim that people had cluttered up such a beautiful river.

Soon he bumped into his first fisherman. Maxim's entire

attention was glued to the riverbank, that's why he started when his gaze suddenly caught a rubber boat that was hiding on the opposite bank. A fisherman was in the boat. Maxim immediately bent down. Having realized that the fisherman didn't see him, he ran over behind the bushes still bending down.

He watched the fisherman for a couple of minutes. Then he started slowly walking downriver and immediately bumped into a motorbike. Next to it was a tent with no one inside. Apparently, the motorbike and the tent belonged to the fisherman in the boat.

Perhaps only now did Maxim sense the first flashes of excitement, the feeling Andrey talked about earlier. Having realized that the fisherman was looking at the float, with his mind far away from the motorbike and the tent, Maxim, bending down, went up to the tent, lifted the curtain and slipped inside.

Inside he discovered a layer of fir twigs, a folded sleeping bag; to the left in the corner was a backpack; a little to the side was a radio – it occurred to Maxim that if some petty thief had been in his place, the fisherman would no doubt find a thing or two missing.

He slipped out of the tent just as unnoticed as he entered. He ran off to the side, feeling a noticeable shiver in his body. Still, Maxim was quite pleased with himself. Now he knew that there was some meaning in Andrey's words about the feeling of power; it seemed to Maxim that he was truly on to something. There was something about this shadowing, attractive and exhilarating, something spirit-stirring. He glanced at his wrist watch – it wasn't even noon yet – Maxim went further down the river.

He found another group of campers about a kilometer away. At first he heard some children shriek and someone laughing then he heard the sound of an axe. Having bent down somewhat, Maxim carefully went towards the sound, trying not to step on any dry twigs. Something bright flashed ahead. Maxim squatted. The spot didn't move – Maxim listened closely for any sounds, and then walked on.

The bright spot turned out to be a car on a glade. Next to it, a man and a woman were putting up a tent with two children playing right next to them. Maxim reckoned that today was Friday. That means they're here for the whole weekend.

A crunch of twigs was heard nearby; Maxim instinctively bent down and then lay flat down on the ground, realizing that they could notice him any second now.

Past him walked a young woman about seventeen years old, she was heading for the tent, carrying a pile of dry branches. Evidently, that was the firewood, Maxim guessed.

If it weren't for the branches, the young woman would definitely have seen him; she went by very close. Maxim drew a sigh of relief, thinking that he should be more careful.

He spent about half an hour watching this family. Then, having decided that it was enough for today, he walked back to the cabin.

That's how it started. Maxim checked the riverbank every day; his outings became longer and longer. At the same time Maxim kept discovering new details – he knew what he should do, and what he shouldn't. And if he was literally sneaking along the forest the first day, later he realized that it was stupid. After all, while he is just walking around in the forest, he is not doing anything illegal. Even if he'd get noticed, they'd probably take him for just another camper. But if someone would notice a person sneaking about, that surely would arouse suspicion. From that moment on Maxim tried to act as natural as possible, starting to sneak only when there was no other way of getting closer unnoticed.

The first week was very rewarding; Maxim clearly sensed his consciousness change. Having experienced the feeling of power, Maxim started cultivating it consciously. He was usually gone in the woods until noon, then, after lunch, he had a small break. After the break he'd do some exercise – Maxim felt that he lacked strength and agility, that his body should match his new tasks. And he kept working out – until he was covered with sweat and totally exhausted.

Just as promised, Andrey arrived a week later. Having heard Maxim's reports, he was left pleased with his progress.

'You're doing a good job,' he said after lunch, when they were sitting on the bench outside the house. 'You were able to feel the power, and that's what matters. Now you'll do the same thing, but with one small change: from now on you'll go hunting at night.' Andrey went quiet, waiting for Maxim's reaction.

'Fine,' Maxim agreed. 'I'll give it a go.'

'You do that,' Andrey smiled. 'The most important thing for you now is to learn how to not be afraid of the night. Why do people fear the night?' Andrey looked at Maxim.

'People have always feared the night,' Maxim shrugged. 'It's a natural fear.'

'Yes, but what is it based on?'

'Maybe, it's based on the fear of bumping into some predator or just something scary,' Maxim surmised.

'That's right,' Andrey agreed. 'But if we were to dig a little deeper, we'd find the fear of dying at the base of every fear. Man is not simply afraid of something dangerous waiting for him in the dark – he is afraid of getting killed. The fear of dying makes him hide at night. You will have to conquer that fear. Don't feel like a victim, feel like a hunter – not a guest, but a master. The night belongs to you, there's no one scarier or more dangerous than you. You're not the one to be afraid – others should be afraid of you. Do you understand what I'm saying?'

'Yes,' Maxim nodded. 'Kind of.'

'That's good. And the most important thing – don't think of the dark as a hostile environment. The dark is your friend, your defender, your protector. Become friends with it, and you'll see how much it will be able to give you. Try doing this exercise one night: sit down in the dark, best of all if you'd get into the lotus position – if you can. The dark must be absolute. After that stretch out your arms and try to feel the dark on the tip of your fingers.

Feel its power, its might. Then take a slow breath, drawing the power of darkness through your fingertips inside of you. Once you feel the power enter you, you may lower your arms and just breathe the dark, drawing it in not only with your lungs, but with the whole surface of your body. Try it, and you'll see how great it is.'

'I will,' Maxim replied. 'For sure.'

'To get acquainted with the dark, I'll give you two weeks. It's a difficult assignment. Then you'll leave and practice the rest of the techniques at home.'

'And what techniques are those?' Maxim inquired.

'There are quite a few of them; I'll send you detailed instructions. But your next assignment will be getting acquainted with a city. I know, you spent all your life living in a city, but that doesn't mean a thing. You will have to study Rostov from new perspectives. For example, do you know of places in Rostov where you could shake off someone following you?'

'No,' Maxim hesitatingly drawled. 'I never really thought about that.'

'My point exactly,' Andrey agreed. 'You just didn't need it. Now you'll have to find places like that. It could be subways, entryways with a through-passage, crowded places like markets, big malls with several exits. And it's not the amount of such places that's important, but their quality. Let there be only three places in the whole city – on the other hand, you know that you'll definitely be able to shake off someone following you. And that is just a small part of what you will have to learn and master. I'll teach you to enter closed premises; I'll introduce you to operative chemistry. You'll learn everything there is to learn about weapons; you'll master the shadowing technique, the technique of tapping. There is a whole bunch of people who know how to make war in a forest or in the jungle. And there are much fewer persons able to wage war in the concrete jungle of a city. You'll be one of them.'

'You think I need it?' Maxim hesitantly drawled.

'You do. Understand, Maxim, the point is not to make you a professional killer. It's about altering your consciousness. Every new area of knowledge is just a corresponding mindset. Do you remember being chased around the woods not long ago? You were the victim, they were the hunters. If you had my skills, not one of them would have left that forest alive. You could talk a lot about non-resisting evil with violence and other lofty topics, but when you've got an enemy in front of you, who wants to destroy you, you've got little choice – to kill or to be killed. Those are the realities of life. You must know how to defend yourself and those dear to you, in any situation.

'I agree,' Maxim nodded. 'But is it necessary…' he faltered, looking for the right word, '…to go so deep? Night? The power of dark? The art of killing? All of that smells kind of devilish.'

'And what is the devil?' Andrey asked.

'I don't know,' Maxim quietly answered. 'Rada thinks that everything we can do in life is to choose between God and the devil. And I'm afraid that in this case we're moving away from God and getting closer to the devil.'

'Perhaps,' Andrey tactfully agreed. 'Rada is a smart girl and she's rarely wrong. But I've got my own outlook on things. There is no weapon that is bad in itself – it's a matter of whose hands it is in. And even if the dark side of the power belongs entirely to the devil, then that means I'm fighting the enemy using his own weapon. If you remember, I've already told you that the most important thing is not to cross the line, beyond which the power of the flow will change you to such a degree that you will no longer be able to go back. That is the art of a magician – to take what you need, and nothing more. You just enter the flow, do your thing – and exit. You go down to hell – and bring out trophies. You wage war on enemy territory. The important thing is not to let evil into your heart. Remember the saying – fight fire with fire. That's why in your life there must also be a dominating good side, and that side is what will keep you from rolling into the devil's arms.'

'All right, fine.' Maxim made himself comfortable on the bench. 'But can't you obtain fighting skills through the powers of light?'

'And how do you imagine doing that?' Andrey grinned. 'A kind of "Maxim The Thunderer," striking down his enemies with arrows of lightning? A knight in shining armor? There are dreams, Maxim. And there is reality. Reality tells us that you need to survive here and now, and to do that anything goes. A Warrior of Light will hardly sink to stabbing his enemy in the back. I'll do that without a shadow of doubt – because my life and the lives of my friends are at stake, because that will allow me to win. Those are the facts of life.'

Maxim didn't reply. With his back pressed against the timbered house wall, he thought about that Andrey was right about many things – just like Rada. There must be Light in his heart, but when it comes to fighting, the only thing that matters is what helps you win the battle. And if the weapon of war belongs to the devil – well, so be it…

Just like last time, Andrey left at sunrise. Now, after his departure, Maxim once again tried to evaluate this man. Was there something diabolical about him? No, Maxim could swear that there wasn't – a pure, light gaze, a kind smile. True, you could sense power in this man – but what's wrong with that? It's not about what power you have, but how you use it.

That day Maxim stayed at home, getting ready for his first night outing. Andrey brought him some clothes – black pants with laces at the bottom, a black shirt and thin black gloves with no fingertips. Although, Maxim didn't find the usual black ninja mask.

'You don't need it,' Andrey told Maxim the evening before. 'And this outfit is only to help you get into the role, not more than that. You live in the city, and you won't need a black uniform there.'

'Why not?' Maxim didn't understand.

'You must not attract attention. Your clothes can have special qualities, but none of them should be eye catching. It could be turned inside out and assume a different color; it could be adjusted to hide weapons and other useful things. But on the outside you must look just like any other guy, one out of a thousand. You did your thing, slipped out – and you're gone with the wind. Being dressed ordinarily you have an excellent ability of blending with the crowd. And imagine how people will react when they see an idiot in a black overall. Best case scenario people will start laughing.'

Maxim tended to agree with these arguments. Still, here, in the forest the black outfit really did add a notable secrecy to what he was doing.

Before leaving, Andrey dug in his backpack and drew out a knife in a black leather sheath.

'Here you go – a gift,' he said and gave the knife to Maxim. 'It's a very good blade, made by one of the best Russian masters – Damask steel, sharp like a razor. So be careful with that.'

Now, all alone, Maxim could examine the knife more closely. By the looks of it, the master who made the blade wanted to make the knife as practical as possible – there was nothing superfluous about it. The narrow voracious edge was what attracted the main attention; its somewhat greenish metal had a clear layer-like structure. It really had been sharpened much like a razor. Thoughtfully examining the cut on his finger, Maxim was thinking that he should be more careful with the knife. After all, he didn't even run his finger along the edge, but only touched it.

The handle was assembled out of thin plates, rough to the touch. Either bark or leather – Maxim never figured out what it was made of. In his hand, the knife fit like a key. Maxim knew that his hand would not slip from this handle. A blue, cut aslant, steel knob finished off the handle. On the whole the knife created the impression of a very high quality, durable weapon. The sheath turned out to be rather simple and functional; the knife fit into it with ease and got neatly fixed. Maxim loved Andrey's gift; it was a real combat weapon.

When it got dark, Maxim started getting ready for his first night journey. He arrayed himself in the uniform then turned off the light and for about an hour tried breathing darkness – just as Andrey had advised. Some things worked, others didn't. Maxim thought he felt the dark, but it wasn't in any hurry to accept him.

He made his first outing just nearby the cabin – he didn't want to go far, afraid of getting lost. On the whole Maxim didn't consider the trip a pleasant one. He kept catching on branches, stumbling on snags. Maxim listened closely to the darkness of the night and didn't understand what he was doing there. After an hour of wandering in the vicinity of the cabin, Maxim went back, towards the light of the kerosene lamp that he had left burning on the porch.

The following morning he felt annoyed by his failure. He really didn't manage, and he was aware of that. After lunch he went outside and spent a long time working the knife, polishing all kinds of stabs. That calmed him down a little. Past six in the evening Maxim lay down to rest – he didn't think he'd fall asleep, but he did. He woke up sometime around ten in the evening to head out into the forest after midnight.

This time around he got some results. First off, Maxim changed his strategy. Now he no longer tried to be someone – he simply tried to merge with the night. He listened to its sounds and carefully glided along the familiar forest paths – turned out that venturing out into the depths of the forest wasn't necessary at all. At some point Maxim sensed the already familiar feeling of excitement from his daily outings. Or not excitement – Maxim didn't know himself what to call this feeling. Perhaps, it was still too weak.

The following nights put everything right. Like a ghost, Maxim glided around the night forest, in raptures from the newly opened truths. It was great – Maxim felt either like a god, or like a demon; the usual human fear of the night slowly vanished. And who was he to be afraid of? There was no one scarier than him in this night forest.

On the fifth night Maxim finally decided to walk down to the river. Already during the day he had shadowed a group of fishermen, and so he knew where to go. He managed to get very close – Maxim clearly saw the outline of the tent, heard the snoring coming from the inside. His hand was unintentionally touching the knife hanging on his belt. If these people were his enemies, they would never see the sunrise. He left just as unnoticeably as he appeared.

During the remaining nine nights before Andrey's arrival Maxim discovered so many new things about himself that it even scared him – what other surprises did his "I" hold?

Castaneda wrote that our consciousness is determined by the position of the assemblage point. Now Maxim knew for a fact that that was the case: consciousness turned out to be a surprisingly variable thing; here he was sitting at the table and watching the flame of the lamp – it was night outside, the cyclone that swooped down from nowhere had brought heavy winds and rain. He didn't even want to think about going outside. But that was just one side of it. And if you gave it some thought, going outside that door was not so bad. His gaze caught the belt with the knife hanging on the wall; his palm touched the thick stubble on his chin – it had been a long time since Maxim had had a shave. Having retrieved the black uniform from under the mattress, he quickly got dressed and glanced in the mirror. The little jar with his own miracle-working paint – a mix of soot and vegetable oil – was right there; you just had to stretch out your hand. While he was putting the paint on his face, his consciousness altered completely. Now he had to put on the sash with the knife – and where did it go, the fear of the night? Where was that man, who just five minutes ago looked at the dim flame of the lamp and started at the sound of the blasts of wind? He was no more. Maxim opened the door and slipped out into the dark of the night...

He returned only at five am – wet, dirty, tired. He took off the sash, wiped the soot off his face, washed his face and went to bed.

He woke up past noon. It had stopped raining; the sun was shining in the sky again. The world was bright and friendly, Maxim's consciousness was that of an ordinary man. But he already knew that it was just an illusion. And there, under the shell of an ordinary man, lived another Max – predatory, dangerous, mad...

The most interesting in all of this was that his nightly adventures had a very positive effect on his dream practice; Maxim came across a whole cascade of wonderful lucid dreams. Having thought about it, he came to the conclusion that it was not the actual trips that had this effect, but rather the sense of power and aggression that came with them. There, at night, he was god. Or a demon – Maxim was leaning towards the conclusion that it was probably the latter, that that was the infamous dark side of the power. Possessed – Maxim didn't doubt that that would be the "diagnosis" a priest would give him. But was that true? So far everything pointed at that the devil – is just a mindset. But then a saint too – is only a mindset. A man can get as high up as he can fall down. To get the whole scale at your disposal, the entire range – from a saint to the devil. That's what was on Maxim's mind when he got back from yet another of his nightly walks. He glanced at the watch – four am: just the time for some lucid dreaming.

That night he managed to find Boris in his dream. Everything happened on its own; Maxim didn't even have to resort to any tricks. He just wanted to see him – and so he did.

'Hello,' Boris said. 'Something wrong?'

'Not really,' Maxim shrugged his shoulders. 'I just wanted to talk. You know, lately I keep thinking that there is nevertheless too much from the devil in our path. I spoke to Rada about God, I really liked her words – they are close to me. But now, doing martial arts, familiarizing myself with the power of darkness...' Maxim fell quiet for a second. 'I think that when I try to find the dark side in me, I betray God.'

'You don't say?' Boris smiled. 'Let's take a seat.' He took Maxim by the hand, and a moment later a familiar riverbank with a plank for a bench appeared before them. Boris lowered himself on the bench and Maxim sat down beside him. 'About the dark side,' Boris began. 'The idea is that the world around you is assembled by your consciousness. Remember the pictures in a kaleidoscope and imagine that each and every one of them is a separate world. You turn the kaleidoscope, and the image changes. The dark side is just one of these pictures; it is not better and not worse than the others. Assemble it, and you'll become a demon, a devil, a killer. You could just as well become a politician, a priest, a teacher, a doctor – the list is endless. You yourself put together the world you need – see what I'm saying? The question is – what kind of a world do you need? You could become a killer, or a man of knowledge. Any exhortations in this case are useless; you must find out who you are and what you want on your own. To understand what's closer to your heart: what is really worth striving towards.'

'Boris, I know all of this already. And I've made my choice – the path of evil is not for me. But I also noticed something else: if you were to call the path of evil and aggression the dark side, then the dark side gives you real power. Even the fact that I'm here now, with you, is explained by the dark power. It is in me – even if it's somewhere very deep down, but it is there. Thanks to Andrey I've learned to let it out, but I still have my doubts whether it is a good thing or a bad thing.'

'The dark side is in every one of us,' Boris answered. 'So you're not unique in any way. Just like we've got all of the other sides. You could fear that. Or you could use it to your advantage. Think about it – people have learned to use the energy of water and the energy of the wind, the energy of fire and the energy of the atom – but they still haven't learned to use the energy of consciousness. Remember, we've talked several times about the flows. To connect to the flow, you need to tap into it. Once you're in, the quality of your consciousness changes at once. You could get scared. Or you could use it for your aims. Now for the first time you've touched upon the combat methods of dream searchers, they have perturbed you. And that's good – if these kinds of methods scare you; that means that you'll never be their slave. Think of them just like an instrument, not more than that. And always have a counterweight in the shape of something good and pure.'

'Andrey said pretty much the same thing,' Maxim nodded. 'So, by themselves these methods are not dangerous?'

'With an axe you could build a house or kill a man. I think that's elementary. Just keep an eye out for the effect a flow or a practice has on you. Know how to watch yourself from the outside.'

'But won't the altered state of consciousness influence my assessment ability?' Maxim inquired. 'If consciousness changes, then the rating scale changes too?'

'It does,' Boris agreed. 'However, inside of you still remains some kind of a core, a kind of a second – or a first – "I". And this "I" is what stops the assemblage point from getting fixed in a new position. You just put on a guise, use it, then take it off and become yourself. It's just imperative that you don't stay in an alien flow for too long – so that you don't start feeling at home.'

'You've set my mind at ease.' Maxim looked at Boris and smiled.

'All the better.' Boris got up. Maxim stood up from the plank as well. 'Good luck, Maxim. See you soon.' Boris winked at Maxim, turned around, took a step forward and vanished.

Andrey was supposed to arrive today. In the morning, Maxim

cleaned the house, made some buckwheat porridge. About two in the afternoon, he heard footsteps. Maxim smiled – that must be him.

But it wasn't Andrey. There was a knock on the door, then the door opened, and Maxim saw a young fellow of fifteen on the threshold.

'Hello,' the boy said, closely looking at Maxim. 'Are you Maxim?'

'Yes,' Maxim answered, closely looking at the lad. 'Hi there.'

'Andrey couldn't come; he's got some urgent business. He asked me to follow you to the station.'

'Come on in,' Maxim suggested to the boy. 'Want some porridge?'

'No.' The young lad shook his head. 'We need to hurry, or we could miss the train. Andrey asked me to tell you to go back home. He'll explain everything later.'

'Fine,' Maxim agreed. 'I'll get dressed. Wait for me then, ok?'

'I'll wait outside,' the boy nodded and went outside.

Maxim had to quickly get his things together – he didn't think he'd have to leave so quickly. He changed his clothes and put his things into the backpack. He put the knife at the very bottom of the backpack, so that no overly zealous policeman would reach it. That seemed to be all... Oh right – the porridge.

He shook out the porridge outside, by the closest tree. Having quickly rinsed the kettle, he washed his hands and looked himself over in the mirror – looks ok. Only he still hadn't managed to shave.

Maxim locked the door, hid the key on top of it and glanced at the boy.

'Well, shall we? By the way, what's your name?'

'I'm Pavel. Let's go.'

Pavel turned out to be a reserved young man, even somewhat morose. They couldn't get to talking, so they walked all the way to the station in silence. Sometimes Maxim imagined that Pavel was afraid of something; the boy's gaze was sliding, closely watching the bushes around them. At the same time Pavel almost didn't move his head and didn't look around – that was clearly Andrey's teaching.

Finally they reached the station; the boy looked up at Maxim. 'I've got a fare card,' he said, 'but you'll have to buy a ticket.' 'Of course,' Maxim agreed.

The train arrived twenty minutes later. All the way to St. Petersburg they travelled in silence, like before; Pavel seemed to be complete turned in upon himself. Still, he clearly controlled the situation in the car, unobtrusively watching the passengers coming and going.

And so they reached St. Petersburg; the train stopped at the Baltiysky Rail Terminal. The young fellow got off first then he glanced at Maxim who followed.

'Good bye.' Pavel took his leave and for the first time a ghost of a smile slipped across his face. 'Happy to meet you.' The young lad turned around and walked off in haste.

'Good luck to you,' Maxim said to his back. But the boy didn't even turn around, moving towards the exit together with the rest of the passengers. Maxim followed him with his eyes, then adjusted his backpack and headed for the metro station.

He reached Rostov without any problems. Once at home, first of all he took a look at his plants – how were they doing without him? He examined the conservatory and was pleased with the state it was in. Then Maxim called Oxana and thanked her for taking care of the plants. But actually he just wanted to hear her voice.

The next week didn't bring any surprises. Maxim was resting from being on the road, took care of some business. He checked his mail a couple of times, but there was no news from Andrey. Apparently, he really did have urgent business. Nevertheless, Maxim wasn't worried; he had things to do.

A couple of more weeks went by, and it got very busy at Maxim's place. At first the plumbers had the conservatory connected to the water mains and set up a water drain then they laid a foundation beneath the future conservatory. A couple of days later a mason made a plinth out of bricks. Once the "dirty" work was done, it was time to mount aluminum elements – Maxim watched the workers put up the specially made frames, and rejoiced. This would no longer be a room with shelves for plants, but a very real conservatory.

All the main works took about two weeks. Finally came the moment when Maxim could go into the conservatory and take a look around. True, so far the place was completely empty. He had long hours of work to look forward to arranging the conservatory, but that very fact made Maxim thrilled. This was what he liked doing. This was what he had been dreaming of for so long.

Chapter Six

Back In Captivity

Yana received the report about the established location of the Petersburg group around midnight. Once she had all the details, Yana ordered to continue watching the group then she put down the phone and spent half an hour thinking about what she could gain from this situation.

She could gain quite a lot. Yana knew that the Petersburg group was one of the most powerful ones; there were at least eight experienced searchers. Back in his days, Kramer tried to find this group, but failed; the searchers didn't make mistakes, and the Legion didn't have a single lead. And now they were in luck.

However, Yana didn't believe in luck. Fools are usually the ones to have luck; in her case luck was always a result of competently organized work. And so it was this time, when in St. Petersburg that one of the Legionaries met Andrey Novikov, who had run off from Krasnoyarsk four years ago – he bumped into him by pure coincidence in a tax inspectorate office. The Legionary had enough wit not to shadow the searcher. Rather, he was simply scared of doing that – he knew too well, who he was dealing with. Back then, in Krasnoyarsk, the attempt to catch Novikov ended with the death of five fighters. Two were hurt, but those who survived said later that even a round fired point-blank didn't stop the searcher. Right after that Novikov disappeared; he even managed to get his wife and son out which, by the way, cost the lives of two more fighters.

And now Novikov was back in Petersburg. The Legion had their people in the tax inspectorate; finding out Novikov's new address and last name was easy. Already later that evening the Legionaries knew everything about where he lived, where he worked. All Andrey's phone numbers – his home phone, his and his wife's cell phones – were immediately tapped. Right after that the Legionaries reported to Yana.

Now she had to decide what to do next. Capturing Novikov was out of the question – Yana knew perfectly well that this man was too tough for them to handle. Still, Yana already knew what to do with him. First they had to track all his connections, uncover the whole group, and then…

True, Novikov was a very good searcher. But no one is immortal on this earth.

In the morning Yana told Dags everything. The Sovereign was pleased, and even deigned to give a few valuable guiding instructions. Yana thanked him respectfully. However, secretly she rewarded the Sovereign with a dozen bad words. The fact that Dags advised her and lectured her like a little girl wasn't what annoyed her the most. It drove her crazy that she didn't have any levers of influence with Dags. She had Kramer wrapped around her finger; it was enough to get him into bed. Unfortunately, Dags in this sense preferred very young men, and thus had a pronouncedly cold manner towards Yana.

To keep the strings of events in her hands, Yana immediately headed for Petersburg. Dags gave her permission to use his jet. It seemed that she should be happy about going on the Sovereign's jet, but in reality it only irritated her. Yana wanted to take the jet when she wanted, and not when she got permission to do so.

Careful shadowing of Novikov continued for two weeks; during that time they managed to uncover several of his contacts. But, to Yana's great disappointment, all of these people had nothing to do with the searchers; the scrupulous background check didn't reveal any leads. During the whole time of observation she discovered only one fact that deserved attention – on Sunday Novikov left town on a train. He got off at a little station and went deep into the forest. They feared shadowing him, afraid of getting discovered. He reappeared at the station only the following morning; he waited for the train and returned to St. Petersburg. All attempts to find out where he had been failed.

Days dragged on; however there was no encouraging information coming in. Gradually, Yana started to get the impression that Novikov had broken up with the searchers to focus on his family. His wife Anna was staying at home with a one year old baby girl Olga; their son Pavel was a high school student. Novikov himself spent all his days working in his company, which specialized in IT.

Still, Yana didn't want to give up. It was possible that Novikov simply sensed that something was wrong, and thus switched onto "quarantine" mode, cutting all communication with his group mates. Having assumed that Novikov could transfer some information through his son, the seacher's son too was being shadowed. And it paid off – two weeks later Pavel departed on a train towards the already familiar station. This time they managed to shadow the boy and he brought two field investigators to a log hut. Inside was a guy about twenty five years old. Half an hour later he and Pavel set out back to the station. They decided not to go after the guy, contenting themselves with careful observation.

On the Baltiysky Rail Terminal the stranger and Pavel went their separate ways. Pavel went back home; the stranger took the subway to the Moscow Rail Terminal and bought a ticket for Rostov on Don. He was, of course, accompanied by field investigators all the way to Rostov. Once in Rostov the guy was handed to the local team for observation.

Who that man was, Yana knew already before the Rostov report. She simply had to look at the photographs. When she saw the stranger's unshaved face, Yana raised her eyebrows in surprise. Although, a couple of seconds later her lips broke into a smile.

'Oh, so that's how it is?' she mumbled, looking intently at the photographs. 'Our golden boy has turned up.'

She spent a couple of minutes examining the photographs,

becoming more and more certain that it was him. Now she could bring the good news to Dags – Yana smiled and reached for the phone.

From early morning Maxim was painting pipes and radiators in the greenhouse. He enjoyed working – everything he was able to do, he preferred doing himself. Today it was painting, tomorrow – the lighting. Then – putting together the racks. And once that's done, it will be time for the best part – he could start moving the plants.

Maxim felt his good mood gradually coming back to him. The only thing that he still didn't feel good about was his relationship with Oxana. She wasn't really rejecting him, but at the same time she wasn't saying "yes" either. Perhaps she just needed some time. Now Maxim knew that Boris had made the right decision, sending him to Andrey. A different environment and a new hobby helped him get his mind off things. Maxim didn't blame Oxana; he understood that she was a free young woman and had the right to make her own choice. All he could do was wait.

Nevertheless, his next meeting with Oxana made Maxim once again feel aching sadness – he was drawn to the girl and he couldn't do anything about it. He met her around three in the afternoon, close to the Book Centre. He got up the stairs of an underground passage and saw Oxana next to a newspaper stand. She was examining something in the stand then she took out her wallet.

The young woman was buying a SIM card. While Oxana was paying for the card, Maxim stood a short distance behind her, pondering whether she'd agree to go with him to the movies, or to the theatre, or to an art museum – it didn't matter to him where they'd go as long as she'd be with him. Oxana hid the card and the wallet in her bag, turned around and her eyes met Maxim's.

'Maxim!' Maxim caught sincere joy in Oxana's voice. That was promising.

'Hello,' Maxim greeted Oxana. 'Happy to see you. What's up?'

'I had a walk in the park, now I'm going to the bookstore.' Oxana nodded at the open doors of the store. 'How did you get here?'

Maxim didn't answer; for a moment he got a very unpleasant feeling. And that feeling was caused by a man about forty years of age – right then he was just buying roasted peanuts from a street vendor a few meters away from them. Maxim could swear that only a second ago that man was closely watching them. What's more, Maxim realized that he'd already seen him about half an hour ago. Maxim had gone inside one of computer stores – when he left the store that man was smoking some distance away. A coincidence? But the last couple of days there had been several occasions like that. True, it wasn't anything obvious, but on the whole it all painted quite an unpleasant picture.

'Maxim?' There was concern in Oxana's voice.

'Let's take a walk,' Maxim suggested. He smiled demonstratively and bent down to the young woman's ear. 'I think we're being shadowed. Don't be afraid, I might be wrong.'

Oxana grew pale and caught on to Maxim's arm. He frowned a little – her rash movement was not the best thing to do right now. On the other hand, they wouldn't leave Oxana alone now anyway.

'I know a great coffee shop,' he said in a loud enough voice, looking at Oxana with a smile. 'I suggest we go there – my treat. We'll have a chat – celebrate the occasion. What do you say?'

'I'd love to,' Oxana answered and smiled too. 'Is it far?'

'Not really,' Maxim replied and headed for the underground passage, holding Oxana's hand.

The suspicious man didn't follow. False alarm? Perhaps. But it's better to be sure. They crossed to the other side of the Bolshaya Sadovaya Street. Maxim, still holding Oxana's hand, was heading for the bus stop, thinking what to do next. If he was being watched, then they no doubt already knew about Oxana. He had called her a few times recently – just as she had called him. Then why didn't they take them before? Evidently, they tried to uncover all of the group's connections. He didn't have anything compromising at home; he didn't have to destroy anything – that meant that in case of an emergency he needn't go there. Again, he shouldn't go back there no matter what: the Legionaries would prefer to take them in the house, without a fuss. Perhaps, it was already a matter of hours, and not days. What to do? To separate, as if nothing happened, and then try to hide unnoticed? He would manage, but what about Oxana? If he was quite inexperienced in these matters, then Oxana hadn't had any training at all.

Only now did Maxim really appreciate Andrey's advice – to find a place where he could shake off his pursuers. So far Maxim had only one suitable spot, and he only found it by accident. Now Maxim regretted that he didn't give more attention to Andrey's assignment. He kept waiting for Andrey to write him.

'Where are we going?' Oxana whispered without turning her head.

'We need to get to Selmash,' Maxim answered just as quietly. 'There we'll be able to get away. That's our bus – hurry.'

The doors closed just as they jumped into the bus. That's good – not a single eavesdropper had time to follow them. And it happened quite naturally: no one would ever suspect an attempt to escape.

Standing in the bus, Maxim kept closely watching the cars going after the bus. First stop – most of the cars passed the bus and drove on. One car stopped on the curb; no one went out of the car. A coincidence?

The bus was off again. The black jeep that had attracted Maxim's attention followed. Then it overtook the bus and dropped out of sight.

Standing next to him, Oxana said very quietly: 'You know, I've also noticed a few suspicious things lately. A couple of electricians have been fiddling about in our house, on my floor.'

'Did you call the landlord?' Maxim asked, 'to find out whether anyone had called them?'

'That didn't occur to me,' Oxana lowered her eyes.

The next time Maxim noticed the jeep that had aroused his interest next to the "Olymp" stadium, right by Oxana's house – and that told volumes. Perhaps, the Legionaries decided that they're going to Oxana's place, and that's why they were waiting for them there. The bus drove off from the station; the black jeep crawled out on the road and followed.

'That's them?' Oxana asked quietly.

'Possibly,' Maxim answered. 'But there must be another car. There's too much traffic; it's hard to figure us out.'

'What do we do?' There was fear in Oxana's voice.

'We'll try to get away.'

Soon the bus drove up to Selmash. It dove under the railway crossing and turned to the right. Maxim glanced at Oxana:

'We're getting off now.'

They left the bus through the front door, paid the driver and quickly crossed the road. Now Maxim held Oxana's hand and calmly walked towards the factory checkpoint; a smile was playing on his face – Oxana had just told him a joke. That was the right way to do it: they mustn't show that there's something troubling them.

They were being watched; Maxim realized that when he saw the already familiar jeep. It stopped about fifty meters behind them and two well-built brawny fellows exited the car, slowly going after Oxana and Maxim. The pursuers almost didn't hide anymore, and that said it all.

'Where are we going?' Oxana asked in a whisper.

'There's an underground passage by the checkpoint,' Maxim answered. 'It leads right to a small market. There are a couple of turns there; the Legionaries will lose us. Then we have to run forward, past the bus stop and immediately to the left. There we'll be able to get away.'

'And then?' Maxim felt Oxana's hand shake.

'Then we'll get out of town and hitchhike our way to Belgorod. Do you know where Iris lives?'

'No, but I have her number.'

'Just don't call her from your cell phone. Actually, you know what – throw it in to the next garbage can. Otherwise they'll track you down. Got it?'

'Yes, but… You're saying this as if I'll have to go there by myself.'

'Oxana, I don't know what will happen. If we'll be able to get away together – great. If not, you'll go without me. And don't argue.' Maxim stopped Oxana, who was ready to object. 'If you manage to get away, I'll definitely be able to run off. It'll be easier without you, do you understand? Just don't get offended. You know that I love you. And I don't want anything to happen to you. Just believe me, and everything will be okay.'

Maxim hoped that is how it would be. But it all happened differently. There were still about twenty meters left to the underground passage, when a white Toyota appeared right in front of them, screeching with its breaks and cutting them off from the underground passage. The brawny fellows immediately darted towards them.

'Run!' Maxim screamed, kicking the opening car door as he passed. It was a hit – the door pinched the leg of the fighter about to jump out of the car. Maxim grabbed Oxana's hand and ran towards the underground passage. Behind, they could hear swearing and the tramping of someone's feet – they were being pursued.

That they would not be able to get away, Maxim realized already on their way down the underground passage. He would have managed to run away on his own, but Oxana… She couldn't run too fast; together they would never be able to hide from these cutthroats. Then Oxana looked back at the pursuers, Maxim noticed her desperate gaze and made up his mind.

'Tell Boris everything!' he shouted, then he let go of the girl's hand, stopped and turned to face the pursuers.

'Maxim!' Oxana screamed, halting.

'Run!' Maxim bellowed and took a step towards the closest fighter.

He stopped the first pursuer by throwing one of the sellers' stands under the fighter's feet – there were quite a few stands in the underground passage. He knocked down the second pursuer with a punch to the bridge of the nose – he hit him hard, not holding back for the first time in his life. He couldn't get the third fighter, who showed surprising agility. Nevertheless, Maxim delayed both him and the two remaining fighters. Having jumped back a couple of steps, Maxim knocked over a nearby stand under the feet of his pursuers, not minding the swearing of its angry female owner. He looked back for a moment – Oxana was no longer in sight. A thought flashed in his mind – run, hide; however, Maxim suppressed that desire and kicked another fighter, who tried to get past the knocked-over stand. He had to buy Oxana some time to get away.

It couldn't go on like that for very much longer. One of the fighters grabbed his sleeve. Maxim lounged forward, trying to free himself. He defended himself with his knee from a kick in the groin and at the same instant he missed the punch of a tall broad-shouldered strapper – everything went dark before his eyes, his legs turned to jelly at once. In order not to fall, he grabbed hold of the bull and noted in the corner of his eye that one of the Legionaries had managed to break through and was now running along the passage, trying to run down Oxana. Unable to remain on his feet, Maxim fell down, pulling the bull after him, who with all his weight pinned him to the ground. There was hate in the eyes of the fighter – the Legionary grabbed Maxim by the collar and hit him twice with his free hand; Maxim's consciousness grew dim once again. The last thing he saw was a small black box in the fighter's huge paw. A thought that it was probably a cell phone had time to appear in Maxim's mind, when an electric discharge stabbed into his side, depriving him of what was left of his consciousness.

Maxim woke up because he was shaking. He opened his eyes, moved – a burning pain pierced his side. He moved his hands – they were locked behind his back. Seemed like his feet were tied too.

There was another jolt; Maxim realized that he was lying in a car – perhaps, in the trunk of that very jeep. His mouth was taped over – he wouldn't be able to scream or call for help. Besides, they had covered him with something dense – felt like a piece of tarpaulin. More likely though, it was the car case.

There was a short stop. He could hear the jeep engine run; he could feel the vibration with his body. Tried to turn – didn't work. Needless to say, they had done a pretty good job swaddling him.

They were moving again. A couple of bumps – felt like a railway crossing. A turn, the car started to accelerate. 'Where are they taking me?' he wondered.

They drove for half an hour. At first Maxim tried to count the turns, then, at the very end, he lost count – apparently, the car was driving along some narrow streets. Then it made another turn and stopped. A dull metallic clank came from the outside – seemed like the gates were being opened. The car moved again, but this time not for long – Maxim felt the car tilt down and drive into an underground space, then the car assumed its original position and stopped.

Doors slammed shut, Maxim felt these sounds with all his body. Finally the back door opened and someone pulled the tarpaulin off him.

'Take him out,' someone commanded. They pulled Maxim out of the car, took him under his arms and dragged him along. Still, Maxim tried to remember everything he saw – an underground garage, a hallway, a room with a sofa, a pool table and a TV, another hallway, a couple of metallic doors with huge bolts. One door was being opened, thus, he was going that way.

A couple of minutes went by. Maxim was sitting on a built-in metallic chair, firmly chained to the seat with a pair of handcuffs. Standing next to him were two guards. Right nearby, a short little man in a white robe was bustling about – evidently, that was the doctor. The little man was clanking his bottles, Maxim made out a syringe in his hands. By the looks of it, that was aimed for him.

Someone entered. Maxim turned his head a little and saw Yana.

Yana had a smug smile on her face. She was dressed in black jeans and a black shirt to match. Even in this situation Maxim noted how attractive that bitch was. With a casual movement she threw her handbag onto a chair standing in the corner and went up to Maxim.

'Remove the tape,' she ordered. One of the guards pulled off the piece of tape from Maxim's lips. It was surprisingly painful. Having pulled up another chair, or rather a stool – high and round with three legs – Yana sat down in front of Maxim, looked him in the eyes and smiled again.

'Gold, you say?' she asked, a sneer flashed in her eyes.

'Gold,' Maxim confirmed, coolly looking at Yana.

For some time Yana was silent, closely staring at Maxim. Then she opened her lips again.

'You're not a stupid guy. And you must know that this time you won't get out of this mess.'

'So?' Maxim said with a crooked grin. The broken lip didn't allow him to grin normally.

'Leave us!' Yana told the guards; they silently obeyed. When the door closed behind them, Yana turned back to Maxim.

'Look at me,' she said. 'I too was with the searchers, but I left. And I did it out of my own will. Now I have it all: power, money, respect. But what's most important of all is that I belong to the people who actually rule the world. They actually rule the world; do you understand what I am saying? Russia will never get up from her knees – her fate is predetermined. Now a new Russian elite is being formed – one that will rule the former empire. You've got a choice: you can die. Or you can join us. You've got talent; you've got huge perspectives. Don't miss your chance.'

'I know you're a smart girl,' Maxim quietly answered. 'Boris had a very high opinion of you, and you have to earn his praise. You left, having betrayed those who trusted you. Sure, you got money and power, but was it worth what you've lost? Tell me honestly – there are only two of us here.'

Yana was silent; her lips squeezed together; her eyes growing narrow.

'You know I am right,' Maxim said, continuing to look at Yana. 'True, I could go with you, and get my life and thirty shekels as a reward. But what's the point of living then? And how do you live with the knowledge that you are a scumbag? You do know that Judas hanged himself. Why do you think that is?'

'We're getting off topic,' Yana said coldly. 'I need a clear answer – are you with us or not?'

'There was once a movie with Vysotsky on TV,' Maxim continued. 'There, he and a young woman were taken prisoners. Vysotsky's character explained to her: you'll be asked into an office and offered a cigarette. Then they'll offer you your life. You can take the cigarette, but you'll have to say no to your life.'

'Fool!' Yana lost her temper. 'Don't you understand that you don't stand a chance? Not a chance. Do you understand? You will all die – you, Boris, Rada... Here, look...' Yana quickly went up to the table, hurriedly opened her handbag. She searched nervously and took out a few photos. Having walked up to Maxim, she shoved them into his face. 'Look here – you see? Not even he could do it, even he got killed! With all his talents, with all the things he could to! You haven't got a chance!'

Maxim moved away a little, looked at the photos – and twitched. It was Andrey. He was lying on a metallic table; it was clear from the very first sight that the searcher was dead. Yet

Andrey's face had an amazingly peaceful expression – seemed like he just fell asleep.

'There's no way out. Do you understand that?' Yana was almost shouting into his face. 'No way out!'

'There is always a way out,' Maxim answered. 'Haven't you realized that yet?'

Yana didn't reply, silently looking at Maxim. Her gaze slowly filled with hate.

'And don't tell me later that I didn't try to save you,' she said coldly, heading for the table. She picked up her handbag and put the photographs back. Then she maliciously hit the door.

The door opened, two fighters entered.

'Get to work,' Yana ordered. 'But don't kill him; he's needed tomorrow alive.'

Yana left; in her place entered the doctor. With an unpleasant smile on his face, he approached Maxim, a syringe flashed in his hand.

'Better if you answer all of the questions right away,' the doctor said, bending down to Maxim. 'Trust me, it will be much better.'

The needle penetrated the vein; Maxim winced. He tried to twitch, but the guards immediately pressed him down on the chair, letting the doctor finish his job.

'There you go,' the doctor said with a smile, moving aside. 'Give him fifteen minutes and then you can start.'

At first Maxim didn't feel anything. Not even five minutes had passed before the first changes appeared in his consciousness. Maxim caught himself chatting away – so far – to himself. Thousands of thoughts were crowding in his head. At some point he felt like laughing and he did so involuntarily. Apparently that served as a signal for the fighters to start working.

At first they didn't beat him too hard. They'd ask some question, then, without waiting for an answer, they went to work on him. An hour passed by and the fighters gradually started to lose their tempers. One of the punches broke Maxim's nose: the pain was excruciating. Before that Maxim lost a couple of teeth, then came the turn of his ribs. When they broke a second rib, he lost consciousness.

He woke up from a pungent asphyxiating smell. He shook his head and started coughing, wincing with pain. His gaze caught the doctor's white robe.

'Watch him,' the doctor ordered. 'And don't do anything stupid. I'm responsible for him.'

The door rattled as the doctor left the cell. Maxim slowly looked around. It was the same cell. In the middle of the room was the already familiar metallic chair. Next to it, two guards were sitting on two stools. Turns out they didn't risk leaving him alone even in his present condition.

There were clots of blood in his mouth. With a shudder Maxim remembered spitting out the knocked-out teeth. The bloody stains next to the chair were gone – they had wiped them off. Only now did Maxim realize that he was lying on the floor, in the very corner of the cell, on a dirty mattress. His hands were still in handcuffs. He raised himself with difficulty and sat down, supporting himself with his back against the wall. The guards controlled his every move. Two completely different guys had been beating him; having realized that, Maxim looked at the guards with one open eye, the left one was swollen shut.

'I need to wash my face,' he wheezed, nodding at the sink. 'Please...'

'Fine,' one of the guards agreed after a moment's hesitation. 'And don't you try anything; you don't want to go looking for trouble.' The guard got up from the stool and went up to Maxim. He retrieved the handcuff key and with a quick and agile motion replaced the handcuffs – now Maxim's hands were locked in front of his chest. 'You can go and wash your face.'

Maxim got up with great difficulty; now and then wincing with pain he limped to the sink. He turned on the tap and splashed some water on his face – the water immediately turned pink. He touched his nose – just as he thought – it was broken. And a couple of broken ribs on the left side. Maxim felt the flinders brush against each other on every inhale, it caused piercing pain. That was bad; he wouldn't last long like this. Once Maxim was finished washing his face, he sipped some water and limped back to the mattress, then carefully lay down, grimacing with pain.

'Hey, don't you lie down!' The guard that had allowed him to slake his thirst was fat and solid, and was getting up from the chair. 'You can't sleep. Sit up and stay there. Come on!'

Maxim was forced to get up. "Of course, they won't let me sleep… Afraid that I'll disappear again. Should I try to fall asleep? Inconspicuously?"

He couldn't fall asleep – he only had to close his eyes to hear one of the guard's shouting. Sometimes the guards left the cell – taking turns. Maxim noticed that the door opened when a guard knocked twice. Turns out there was another guard keeping watch outside. Could he escape? Even in a normal condition that would be a hard thing to do, and in his present condition it was simply out of the question. But did he have a choice? The Legionaries had taken into account all their previous mistakes; they wouldn't let him fall asleep. Apparently, it was already night. Tomorrow they'd go to work on him again. The effect of the drug – or whatever it is they injected – was gone, but that was clearly just the beginning. He wouldn't live through tomorrow, Maxim was sure of that. And that meant that he had only tonight at his disposal.

So, what did he have? They had taken off his boots – on the one hand, that's bad, but his kick, if need be, would be quicker. What else? Chairs – quite a decent weapon for those who know how to use it. The second fighter – the taller one – has got a gun. You could tell by the bulge on his jacket. But he couldn't shoot in here; the guard standing outside would not let him out. So, he had to act more cunningly. But how? It was an almost hopeless situation.

Nevertheless, anger gradually started stirring in Maxim. And also, determination – if he was meant to die, then let it happen in a fight. When the escape plan had taken shape, Maxim set it into motion.

To begin with, Maxim started dozing off more and more often, forcing the fighter to yell at him. Then he stopped opening his eyes when they yelled at him, each time such willfulness ended with a kick or a hard box on the ear. Finally, the tall fighter pulled the chair closer to Maxim to be able to kick him without getting up.

That played into Maxim's hands. Sitting a meter away from the fighter, he tried to calculate everything to the smallest detail, understanding that there wouldn't be a second chance. It was time – Maxim swayed and collapsed with his face down right onto the fighter's feet.

'Get up!' The fighter bent down and turned Maxim over. He tried to get him up. The prisoner's head hung limp, the empty eyes stared ahead. 'Did you pass out or something?'

That was the moment Maxim was waiting for. He gathered all his strength, grabbed hold of the fighter and jerked him forward. The guard lost his balance and flew over Maxim. He collapsed on the floor and a moment later a heavy blow in the chin caught up with him. The second guard jumped off the chair and froze upon the sight of the barrel of a gun aimed at him.

'Make a peep, and you're dead,' Maxim told him very quietly. 'You know that I've got nothing to lose.'

The guard stood there, giving Maxim a piercing look. It wasn't a fearful look – Maxim noted that. The guard was clearly trying to figure out what to do.

'Sit down on the chair,' Maxim commanded, squeezing the gun with his two hands. 'Not this one. Over there.' He pointed at the metallic chair built into the floor. 'Take out the handcuffs and the key... Good boy... Throw the key on the floor over to my feet... Now cuff yourself to the chair.'

The guard obediently carried out all of the instructions. With his eyes fixed on the guard, Maxim picked up the key and freed himself from the handcuffs.

'Turn away… I said, turn away!'

The guard unwillingly turned away. Maxim slid up to him and hit him hard on the back of the head with the handle of the gun. Without even a shriek the guard slipped down on the floor like a sack of potatoes.

Maxim approached the door and knocked twice – the way the fighters did it. A couple of seconds later he heard the sound of a bolt moving.

Apparently, the last thing the guard behind the door expected was to see the prisoner – his eyes widened in surprise. A moment later – when Maxim kneed him with all his might – the guard's eyes became completely round. He let out a moan and quietly sunk to the floor.

Maxim remembered the way; however, he didn't manage to get away quietly – in the room with the pool table he bumped into three fighters at once. Two were playing pool; the third one was watching TV. Maxim heard the sound coming from the TV already in the hallway, but he had no other choice – he entered the room, saw the fighters and without thinking, drew his gun.

They turned out to be trained men. Maxim managed to get two of them; the third one darted to the side and hurriedly pulled out a gun. Their shots almost coincided; Maxim felt a sharp blow to the side. He swayed and fired two more times. The fighter that had injured him froze and dropped the gun.

The roar of the gunshots was still ringing in his ears. Maxim touched the wound on his side with his left hand then looked at his palm – it was all bloody, the bullet hit him right between his broken ribs. He wondered how long people live with such an injury. Although, now was not the time to think about it. So, where to now? That way…

To Maxim's surprise he didn't meet anyone else in the house. He pressed the wound with his palm and reached the garage without any difficulty. He got up to the lifting gates, found the control buttons on the wall – the gates twitched and started slowly going up.

The gates had opened about half a meter when Maxim saw someone's legs behind them. He decided he didn't want to find out who they belonged to – he aimed at the knee and pulled the trigger. When the man collapsed, he pulled the trigger once more; the stranger jerked and stopped moving. Now Maxim could examine him properly; it was a guard armed with an automatic weapon. The temptation to take the automatic with him was big, but it occurred to Maxim that he couldn't bend down. And never mind getting up after that. That's why he stepped over the guard and limped towards the gates.

He didn't know how to open them, so he tried simply climbing over to the other side, having put the gun in his belt. It turned out to be an extremely difficult thing to do; Maxim thought he'd faint any moment now. Somehow he reached the top and was ready to jump over, when the house door opened and someone rushed out. Maxim took out the gun and fired a shot, but missed. He pulled the trigger one more time – the charger was empty. Clutching at the fence, he slipped down on the ground and dropped the gun. He turned around and slowly started running away from the house, trying to figure out where he was exactly.

The place was reminiscent of a holiday village or a suburb, built up with private cottages, a proper road and street lamps. Having run a hundred meters, Maxim turned into the closest alleyway.

He ran – or rather, limped, swaying from side to side. He kept seeing double the amount of street lamps. The shirt under his palm had long ago turned slippery with blood, but Maxim tried not to think about it. If he was meant to die, then better to do it when you're free.

Still, Maxim knew that he wouldn't last long – no doubt he

was already being pursued. And he was a poor runner right now. But the worst thing was that he had absolutely no one to count on. No one would help him – not the police, not the FSS.

Another alleyway. Maxim made another turn. Now he was walking in a completely opposite direction, hoping to confuse his enemies that way. A car – the Legionaries? Doesn't look like it, an ordinary old Moskvich. This was hardly the sort of car Legionaries would drive.

This was his chance, and Maxim decided to take it. He went out on the road, into the headlights, stopped and raised his arm. The car screeched its breaks and froze. Maxim made out the wonder-struck face of the driver. Slowly, he approached the car from the driver's side, leaned on the roof, leaving bloody stains.

'Please, get me out of here... Or they will kill me...'

The driver, a man about fifty years old, was obviously hesitating. Maxim discerned fear in his eyes. Next to him, on the front seat, was a woman – must be his wife. She was the one to make the decision.

'Yasha, open the back door.'

The man silently obeyed. With great difficulty Maxim climbed into the cabin, thinking that he would get blood all over the upholstery.

'Where to?' the driver turned around and asked.

'Doesn't matter... Please, hurry – if they find us, they'll kill both you and me...'

That had an effect; the car started and was quickly gaining speed.

Maxim leaned back in the seat and pondered what to do. He tried to understand where they were, but couldn't. His consciousness kept "floating away"; Maxim had to cling to a detail of the cabin with his gaze in order not to pass out.

'Should I take you to the police?' the driver asked without turning around.

'No.' Maxim shook his head. 'Anywhere but the police. They'll find me there for sure. They've got their people everywhere.'

'Yasha, he's hurt. We need to take him to the hospital.'

The driver said something back, but what exactly Maxim didn't hear. There was a slow ringing in his ears, everything around him went dark. Then it turned pitch black and everything disappeared.

When he opened his eyes, he didn't understand right away where he was – a white wall, a white ceiling – he could hear some kind of buzzing and soft muted sobs. He tried to get up and at the same moment gasped from the pain in his side. Maxim relaxed again and squinted. This time he was able to discern a door and a bed. On the other bed lay a man that Maxim didn't know. A plastic tube stretched to his mouth; next to him on the stand with medical equipment a respirator was "sighing" in measured manner. That's where the sobs were coming from.

Looked like a hospital. Rather, it had to be a hospital or even more specifically, the emergency unit. That's right; he was shot at yesterday. Besides, he got a little beating before that. The left eye still had almost zero vision, there was something white on his nose – apparently the doctors noticed that fracture as well. But the teeth he would have to take care of himself – one was gone, sharp debris was all that was left of the other. The rest appeared to be intact.

About an hour later a man in a white robe entered the room. He was young; Maxim decided that he's just a hospital attendant. Having met Maxim's eyes, the attendant smiled.

'Aha, you've come around… Do you understand what I'm saying?'

'Yes,' Maxim said quietly.

'That's good. You got to us in time – another hour, and you wouldn't have made it. Now you will get better.'

'Where am I?' Maxim asked.

'In a hospital. Where else!' the attendant cackled.

'That's not what I mean. What city is this?'

'Rostov. What else can it be! What, you don't remember anything?'

Maxim remembered everything, or almost everything. Right up to the moment when he got into the car. But he had a feeling he shouldn't expand on that just yet.

'No... I don't...'

'That sucks. But don't you worry, memory usually comes back. You need a bedpan?'

'What?'

'Do you want to go to the bathroom?'

'No,' Maxim said after a pause. 'Not right now.'

'Then get some rest. There will be lunch soon.'

'Thank you... By the way, who's that?' Maxim moved his eyes in the direction of the neighboring bed.

'That guy?' The hospital attendant glanced at Maxim's neighbor. 'He was also brought in last night. Got into a vehicle accident. He wasn't as lucky as you were. Okay, you stay in bed. I'll come back.'

The attendant left. Maxim closed his eyes. So, by the looks of it, it was just an ordinary hospital. If the Legionaries start looking for him at hospitals, they'll find him for sure. He had to get out of here, but how?

Maxim made another attempt to get up and realized that he wouldn't be able to leave without somebody helping him. Who could help him – that hospital attendant? Or perhaps he should try finding Boris in a dream?

He thought the latter to be the safest option. Maxim closed his eyes and tried to fall asleep – and he did.

Unfortunately, sleeping didn't get him anywhere. When Maxim woke up he realized that not only did he not have lucid dreams, he didn't even have normal dreams. You need power to have lucid dreams, and that's something he had too little of right now. Thus, all he could do was wait and hope for the best.

The following morning Maxim felt much better. A doctor examined him before breakfast and gave a few injections. There was still agonizing pain in his side; however, according to the doctor, it wasn't so much his wound that was hurting, as the broken ribs.

Maxim already knew that not only did he have surgery yesterday, but that he had been given almost a liter of blood. He also knew how he got here; someone put him on the porch of the hospital and knocked on the door. No one saw the person who brought him in.

That suited Maxim well – apparently, the owner of the Moskvich and his wife didn't want to have any questions asked. Quite possible that the Legionaries still didn't know where to look for him. Sure, they probably had found drops of blood – both on the fence, and on the gun. But simple logic says that if a man has run off, then he's not seriously injured. And going to the hospital with a gunshot wound, even a minor one, means drawing a lot of trouble upon yourself. Hence, everything indicated that he was not in a hospital – he's not an idiot after all. And Yana didn't think him to be one. Did he dare to hope? Sure, even if it was a small hope. What if there was someone particularly meticulous among the Legionaries. Besides, they were probably going ballistic right now. How many did he take down – three, four of them?

It was odd, but thinking about the killed enemies didn't make Maxim uneasy. He was even surprised; Maxim advisedly tried to summon a feeling of remorse, regret. After all, it was not some garden bugs – it was people. He tried, but it didn't work. There was no compassion in his heart – not after having seen photos of Andrey.

Maxim didn't know how the Legionaries managed to get to him. Perhaps, they just caught him off guard.

After lunch Maxim was transferred to another ward – a very small one. There were only two beds in the room. One was empty,

Maxim got the other one. Why he was to be kept in isolation, Maxim figured out only when an investigator entered the ward.

The conversation lasted almost forty minutes. Maxim didn't tell him anything about himself, rather convincingly imitating a complete memory loss. All he said was that he remembered a brick wall, train tracks, a train car of some sort and nothing else… All the attempts of the investigator to establish his identity and find out where and under what circumstances Maxim received his injury failed. Finally, the investigator left, having promised, however, that he'd be back.

Maxim was perfectly aware of the gravity of the situation. Should the Legionaries find out about him, nothing would save him. His only comfort was that Oxana managed to get away; otherwise Yana would have definitely tried to take advantage of that. Well, as for him – he only had to wait.

The next day began with trouble – the already familiar attendant came into the ward and said that someone's come for him.

'You're being transferred to the infirmary of the pre-trial prison,' he said. 'They're signing the papers just now.'

Maxim pursed his lips. So, they got to him anyway. There could be no other explanation to what was happening.

'Help me escape,' he asked, staring at the attendant. 'I'll give you twenty thousand dollars. Honest, I won't cheat you.'

'What, are you nuts?' the attendant grinned. 'I'm not an enemy to myself. I don't need trouble. So, sorry.' The attendant turned around and left the room.

Maxim looked around – as ill luck would have it, there was nothing he could use as a weapon. He couldn't fight with the bedpan now, could he?

So he had to admit that he has lost. He couldn't run in his present condition – so he just had to accept the inevitable with honor.

He lay there and waited; the investigator still didn't show.

Finally he heard footsteps down the hall and the door opened.

It was a man he'd never seen before, forty years old, dressed in a classic grey suit with a white robe thrown over it. A couple more people stayed in the hall.

'That's him?' the stranger asked the hospital attendant who had just slipped into the room; he obviously didn't want to miss any details.

'That's him, alright,' the attendant said in a cheerful voice. 'He even offered me money, so that I'd help him run away – twenty thousand dollars.'

'Really?' A smile touched the stranger's lips. 'You should have taken it... I'm joking, of course. Leave us alone, please. And close the door.'

The attendant left at once. Maxim lay in bed, thinking whether the man would kill him right away, or take him somewhere. Probably the latter; no doubt the Legionaries had more questions to ask him.

'Well, hello, Maxim Viktorovich.' The stranger reached into his pocket. Maxim tensed up. But instead of a gun, in the hands of the guest appeared a red ID folder. The stranger unfolded it and carefully brought the identification to Maxim's eyes – Colonel Marchenko. Federal Security Service.

The minibus with tainted windows was driving him along the city street. Lying on a stretcher, Maxim looked askance at the guards – three hefty guys in black masks and uniform overalls with the letters "FSB" on their backs. All three of them were armed; the barrel of one of the automatic guns was aimed right at Maxim's face. Colonel Marchenko had made himself comfortable on the front seat next to the driver; he didn't turn around even once during the entire journey.

The trip took about twenty minutes; Maxim couldn't make out, where exactly they had taken him. By the shadow that slipped above the car, he could tell that they went under an arch, the minibus stopped in a small yard. At some distance behind them was the sound of an operating mechanism of the closing gates. At the same instant the back door opened wide, Maxim was carefully pulled out of the car and brought to the porch. Then he was taken down a long hallway and brought underground in a service elevator. Maxim automatically counted the floors – third, fourth, fifth. On the fifth underground floor the elevator stopped. Maxim was again taken down a hallway. Lying on the stretcher, he looked at the metallic boxes of the air duct stretching along the ceiling, and sadly thought that there's no way he could escape from here.

He was put in a separate ward – or rather, a cell. Clean and bright, with minimum furniture – next to Maxim's bed was a white plastic table and chair. An austere looking elderly doctor, in the presence of guards and two medical assistants, carefully examined Maxim's wounds and gave him a few injections. Having instructed the assistants, he left the room. The guards retired as well. A couple of minutes later the assistants left too. Maxim was left on his own. His eyes were closing – apparently, they gave him a shot of sedative. Maxim decided not to resist – who knows, perhaps that's just what Boris or Rada were waiting for?

He didn't know how long he slept for, and his sleep was more reminiscent of being unconscious. Having opened his eyes, he saw that same milky lamp shade hanging from the ceiling, and the yellowish walls.

He was obviously being watched, as at the same moment a medical assistant entered the room. To Maxim's request to get something to drink the assistant poured some water into a plastic cup and let Maxim empty it. Then he left, having said that he'd bring some supper in an hour.

Maxim never figured out where the surveillance camera was installed. However, that didn't worry him too much either – let them watch him, if they wanted.

Another twenty minutes went by and the door opened again.

Maxim saw the familiar colonel. The man pulled the chair close to Maxim's bed, took a seat and gave him a close look.

'Let's talk?' he asked.

'Let's talk,' Maxim agreed.

'I think you've already guessed where you are,' the colonel started. 'I won't beat around the bush. This is how it is – you're in a deep mess. There are four bodies on your hands; the police have got a gun with your fingerprints. You're being accused of robbery-related assault. There is a whole ocean of witnesses; you'll never prove that you were brought there by force. So, best case scenario you're looking at twenty years in a maximum security prison. But you're more likely in for a lifetime sentence. That is – on paper.' The colonel gave a gloomy smile. 'In reality, you won't even last a month, and before you die, they'll beat everything you know out of you. That's the downside of it.'

'What, there's an upside too?' Maxim smiled crookedly.

'Rather, an upside is possible. You must understand that there is no going back for you. But I can give you a new life and an interesting job.'

'That's an offer?'

'Yes.'

'And what happens if I say no?' Maxim inquired.

'Nothing good. Just think about it: on the one side – prison and death, on the other – working for the good of the motherland. You'll have everything a person could only dream of – a nice house, a nice car, good money, women – any women, and any way you want them. And most importantly – an interesting job; an opportunity to fully develop your potential. People don't decline offers like that.'

Maxim was silent.

'I don't expect an answer right away; you've got time to think it over until tomorrow. In the morning you'll have to give me an answer. And I really hope that it's going to be the right one.' The colonel rose from the chair. 'Oh, and one more thing – you won't be able to escape. Trust me, I've taken care of that.' A ghost of a smile slipped across the colonel's lips. 'Have a nice rest.'

The colonel left; there was the clank of the door lock. Maxim closed his eyes and started thinking. For some time he lay quietly, then he gave a soft sigh.

'Out of the fire into the flame,' he mumbled. Now Maxim had a pretty good idea about what Boris meant, when talking about difficulties in the relationship between the searchers and the FSS.

Soon one of the medical assistants brought supper. Maxim finished his meal without any appetite and thanked the assistant. Once alone, he lay for a long time, staring at the ceiling. He wanted to sleep, but he was afraid to close his eyes. Maxim knew that should he only press his eyelids together – it would already be morning. And in the morning he would be forced to make a choice.

Alas, the morning arrived nevertheless. Maxim woke from the sound of the door being opened. It was that same austere and reticent doctor. Having checked up on Maxim, the doctor retired. Five minutes later Maxim was served breakfast. Maxim finished eating and started waiting for the colonel. He already knew what he'd tell him. Now Maxim knew that in his case there was simply no choice. The most precious thing in a person's life – is his freedom. And no one has the right to take it away.

Marchenko showed up about an hour later, this time he came dressed in an officer's uniform. Needless to say, he looked pretty impressive; the colonel's chest was decorated with a rather large service ribbon. Having closed the door behind him, the colonel pulled up the chair, took a seat and glanced at Maxim.

'Well?' he asked.

'I think, I'm going to choose the prison,' Maxim answered.

For some time the colonel remained in silence, closely examining Maxim. Then he opened his lips: 'That's your final decision?'

'Yes.'

The colonel spent some time peering into Maxim's eyes, as if trying to penetrate his soul. In response, Maxim even had the audacity to smile.

'You made your choice yourself,' the colonel said then got up from the chair and left the room. Maxim was once again alone.

No one disturbed Maxim for the next couple of hours and he had time to think about his fate. Did he regret what happened? No. He chose the world of dream searchers himself and, if he were given another shot at it, he wouldn't do anything differently. They say that a tiger that has tasted human blood doesn't recognize any other food – the same with a person who has tasted the secrets of magic. He will no longer be able to go back to an ordinary life. It's a somber comparison, but it was what popped into Maxim's head. For a chance to touch upon a mystery you'd give anything. True, he had a bad turn of luck; he was among the losers. It happens.

When the door opened again, Maxim even smiled – here we go…

He was moved onto a stretcher, taken out of the cell and carried to the elevator in the company of armed guards. While the elevator was going up, Maxim was softly smiling. Perhaps, he would have a chance to see the sun one last time.

He really did see the sun – it was bright and warm. Dear to him. However, it was immediately covered by the tainted windows of the already familiar minibus.

He didn't know where they were taking him. Marchenko wasn't on the bus; Maxim was accompanied by some major and three masked guards. They drove for quite a while, at some point Maxim caught the rumble of an airplane. They must have taken him to the airport.

It was indeed an airport. The minibus smoothly drove onto the aerodrome territory and stopped. When Maxim had been carried out of the car, he saw an airplane nearby – by the looks of it, it was a "TU-134". Maxim was carried into the cabin, where a woman doctor expected him. The woman smiled and gave him an intravenous injection in his arm; Maxim didn't protest. He simply knew that should he only start resisting, these fine gentlemen with the fire arms would immediately calm him down. The last one to enter the plane was the major. A couple more minutes went by, and the airplane started taxiing out onto the runway...

Chapter Seven

The Final Battle

This was already getting beyond the borders of decency. Having found out that Vorontzov had escaped and killed four guards in the process, Yana got immensely annoyed. She just couldn't understand how one could escape from a prison cell, being handcuffed and watched by two musclemen. When, however, the ashamed prison guards told her how the searcher managed to get away, Yana went completely mad. She could understand if he had used some kind of magic tricks, then the behavior of the guards could have been justified somehow. But the searcher outplayed the guards on their home field – so there was really nothing to discuss.

Yana was sitting in a luxurious armchair of a Legion deputy of the Rostov region. The Deputy himself, a flabby and visibly balding man about fifty years old, was standing before her, with his gaze lowered. True, his people fell short of their target, and the Deputy was perfectly aware of that.

The Deputy was silent, and so was Yana, thinking about what she should do with this man. She had only to whisper a few words to Dags and this idiot would be gone. Only, who would take his place? Another idiot?

'Look, Konstantin Andreevich,' Yana finally said. The Deputy started. 'You are not directly at fault in the incident. However, you know perfectly well that ultimately, the manager is the one responsible. We'll consider you lucky this time, but another mistake will cost you your career – and that's at best. As for the idiots that lost Vorontzov, deal with them yourself. Is that clear?' Yana got up from the armchair and walked up to the Deputy.

'Yes, Yana Igorevna, I'll take care of everything.'

'Let's hope so. I'm going back to Moscow; if there's any news, let me know at once.' Yana picked up her handbag from the table, walked past the Deputy and left the office.

'Goodbye, Yana Igorevna.' The belated farewell of the Deputy reached her ears.

'Moron,' Yana mumbled and headed for the exit.

A limousine was waiting for her by the entrance to the residence; an obliging guard opened the door before her.

'To the airport,' Yana flung out.

A minute later the limousine was already carrying her down the streets of Rostov. Yana was sullenly looking through the window, but her mind was somewhere completely different.

It was not without reason that Yana was proud of her intuition. Back then, in the distant 1996, she didn't hesitate to cross over to the Legion's side – she simply knew that the future belonged to the Legion. But then a new century began, a new millennium – and what's the result? Despite the titanic efforts of the Legion, Russia was being reborn. At first it was only a matter of timid flashes. The leaders of the Legion thought them to be much like the spasms of a dying giant. No one believed that Russia could rise; that was against any common sense. But it was rising nevertheless. There were more and more confirmations of that; even the Supreme Hierarchs had become aware of the situation – after all, the fact that they hurriedly developed the strategy of the final blow was far from a coincidence. The collapse of the Soviet Union was provoked by an artificial fall in oil prices – the empire was robbed of dollar injections and collapsed. Now they had decided to repeat the same procedure with Russia. Having bereaved Russia of the dollar inflow, you could easily provoke a social explosion. Now they even knew who would lead the explosion, who would stand at the head of a new democratic government, loyal to the Legion.

Yes, on the outside everything appeared to be fine – Russia was besieged; its destiny was decided. That's what the Supreme

Hierarchs believed – that's what they'd like to think. But would their plans come true? That's something Yana had all reason to doubt.

Maxim didn't know where they were taking him. What's more, he didn't care. They were taking him somewhere because they had to. After the take off, he spent some time just lying on the stretcher, listening to the din of the engines then he fell asleep.

He woke up from a hard bump. He involuntarily grasped the edges of the stretcher and realized that the airplane had just touched the landing strip.

Ten minutes later they carefully carried him out of the airplane; it was already night outside. So, they've been flying east, Maxim guessed.

Next to the airplane was a white medical minibus. Maxim was carried inside and put on a couch. The major and two guards had made themselves comfortable nearby. The back door slammed and the minibus slowly took off.

The trip lasted for about twenty minutes. When the minibus finally stopped, the back door opened again. The major climbed out and went away; the wearisome minutes of waiting dragged on. Then there was a sound of an engine and another car stopped not far from the microbus. The major went up to the car.

'Take him,' he said to someone; some person immediately climbed into the minibus. Maxim glanced at him and started. It was Boris.

'Hi there,' Boris said, grabbing hold of the stretcher's handles. 'Don't get up, everything is okay.'

'Boris,' Maxim whispered and sighed with relief.

Then Denis appeared in the doorway, together with Boris he pulled the stretcher out of the car.

Nearby was a yellow emergency minibus. They loaded Maxim inside. For some time Maxim could still hear quiet talking outside then everything ended. Denis took the driver's seat; Boris got into the cabin and shut the door. The engine started softly spinning; the minibus was slowly gaining speed.

Boris looked at Maxim with a smile: 'Still alive?' he inquired.

'Partly,' Maxim answered and smiled in response. 'Is Oxana okay?'

'Yes, yes. She's safe and sound, don't worry,' Boris grinned. 'You'll see her in a couple of hours.'

'We're in Novosibirsk?' Maxim guessed.

'That's right.'

Maxim sighed wearily. He lay there for a little while then glanced up at Boris. 'What happened? They promised to send me to prison. I thought that's where they were taking me.'

'They probably offered you a job?' Boris guessed.

'They did.'

'And you declined?'

'That's right.'

'That's why you're here. You'd be of no use to them in prison; they just wanted to scare you, trying to persuade you to come work with them. When that failed, they resorted to plan B. Marchenko called me – we go way back. Told me that they've got you and offered to make a deal.'

'What do you mean?' Maxim didn't understand.

'You know, tit for tat. They let you go. We help them out with something. We had to agree.'

'And what was that something?' Maxim asked worriedly.

'We will have to work with a man, a member of the White House staff. That is, the American White House, not ours. The special agencies need that man; we will help them pressure him.'

'And how will you do that?' Maxim asked. He really didn't like this whole story.

'We're going to put his wife into a coma. Once he'll agree to work for our special agencies, his wife will regain consciousness.'

For some time Maxim was silent, trying to grasp what he had just heard.

'But you can't do that,' he said. 'It's wrong.'

'It is wrong,' Boris agreed. 'But that's the price we had to pay for your life; we had to agree. Besides, that woman is in no real danger. She'll spend a couple of weeks in a coma then we'll pull her out of there.'

'Can you really put someone in a coma?' Maxim inquired.

'You can. You just need to find that person in a lucid dream and get him into a place where he won't be able to get out of himself. In the real world it will look like the man just fell asleep, went into a coma. A lethargic sleep, more specifically.'

'Then that means that a lethargic sleep is when a person gets lost in his dreams?'

'Something like that,' Boris agreed. 'Usually, it happens quite rarely; man has got innate defense mechanisms. But an experienced dreamer could knowingly get someone into such a wilderness from where you wouldn't be able to get out on your own. As a result, you simply won't wake up.'

Maxim didn't answer this time either. For some time he lay there, then glanced back at Boris. 'I'm sorry about this,' he said. 'It's my fault.'

'Forget about it,' Boris smiled. 'We'll wiggle out. And you are not at fault for what happened – you did everything right. The Legionaries were watching you all the way from Petersburg; you had no chance of escaping them.'

Maxim frowned.

'Yana showed me photos of Andrey. He's dead... Is it true?'

'Yes, Maxim,' Boris sighed and lowered his gaze. 'It's true.'

'But how could it happen? How can you kill someone that can't be killed?'

'You can kill anyone, Maxim. They simply poisoned Andrey. He sensed danger and had time to hide his wife and children. But he couldn't get away himself.'

'He's got children?'

'Yes. Pavel, he's fifteen. And Olga, she'll be one soon.'

Maxim started thinking. Turns out that young fellow was Andrey's son. And they poisoned Andrey – it's so like the legionaries.

Boris glanced at Maxim. 'Let's not talk about the sad stuff,' he said. 'Get some rest, we'll be home soon.'

Apparently, he dozed off again. When Maxim woke up he realized that the minibus was making a turn; the city lights were shining around him. A couple of turns along the narrow lanes, then a stop and he could hear the gates open and the engine spin again. That's it...

'We're home now,' Boris sighed with relief.

'Yes... I'll get up...' Maxim tried to get up, but Boris held him back.

'Lay down. We'll carry you over.'

Maxim didn't object, feeling that he could lose consciousness any minute now. He was carefully carried out of the car then there was the sound of Oxana's voice nearby:

'How is he?'

'He'll live,' Boris replied. 'He just needs some rest.'

Maxim opened his eyes and saw Oxana bending over him. He tried to smile. 'Hi,' he said quietly. 'Happy to see you.'

'Hi, Maxim.' Tears glimmered in Oxana's eyes. 'Everything will be ok.'

'I know that too,' Maxim answered. With pleasure he glanced at the searcher residence towering before him – the familiar house, the porch that was already like his own. And here's Galina...

'Hello, Maxim-boy! You are allowed to eat, right? I've made some soup.'

'I'm allowed everything now.' Maxim smiled and closed his eyes.

He felt very good about being back in his room. Maxim was lying in his bed, feeling the tears rolling from his eyes. He started blinking hastily – Galina had just entered the room.

Maxim rejected Galina's attempts to feed him off the spoon

right away. He ate on his own, enjoying not only the quite delicious soup, but also Galina's incessant chattering. Listening to her was nice. Then he fell asleep, and when he woke up it was already morning.

The first one to enter Maxim's room was the doctor who in his day examined Kostya Prilukov. Having assessed Maxim's condition, the doctor was left very pleased.

'Everything is great,' he said. 'You were lucky; it's quite a fortunate injury. I mean, it could have been much worse.'

Maxim ate breakfast again in Galina's company. It was past eight o'clock in the morning, all the searchers had left – they all had business to attend to. Maxim finished his breakfast and for some time just lay in bed, thinking about the last events, then he fell asleep.

Closer to lunch time Boris walked into his room. He just got back and had two beer cans in his hands.

'You're being too quiet,' he said with a grin. He threw one can to Maxim – no allowances for the disabled – and sat down in an armchair. Maxim caught the can, and felt a piercing sensation in his side. He involuntarily smiled – Boris was true to himself. Nothing could throw him off balance.

'We haven't actually got anything to talk about, really,' Maxim shrugged. 'Everything is kind of clear anyway. Thank you for getting me out – for the second time now.'

'Oh, stop it.' Boris opened the beer and foam spurted out of the can. 'Damn it! Is it old, or something?' He took a sip and gurgled the beer in his mouth. 'Nope, seems fine.' Having made himself comfortable in the armchair, he looked back at Maxim. 'I've got good news – we've finally managed to figure out Dags. And it's all thanks to you.'

'And we'll be able to get him?' Maxim inquired.

'We will. But not the way you think. Rada and I have recently developed a new method – remember I've told you about programming events?'

'Yes,' Maxim nodded. 'Only, I never really understood how it is done.'

'We just haven't really talked about it, that's all. You see, there are two levels of influencing events – for now, we'll name them the external and the internal levels. The external one is when you work with what is around you. Your whole toolset, all of the elements of the chains of events are in front of you. Using your intention, you can weave these elements into a chain of your liking; you can play with them like with a toy construction set. Of course, at the same time you would have to take into account the flow of events, the nature of the further development of the situation. A searcher in this case is like a switchman, moving the situation into the needed channel. The switches are the key elements of the situation. For example, someone is aiming a gun at you – sorry, if it's a bad example.' Boris sipped some beer. 'To avoid the bullet, you can make the cartridge case the key element of the situation. It simply won't work – it won't fire. Your intention will direct the development of the situation into the right channel. After all, a cartridge may fire, and it may not. The odds are against you – about ninety-nine to one, if not less. But your intention allows you to draw that particular chance – do you understand?'

'More or less,' Maxim nodded. 'And what if he readjusts the lock and pulls the trigger one more time?'

'Then you're a dead man,' Boris shrugged. 'But that's the whole point – that you will have time to take adequate actions. To run away or get him and not let him fire again. Your magic know-how in this case gives you a chance to escape. But you will probably not be able to repeat this trick because there are no miracles.' Boris sipped some more beer. 'To practice this level of interacting with reality, try working with little events – the ones for the realization of which everything is ready. The probability of such events is pretty high in itself; it's the ideal testing area for polishing the technique of intention, especially if you take into account that a beginner's intention is very weak, practically unworkable.'

216

'And what does it look like in practice?' Maxim inquired.

'Very simple. For example, you could want a bird to fly by you. Shape a picture of this event in your mind – imagine that bird fly you by. The clearer you'll see the picture with your inner eye, the better. Then calmly await the results. And don't get too worked up about this exercise: if it works – great, if not – well, to hell with it. This kind of indifference is one of the keys to success. I've already told you that when you really want something, your desire immediately launches a counteraction from the real world. But when you are indifferent, everything works out. Again, there's another detail – being indifferent to the result, you still have to know that there will be a result. It's a sort of undisputable knowledge that your order will be fulfilled. After all, you are a magician, and a magician's intention is the law. If everything is done right, the bird will fly by you in the next ten or twenty seconds. Of course, if there is a bird nearby.'

'When we met in Rostov, was that the method you used? That is, you imagined a sparrow sitting on the bench?'

'Not quite. The truth is that you only need the picture in the beginning, while you are still learning. With time, your intention alone will be enough. By doing this exercise, you learn to interact with the Nagual. For an ordinary person the Nagual doesn't exist. Consequently, in his life there is no room for miracles. A magician enters the Nagual into his cosmography charts as an element responsible for miracles. Castaneda's teacher said that the Nagual is the place where the Power resides. A magician learns to interact with that power, to control it. Notice this: if you just enter the Nagual into your inventory list, it won't be of any use. At this point you need to apply effort like you would when training muscles – the Nagual becomes an actual existing element in your life only when you start using it. The exercise I described to you is meant precisely for such a practice. Lots of little events are happening around you all the time; you are learning how to influence them. Usually, the first couple of experiments go pretty well then comes the period of calm – the world stops answering your efforts. It's a normal reaction of the real world to interfering with its subtle mechanisms – a manifestation of its immunity. With time your ability to influence the events going on around you will resume – you could say then that the system has upgraded your status. Only once that's been done you'll be able to truly develop your skills; to get a result you would only need the intention to get it. But, as I've already mentioned, you need to start with something simple – with the flight of the birds, butter-flies, with falling leaves, dog barks, car honks and other events like that.'

'I get the general idea,' Maxim nodded. 'Okay, that's the external level. And what's with the internal one?'

'The internal level is actually the mystery of mysteries. Has Rada told you about labyrinths?'

'No,' Maxim drawled hesitatingly. 'She mentioned it once, saying that you could end up in a labyrinth when having a lucid dream. But we never spoke about it in detail.'

'Then we'll talk about it now, thankfully we've got enough time. First off, what are labyrinths? They are a sort of energy structures that have a direct influence on our life. There are three types of labyrinths.' Boris became thoughtful for a second. 'The first labyrinth is the labyrinth of life. It could also be called the wheel of fate. Interestingly enough it is not a metaphor. The labyrinth of life is a specific energy formation, and all of us, from birth do the very death, are bound to move in it. The most notable thing is that our being in a particular section of this labyrinth has a direct impact on our current life. You could say that the labyrinth of life is a template: a program that determines the course of our life. You could reach the labyrinth of life in a lucid dream or during deep meditation. The labyrinth is hard to describe – it is something that's permeated with a complex web of interconnected tunnels. Once in the labyrinth, you can try going to another place – it feels like flying, like moving along a tunnel.

Usually, you are trying to get out to a brighter place. If you've managed to move in the system of the labyrinth of life, your life in the real world will change as well – something will happen that could change your life dramatically. That's why the labyrinth of life is responsible for big, determining events in our life.

'The second labyrinth' Boris continued, 'is the labyrinth of events. On the one hand you could consider it subordinate to the labyrinth of life, because if you moved in the labyrinth of life, the labyrinth of events will immediately "work off" this movement with specific events. But there's another side to it: everything that happens in the labyrinth of events moves us along the labyrinth of life as well. It could be likened to a mechanical clock, where the labyrinth of life is the hour hand, while the labyrinth of events is the minute hand. You move one hand, the other moves too. That is, a magician can work with one labyrinth as well as with the other. The difference is only in the level of hierarchy, in the scale of events. The labyrinth of events is that cause-effect matrix that connects millions of big and small events. And for the most part we're ordinary extras in that matrix. Each of us lives in the whirlpool of events; we are thrown from side to side, and for an ordinary person to foresee where we'll get carried off next time, is practically impossible. Man tries to fight, tries to achieve something, but in most cases he's left with nothing. And the main cause for that is that he doesn't understand the nature of this mechanism.

'The third labyrinth,' Boris continued after a short pause, 'is the labyrinth of attachments, the labyrinth of interests. In our diagram with the clock we can think of it as a second hand. Our attachments to some things are what shape the lion's share of our actions – and that means, at the end of the day, they also shape our life. Someone likes sports, someone likes books, someone is crazy about dogs, someone else prefers drugs, another thinks there's nothing better than intrigues and politicking. And there are millions of such attachments, at the same time they are characteristic of most people. Moreover, the harm of all of this is also in that attachments take a lot of energy away from us; they demand our constant attention. These are real attention traps. At the same time, the life of an ordinary person consists mostly out of such traps; he moves from one trap to another, sacrificing a part of his power to each one. This drains us in the most monstrous way – and if a person has no energy, consequently, he is unable to influence his life. The labyrinths have a firm grip on him, not leaving the man a single chance. That's why don Juan advised Castaneda to get rid of attachments, to clear his life of excessive rubbish. Only then do we get power, only then are we able to have a real impact on our fate. Do you get the idea? Roughly?'

'Roughly – sure,' Maxim nodded. 'But I'll have to work on this, and work pretty hard.'

'Of course,' Boris agreed. 'Now we only have to look at one more detail: namely, how a man can get into the nets of the labyrinths. As I've already mentioned, all three labyrinths form a well-defined hierarchic structure: the labyrinth of life, the labyrinth of events and on the lowest level – the labyrinth of attachments. You could even say that it's all one labyrinth, made out of three parts – three sublevels. But the most interesting thing for us is that the labyrinth keeps spreading certain spores, embryos, points of future growth. And these spores can become embedded in our consciousness. Each such spore represents an embryo of a future attachment. If a person is weak, the spore sprouts and that person becomes addicted. That is, he starts smoking or suddenly takes to drinking – these are the simplest examples. Such an embryo of a future labyrinth, having become embedded in the consciousness of a person, starts developing very rapidly. For example, at first the man smoked a cigarette a day, then more and more. He reaches a level – say, a packet a day. That is the level of satiety of the labyrinth of attachments. The second hand has completed the circle, now the minute hand starts moving. Then, with time, the hour hand. The movement of the minute hand manifested in spending money on cigarettes, in fighting with his wife who cannot stand cigarette smoke. Already the movement of the hour hand influences the entire course of a man's life: our smoker gets lung cancer and dies. That is a graphic diagram of how labyrinths develop, and what influence they have on our life.'

'But then that means that each person has got his own labyrinths?'

'In some sense, yes. At the same time, these labyrinths are characteristic of all people. That is why they are also called archetypical. It's like with a flat: you are kind of living by yourself. But at the same time, next to you, there are hundreds of people that live in flats just like yours, while all of you live in one house.'

'All right, but not every labyrinth leads to such tragic consequences – like cancer?'

'Of course not,' Boris agreed. 'But each labyrinth is potentially striving towards its development. And if there is a possibility of growth, it grows.' Boris fell silent for a couple of seconds. 'Now, about the most important thing for us, you see – there are also artificial labyrinths. That is, labyrinths created by someone with a specific goal in mind. First, you create a spore of a future labyrinth, a spore that has a fully specified program of development. You can embed it into the consciousness of a person in a lucid dream, and the spore itself is created there too. This is more or less how it works: you find yourself in a lucid dream, create with the help of intention the canvas of a future situation – to describe how it's done using words is very difficult. But in practice everything is rather simple. Then you dissolve the obtained image, leaving only the lines of intention. You roll them up into a seed, a spore, and place it into the body of a person – of course, to do that you'd need to meet that person in a lucid dream. That's it, it's done. The man wakes up, quite unaware that there is already an embryo of a future labyrinth inside of him. The embryo sprouts, directing the chain of events into the right channel. What exactly will happen to that person depends on the program you've put into the seed. It could do good to him or it could have negative consequences – for example, it could be aimed at the appearance of a disease. However, I'd caution you against using this technique, even if you mean to do good – you cannot influence people without their consent, because then it would be black magic, and for a man of knowledge that would be unacceptable.

'I think, I understand,' Maxim said thoughtfully. 'You want to embed an embryo into Dags's consciousness?'

'Yes. But it will be a special kind of embryo.' Boris went quiet for a second. 'Some time ago we did some research, trying to find efficient ways of prolonging human life. We haven't gotten the result we were looking for yet, but when conducting this research we've come across some rather interesting details. Have you ever heard anything about progeria?'

'I don't know, to tell you the truth. It sounds kind of familiar.'

'Progeria is a disease characterized by a very fast aging process.'

'Right, I remember,' Maxim nodded. 'I've heard about this.'

'All the better. When afflicted with this disease, a ten year old child could look like an old man – or, to be more specific, he is an old man. The biological clock of someone afflicted with progeria has got a different rhythm, much faster than that of an ordinary person. As a result, a man very quickly grows old and dies. We managed to find someone with that disease; we worked on him a little, trying to figure out the mechanisms of this illness. Because, if you manage to find out how the human biological clock works, you get a chance to slow it down and thereby prevent aging. It turned out that the energy body of those afflicted with progeria has one characteristic feature. We couldn't remove this anomaly; it proved to be surprisingly stable. But creating it in a healthy individual turned out to be quite doable.'

'And have you tried doing that?'

'Of course, not,' Boris shook his head. 'We found out about a potential possibility of such an impact on a human being, and Rada did a few experiments on mice. That's, actually, much more difficult to do than with a human being. The effect was staggering – right after having been exposed to Rada's manipulations, a young mouse grew old and died only in a couple of days. Now we are planning on doing the same thing to Dags – I think that after Andrey's death we've got a perfect right to do that. Rada will form the right embryo and embed it into Dags's body. If everything goes as planned, Dags won't last a month.'

'Magic is starting to scare me,' Maxim said, having smiled apologetically. 'What if techniques like that will get into the hands of the villains?'

'That's why we keep these techniques a secret, so that something like that won't happen. We don't even write them down, but simply pass them on from person to a person. That's the safest way.'

'Yes, perhaps... Can I be of any help?' Maxim inquired.

'Don't think so,' Boris smiled. 'You've done your part – you helped us find Dags. Are you going to get some rest?'

'Yes, a little.'

'Then stay in bed. We'll have time to talk.'

Maxim was forced to spend eight days in bed, all this time he was being looked after by Anna Andreevna, an elderly assistant nurse – the doctor brought her. The doctor himself visited Maxim twice more. The last time, he carefully examined Maxim then smiled:

'Wonderful,' he said with satisfaction. 'You can gradually start getting up; you only have to bandage the wound more tightly – for the ribs. I think, Anna Andreevna can go home, you don't need her anymore.'

When the doctor left Maxim felt like a mummy – that's how tight the bandage over his ribs was. Still, the bandage was what allowed him to get up on his feet. Clutching at the bed-rail, he sat down then slowly got dressed – his clothes were lying on a chair right next to him. He carefully got up – it wasn't too bad, he'd survive.

By the end of the second week Maxim felt much better, and after yet another week he was able to start doing some light exercises in the sports hall. Roman obtained a new set of documents for him and Maxim started going out to town. The first couple of visits he paid to the dentist: he had to remove the consequences of getting acquainted with the Legionaries' fists. He went a couple of times with Oxana to the movies, happy that their relationship was slowly improving. At first he was a little apprehensive, thinking that Oxana was just trying to somehow thank him for helping her get away – back then, in the underground passage. But little by little that worry dispersed. There was no gratitude in Oxana's eyes; something greater was shining in them. Love? Maxim really wanted to believe that.

There was also another issue that had often been on Maxim's mind lately: his work – his flowers, his house, the company he created. And while he didn't worry too much about losing the company – which was a surprise to Maxim too – the realization that his plants would now die without him caused him pain. After all, they are alive too; they trusted him and he abandoned them. True, it wasn't of his free will. But still...

Nevertheless, gradually Maxim accepted that fact too. Boris told him that a magician doesn't have a destiny. Unfortunately, he was right, as always. And while the Legion exists, while there is an active opposition, all other businesses and cares must be a second priority. Too bad he didn't realize that right away.

He wondered; do magicians ever feel happy? They probably do. Rada told him once that she's happy. And it showed. Her real name was Svetlana – that means light. To understand that you just had to look at her. She's always very calm and gentle. You look at her, and it seems as if her whole body is illuminated with an inner light; take her eyes alone – a very unusual combination of warmth, tenderness – and power. It seemed that in her presence, even the clock on the wall didn't tick as loud as before; the level of her calm was simply contagious as if she was always accompanied by a cloud of soft silence. Maxim remembered how Rada on occasion could put out even the most heated argument by simply appearing in the room. It's just that in her presence any arguments lost their meaning. When looking at Rada, Maxim sometimes got a little dismayed – he simply knew what gigantic efforts he had to apply, to reach her level. She managed – would he?

By the end of June Maxim was fully recovered and actively joined in the work. Now he knew that his only task was fighting the Legion. Everything else would happen later – if it would ever happen.

The searchers' main objective right now was assigning the first mass of graduates of the School of Keepers – female Keepers to be more specific. This time there were twenty three of them. Some returned to their cities, others moved to new ones. The searchers had to help many of them settle in at their new location, provide security – all of that required a lot of organizational work. Maxim was directly assisting in the organization process; sometimes he had to make trips every week. The Keepers, mostly young ones, treated him with great respect; Maxim thought it was both funny and embarrassing. They considered him a searcher, although, in reality, he practically didn't have any experience at all. Nevertheless, he did an excellent job, having safely settled four alumni in a new place. For the time being, they'd be on their own, but with time new teams will start forming around them. What's more important is that already at this point the keepers could have the most favorable effect on the spiritual atmosphere of their cities. When they've managed to involve at least two thirds of the large Russian cities in this project, Legionaries will be in a tough spot. According to Boris, there'll be a domino effect: the good energy of these cities will start affecting other cities. And then

Legionaries would have to get out of the country whether they like it or not. When there's no support in the hearts of the people, any games lose their meaning.

It was past the tenth of August when Boris and Rada told everyone that everything was ready for the decisive duel with Dags. Rada was certain she'd get it right.

'All right, everything is clear with Dags,' Maxim said during one of the evening get-togethers. 'But what do we do with Yana? The same thing?'

'No,' Boris shook his head. 'Unlike the Legionaries, we do not wage war on women. But I believe that one day Yana will still get what she deserves. It can't be any other way – what is meant to pass always comes to pass.'

A group meeting was announced to discuss and prepare the attack on Dags. On the fourteenth of August, the representatives of several groups assembled in the house – eleven people altogether, many of whom Maxim met for the first time.

The discussion of the forthcoming operation lasted more than five hours. As far as Maxim had managed to gather, they planned on attacking from two sides at once – in the real world and in the dream world. Furthermore, the first attack had to take place during the day, the second – at night. The probability of success of the military operation was estimated to thirty percent – Dags's security was made out of former government security men and it was very well organized. Apparently, Dags assumed that someone could set up an assassination, so if there was a need to leave his residence, he used the services of three corteges at the same time. All three were identical – no one could know in advance which one Dags would use. And even if you had the right car it didn't guarantee success – the traffic routes were constantly changed, and the armored frame and windows of the limos could stand the hits of even large caliber bullets. Still, they decided to go through with the attack – even an unsuccessful outcome had its advantages. Dags was expecting a potential attack and, having realized that it failed, would fall asleep confident that he's safe for now. Thus, he would not be prepared for someone to attack him on the same night.

Denis was the one to be most enthusiastic about the upcoming operation; he and his people were entrusted with preparing and executing the military action.

'I hope he won't live until nightfall,' Denis said, when all the details of his assignment had been clarified. 'Well, and if he does, you'll deal with him.'

The following morning the guests departed; the date of the operation was chosen to be the first of September – the Day of Knowledge. There was a point to it – they managed to find out that on that day Dags always paid a visit to one of the Moscow business colleges. The financial and industrial group, officially led by Dags, created this college seven years ago. And it was far from an unselfish act – every second college graduate became a member of the Legion. The fact that they knew Dags's exact destination increased the chances of a successfully executed operation.

The details of the nocturnal operation were also drawn up with the information that had been collected on Dags in mind. His guardians hindered anyone from harming him – thus, it was necessary to create a situation where they wouldn't have time to interfere. Now the searchers knew how to do that.

All last week Dags was in an excellent mood. God knows, he didn't spend so much effort and energy for nothing – his diligence had been noted and appreciated. It was communicated in the letter delivered by secret mail that he was going to be promoted and transferred to the central apparatus of the Legion. In his new position he would curate all of the matters concerning the countries of Eastern Europe and former USSR. Subordinate to him would be tens of ordinary Sovereigns – that would mean something. And who knew, perhaps with time he would get a chance to grow to the level of a Hierarch too.

The new appointment faced Dags with the necessity of finding someone to replace him. Yana would be the most suitable candidate, however the Supreme Hierarchs would never approve of such a choice. Besides, Dags too had his doubts about the advisability of advancing Yana on the career ladder; in his opinion, she had already reached the limit available to a woman. So, after a brief moment of wavering, Dags suggested Rat-catcher as his replacement – the Deputy of the Krasnoyarsk region. Perhaps, he wasn't the sharpest tool in the box, but he was honest and completely devoted to the Legion; a real campaigner – earnest, industrious. You could hardly find anyone better than him. And then Yana would, of course, shoulder all the main work; that's what they were paying her for. Of course, if Rat-catcher decided to leave her with him... Dags knew that in their days they'd had rather strained relations.

Over the last couple of months Dags had been able to carry through several brilliant operations – of course, not without the help of the curators of appropriate sectors. Remembering how skillfully he had managed to play on the disagreements between Russia and a couple of CIS countries, Dags only smiled. Indeed, it was all about divide and conquer. There wasn't a more fertile ground than the ambitions of the political leaders of the post-soviet elite. And there was an interesting trend: the paltrier the dog, the harder it tried to bite its former master. And if biting didn't work, then you could at least bark at him – what else were they capable of doing.

Nevertheless, Dags knew perfectly well that in the present condition the complete rebirth of Russia was only a matter of time. Even with the upcoming revolution in Ukraine, Dags didn't have any illusions; at best, it would be a temporary success. That's why he thought the new appointment to be a godsend: when the tide turned someone else would have to answer for it – Rat-catcher, for example. But no one would ever be able to place the blame on him for anything.

The morning of the first of September started pretty well too. The sun was shining bright outside; Dags was examining himself in the mirror and thinking that he looked exceptionally impressive in a suit. And that's how it should be.

Today they awaited him at the college. It was the little things in life that mattered – they must train the future staff themselves, bring them up from scratch, from the cradle, and nurture them in the spirit of loyalty to new life ideals. And most importantly, keep them as far away as possible from the Orthodox Church – the most dangerous enemy of the new life.

Thoughts about enemies led him to thinking about the searchers – lately they hadn't done anything noteworthy. Had they given up, left the stage? Not very likely, they're not the ones to give up – they were probably scheming again.

That's what was on Dags's mind when he climbed into the armored security jeep. For a while now, on the chief of security's advice, he preferred to travel this way.

The first cortege left the territory of the villa, then followed the second – both were headed for Moscow by different routes. After them followed the cortege with Dags in the head security car.

Sitting in the cabin of the jeep, rushing along the highway, Dags thought about how that in a month or so he'd say the last goodbye to these problems. No matter how you viewed it, the searchers had always been and were the most serious threat. There, far away from them, he would feel a bit safer.

The explosion was heard when the cortege slowed down before making a turn. At first Dags caught the reflection of a flash; a moment later he heard a rumble. Dags involuntarily started. He was immediately pressed into the seat – his driver was leading the car away from the dangerous place. Dags turned around and saw the limousine that had been thrown onto the roadside by the explosion. Right before his eyes from the woods, fire lightning darted towards the car. The sound of several explosions merged into one drawling boom, the expensive limousine turned into a ball of fire. Dags, who had by now gone pale, swallowed the lump in his throat – what if it was him in that car?

'Everything is okay,' the chief of security assured him. Dags thought the man's eyes were too calm. 'We got out.'

Dags decided not to cancel his visit to the college – "no one does two assassinations, one right after the other", he concluded. Besides, his foes were no doubt certain that he was no longer alive. That was a particularly pleasant thought, Dags even grinned, imagining the faces of his enemies – when they found out that he was alive. And they wouldn't even know what exactly had happened. They'd probably think that they had hit the wrong cortege. By the way, he'd definitely have to award the chief of security. Get him a tour on the Mediterranean ocean in the company of some pretty blonde or a brunette – that'd be up to him.

His speech dedicated to the beginning of a new academic year was pure success – and how could it be any other way? Dags spoke with enthusiasm about the new Russia, about its economic development, about a close cooperation with the world community, about that they – young men and women who have gathered in this room today – were to lead Russia forward, that they would be the heads of progressive fields and companies of the new Russian economy.

They applauded him. Dags was happy. It's the little things in life…

He was going home in the most wonderful mood. He was happy with everything: the good weather, his successful appearance. He was even happy with the failed assassination. Of course, his people would find out where the strings of conspiracy lead to. Everyone involved in this matter would certainly get what's coming to them.

He spent the evening in the company of several of the wealthiest people in Russia. They discussed many things: the changing oil prices, the government's attempts to get back once-stolen assets. The latter made Dags's colleagues seriously worried; however Dags hurried to assure them that nothing bad would happen. At most there'd be a couple of notorious and scandalous affairs intended rather for the average citizen. The members of the government and the parliament, loyal to the Legion, wouldn't allow anything more serious than that.

He went to bed after midnight. Before falling asleep, he lay for a long time, thinking about how his new life was going to be. They'd probably place him in Brussels. From there, he'd be able to do a better job controlling the work of his subordinates. Thinking about all these new perspectives made his head spin.

Then he fell asleep. Once in a lucid dream, he looked around, checking if the guardians were there. He ordered them to remain invisible – he didn't like them flashing before his eyes.

He was in a good mood. For about an hour Dags wandered the dream worlds, moving from one dream to another; the guardians glided nearby like shadows. Another dream – neat buildings, a cobblestone road – looked like the Swiss Alps. There were quite a few people, but it wasn't the real thing – just your ordinary phantoms. But here's something interesting...

A tall black-haired youngster was standing next to one of the houses – seventeen-eighteen years old tops, slim, even refined, with a slight fluff of an almost inexistent little moustache. He was dressed in plain blue jeans and a grey shirt with sneakers on his feet. The guy was carefully looking around; Dags got a physical sensation of joy coming from the guy. Compared to the faded phantoms this guy was particularly striking – must be new to this. He probably learned to have lucid dreams not long ago, that's why there are so many emotions.

'I could have some good times with him,' Dags thought. 'First here. Tame him, get him attached to me. Show him how nice it can be. Well and later, if everything goes well, I could find him in the real world. Invite him over to my place, find him a suitable position, for example, that of a secretary. Then I could take him with me to Brussels. That is, of course, if I take a real liking to the boy.'

The guy was about to leave. His awareness was still very weak; it occurred to Dags that the young man could wake up any moment now. And that's what made Dags hurry up.

'Hello there!' he said, having approached the youngster. The guy turned around. 'Don't be afraid. Do you understand me?'

'Yes,' the guy said after a short pause. 'I do. Are you a lucid dreamer too?'

'Yes, I am,' Dags confirmed. 'And I am one of the best in the world. I could teach you a great many things. Take me by the hand – don't be afraid. It will help you maintain your awareness.'

After a moment's hesitating the guy took his hand; it occurred to Dags that the most important thing now was not to scare him off. And then the young man would realize himself how great it was.

'That's good,' Dags said softly, looking the guy in the eyes. 'Now the other one.'

His voice had a calming effect. Dags felt the young man's other hand in his and smiled. Then, without diverting his gaze, he tried to merge their hands together. It worked, the young man turned out to be surprisingly yielding. The sensations were very pleasant. Dags wanted to draw the guy towards him and merge with him. But he tarried – let the lad do it himself.

Having sensed the approaching of alarmed guardians, Dags silently ordered them to move away. They obeyed just as silently. Sadly, these creatures couldn't always properly assess the situation.

'Do you like it?' Dags asked insinuatingly, peering into the guy's eyes.

'It's disgusting,' the guy said quietly, but very clearly; his grip suddenly became very firm. And then something happened that pierced Dags with a needle of terror. The guy's cute face suddenly twitched, became hazy and turned into Rada's. The young woman no longer concealed her power; Dags became terrified – that's how powerful she was.

'You'll come with me,' Rada said firmly. 'Kill these bastards!'

The last words were meant for Sly and another six searchers that appeared out of nowhere. A second earlier Dags felt a jerk – the guardians tried to save their master by pushing him out of the lucid dream. It didn't work – Rada held him very tightly. Having realized the reason for their failure, one of the guards threw itself at Rada, however its path was blocked by two searchers. In their hands they held small mirrors – the guardians had barely come up close, as they were hit by bright blinding rays of light. Dags sensed a low long drone – it was the guardians growling with pain, having experienced the fatal power of the mirrors.

At some point Dags thought to himself that this was the end. Rada's power suppressed and bound him; next to her Dags felt like a pitiful boy. He tried to break free again – and couldn't. A little longer, and they'd win.

They did not win. The power of the mirrors was obviously not enough to keep the guardians away. One of the guardians crumbled Sly – just a moment before the jaws of the shark toothed creature closed together on his body, the searcher disappeared. The second guardian was fighting the other searchers; the third hurried to his master's aid.

Rada didn't wait for the end; apparently, she realized that she had lost.

'You will die anyway,' she said, letting go of Dags's hands. 'I promise you that.'

The young woman disappeared; a moment later Dags jumped out of bed with a whiz.

'Oh God!' he exhaled. He was shaking. 'What was that?'

He sat on his bed for a while, coming around. Then he got up and went up to the bar. He poured himself half a glass of cognac, emptied it in one go and exhaled with a noise. Having closed the door of the bar, he went back to bed.

Perhaps for the first time in his life, he was afraid of going to sleep. Dags knew that it was over, that the cunning attack of the searchers had failed, and yet, he was still afraid. Now Dags knew that if he didn't go away, sooner or later they would definitely get to him.

Already by midday it became clear that Denis and his people's attack had failed – there was a message saying that Dags had held his speech before the college students.

'We probably got the wrong cortege,' Denis told Boris on the phone. 'So he's all yours now.'

'Yes, Denis. Thank you.'

No one really expected Denis and his fighters to finish Dags off, so Denis's message about their failure didn't really come as a surprise.

'Now it's our turn,' Boris said, having told the habitants of the house about what happened. 'Everything will be decided tonight.'

Maxim already knew that there would be eight people taking part in the operation: Boris, Roman, Rada, Iris, two experienced searchers from the Moscow group and two from the Petersburg group. Maxim himself and Oxana didn't take part in any of it – they were too inexperienced.

'It's dangerous, Maxim,' Boris explained to him, when Maxim offered his help. 'Just think about the situation realistically: we are not even asking Oxana, even though she's a much better lucid dreamer than you are. When we go out there, we'll need real fighters that can stand their ground. You don't know how to do that yet. So, no hurt feelings – only "the old guys" are going off to war.'

'I understand,' Maxim agreed. 'Then could you at least tell me how it will all happen?'

'Rada will lure him into a trap by taking on the appearance of a pretty young guy; the Moscow group managed to find out that

Dags has a weakness for them. That makes everything so much easier. When he gets closer, Rada will grab hold of him and we'll perform a distracting attack. While the guardians are busy fighting us, Rada will put the embryo implant into Dags's body. He won't even feel anything.'

'But can we at least watch it?' Maxim inquired. 'From the outside?'

'No, Maxim,' Boris shook his head. 'An encounter with a guardian could end with real physical injuries. You're not ready for such an encounter just yet. So you and Oxana will watch the house.'

'Fine,' Maxim shrugged and smiled. 'We will watch the house.'

Because of the time difference Boris, Rada and Roman went to bed at about three in the morning, all in one room. Maxim knew that at that very minute Iris was going to bed in Belgorod, another two searchers were going to bed in Moscow and two in St. Petersburg. They would meet at the Glade, and then Rada would begin the hunt on Dags.

Maxim and Oxana had settled on the chairs by the door outside the room. They didn't dare go inside – afraid to disturb the searchers, and they didn't want to go too far away either – just in case. Half past three in the morning, four in the morning, four-fifteen – will they succeed?

The hand on the clock was crawling up to four-thirty when they heard a bed creak and voices coming from the room. Oxana jumped off her chair and hurriedly threw the door open.

'Did it work?' Oxana blurted out from the threshold, once she saw Rada sitting on the bed.

'It did,' Rada said and smiled. Then she glanced at Boris. 'They didn't injure you, did they?'

'No,' Boris shook his head. 'I managed to slip away. Man, the teeth on that thing.' He sat up and sighed tiredly.

Roman slowly raised himself on the bed and circled everyone with his gaze. Then his lips widened in a smile. 'That, I tell you, was excellent. It was a long time since I had such good fun.'

'And you didn't take us with you,' Oxana said in an injured voice. 'That's not fair, you know.'

'The important thing is that we succeeded,' Rada answered. 'Dags has no more than a month left.'

'And what if he gets rid of the embryo?' Maxim inquired.

'That's unlikely. After all, he simply doesn't know about it. And once the embryo sprouts, getting rid of it will be impossible. By the way, how about a cup of tea and then go back to bed?' Rada glanced at Oxana.

'You mean I should make some tea?' Oxana specified.

'Sometimes you display the most amazing cleverness,' Rada smiled.

Yana received the news about Dags' promotion with satisfaction. She was simply confident that they would appoint her in his stead. Therefore, it annoyed her very much hearing her subordinates whispering that Rat-catcher would take the place of the Sovereign. The rumors were not groundless: two weeks ago Dags had called Rat-catcher into his office and spent almost three hours talking to him – the Sovereign rarely gave anyone that much time.

Yana had known the Rat-catcher for several years now; they had pretty strained relations. Back in the days, Rat-catcher tried to hit on her; one night in Sochi he even got into her apartment through the balcony – he must have wanted to feel young again. Yana's suggestion that he'd get out of there only made him even more excited; a couple of slaps in the face didn't manage to cool him down either. It all ended with Yana breaking a phone on the Deputy's head and calling the hotel security. Ever since that incident, their relationship was extremely formal; however Yana still caught an unhealthy shine in Rat-catcher's eyes every now and then. Now a Sovereign, he'd get back at her for everything, Yana didn't have a doubt about that. Nevertheless, she still refused to believe it. After all, it was all about the interest of the business – will that stupid martinet really be able to manage the affairs of the Legion? He'll ruin everything that took such time and effort to create.

Sadly, the rumors were confirmed. Having investigated through her own channels, Yana found out that Rat-catcher had already found a replacement and was now packing his things.

The worst part was not the fact that Dags decided to appoint Rat-catcher as his replacement, but that he didn't even consult her in this decision. Practically, she was the last to find out about it – now wasn't that an insult? One might as well regret that the recent double assassination attempt on Dags ended in failure.

Resentment was slowly growing in Yana's heart. She tried to keep a straight face, but that was beyond her. Sitting in her luxurious office, Yana was gloomily looking out the window and thinking that the searchers would never have treated her this way. Indeed, she had lost everything – she lost her friends, lost the excitement and the fun that once lived in her heart. And what did she get in return – this expensive fancy cage with a pool and a tennis court? Power? The opportunity to command people? What's the point of all of that, when there is no more light in your heart?

Soon the date of Rat-catcher's arrival became known; he was expected the twenty eighth of September. There was no point in further postponing the conversation with Dags.

The conversation turned out to be a difficult one. Yana still had a small hope that Dags appointed Rat-catcher only because he decided to take her with him. After all, she's not stupid; she could be of use to him over there too. However, that hope vanished already in the first couple of minutes talking to Dags. He was unusually rude to her, at some point he flew off the handle altogether and started accusing Yana of almost getting killed because of her, that she was the one to blame for the fact that the searchers were still alive. He told her that he was already long fed up with her mind games and that nothing of what she'd promised had been carried out yet. In the end, Dags told her to get lost, having said that he'd make all the arrangements with Rat-catcher concerning her future fate. And that she should pray to God not to end up in some godforsaken hellhole.

Yana left Dags's office feeling like she had just been spit on – she had never before been so humiliated. Some of the visitors standing outside Dags' office probably heard everything; Yana caught someone's evil laughter behind her back. Now she would, no doubt, get quite a different treatment.

The worst part was that Yana was forced to accept what happened – she simply had no other choice, and Dags knew that perfectly well. While he needed her, he tried to be on good terms with her. Now, however, he had spoken his mind. With Dags, she had been his right hand. With Rat-catcher everything would be different. Best case scenario – Yana sadly grinned – was that they would actually send her to Moldavia or Georgia, or they might even find a worse place than that.

Unfortunately, she had to stand it and believe that one day she would be able to get back at that bastard.

There were two weeks left before Rat-catcher's arrival. By Dags' order, Yana was removed from her duties, so when she was once again summoned to the Sovereign's office, sad thoughts were going through her head – he probably had another dirty trick in store for her.

The Sovereign's office greeted her with silence and semi-darkness – heavy curtains were hanging down and the lights were turned off.

'Come in,' Dags ordered. Yana carefully closed the door behind her. 'Sit down.'

Dags's voice was slightly quivering. Yana obediently walked up and seated herself in the armchair opposite the Sovereign.

'I want to talk to you.' Dags' voice faltered again. 'Can you tell me what's happening to me?' Dags stretched out his hand and turned on the table lamp.

Yana glanced at the Sovereign and started. Dags's face was covered in wrinkles; his skin had become flabby and dry. In the five days Yana hadn't seen him he'd gone twenty years older.

'Oh my God,' Yana involuntarily exhaled, looking at Dags with fear.

'Thank you for your kind words,' Dags said gravely. 'I repeat: can you tell me what's happening to me?'

'You're growing old.'

'That's not what I'm asking you!' Dags snapped, although he immediately resumed his calm. 'It's some kind of witchery. Have you ever heard about anything like this?'

'No.' Yana shook her head. 'But who could have done this?'

'Your favorite searchers,' Dags answered. 'It couldn't have been anyone else.' He went silent for a little while. 'Tell me, what should I do?'

'I don't know,' Yana replied quietly, thinking with horror that something like that could also happen to her. 'What do the doctors say?'

'Nothing; they've never seen anything like it.' Dags paused again then gave Yana a hopeful look. 'Help me, and I'll do anything you want for you. Talk to the searchers. Make them some kind of promise. Anything – even mountains of gold. Make a deal with them. Let them remove this curse.'

'Sovereign, they won't speak to me,' Yana lowered her head. 'It's impossible, and you know why.'

Dags didn't reply. He sat for a long time, with his head lowered. Yana saw the vein on his temple pulsate. Finally Dags straightened and glanced at her; in his eyes Yana caught the former cold determination.

'Get out of here,' the Sovereign said distinctly. 'Get lost.'

Yana pursed her lips. She slowly got up, threw the small strap of her handbag over her shoulder. She made a few steps towards the door, then halted and turned back to Dags.

'You know what? I'm even happy that it happened,' she said

with an icy smile. 'You got what you deserved.'

'Out!' Dags shouted, having slammed his fist on the table.

'Old goat,' Yana said resentfully; fire flashed in her eyes. 'You can go ahead and send your bastards after me, I won't hide.' Yana turned around and walked up to the door. In the silence hanging in the office you could clearly hear the sound of her heels. Then there was a creak of the door, and everything went quiet.

No one had ever spoken to the Sovereign that way. Knowing this, Yana expected retribution any moment, however it never followed. Either the Sovereign decided it unworthy to get back at a woman, or he had come up with something else for her. Still, the days left before Rat-catcher's arrival became the worst in the last couple of years for Yana. They took her representative limousine, deprived her of her guards, now Yana was using her Mercedes. She could clearly feel the respect for her drop. If before everyone wanted to be her friend, then now people demonstratively kept away. She was even abandoned by those who she considered to be her closest friends. Unfortunately, the last events clearly showed her that she had no friends.

Yana was sad. More and more often she remember the former Yana, the one who was fun and happy. After all, she had been happy, she had. And she had friends – the ones that would go through fire and water for her. Now her former friends had become her enemies – because of her. And who had her enemies become?

If it wasn't for Dana's death, it could all still be salvaged somehow. Dana's death crossed over everything – there was no way back. Yana was losing hope; she clearly saw her life fall apart.

Rat-catcher arrived precisely on the day and was received with all the proper honors. Tall and thin, Rat-catcher was very calm; Yana caught satisfaction in his eyes. Five people from his team arrived together with him; one of them would surely take her place. Yana looked at their pleased faces and felt the thirst for revenge stir in her chest.

Dags had not appeared in public for two weeks; people said that he was at his last gasp. The Sovereign refused to get hospitalized, Yana knew why – being a magician, Dags was aware of the uselessness of any medical treatment. Having handed all his dealings to Rat-catcher, he returned to his country residence. Three days later came the news of his death.

The Sovereign was buried with full honors; the ceremony was attended by prominent government officials. People spoke of him being the true patriot of the motherland – thanks to him Russia had gotten closer to Europe. One of the prominent human rights activists said that the humanist ideals of the deceased had won him well-deserved respect in life, and the memory of him will forever live in the people's hearts.

Hearing all of this made Yana, who also attended the funeral, smile a faint smile. Only a few of the people that had gathered knew about the man lying in the closed casket; for the majority of the people present he was a politician, a famous and respected businessman. Yana left before the end of the ceremony – she simply didn't want to waste time in a traffic jam made out of tens of expensive limousines.

She was called to the new Sovereign on Tuesday morning. Yana already knew that it wouldn't be an easy conversation, so she prepared in advance for a negative scenario.

Security let her through without any problems. 'I guess I should be grateful for letting me through', she thought. Once on the second floor, Yana went down the hallway then knocked on the door.

'Come in,' she heard the lazy voice of Rat-catcher.

'Hello, Sovereign,' Yana greeted him, entering the office and carefully closing the door behind her.

She didn't hear him greet her back. Having made himself comfortable in Dags's luxurious armchair, Rat-catcher, with a self-righteous smile on his face, was looking at Yana, while tapping his fingers on the desk. He wasn't even looking, he was openly eyeing her – Yana felt his cold, assessing gaze glide along her breasts, hips, legs. Indeed, she was being appraised – the way you appraise a street hooker.

'Well, hello there.' Rat-catcher finally opened his lips. 'And so we meet again. Isn't there anything you'd like to tell me?'

'No,' Yana said with an icy smile. 'I think I told you everything last time.'

'That's a shame,' Rat-catcher smiled. 'I was hoping your heart had thawed just a little bit during the years that have passed.'

'You hoped wrong.'

Rat-catcher sighed. Leaning back in his chair, he was thoughtfully looking at Yana, continuing to tap his fingers on the surface of the desk. 'Well, then so be it,' he finally broke the prolonged silence. 'I would like to congratulate you, Yana Igorevna; you've got a new assignment. You are being transferred to Turkmenistan; we need one of our own there. Warm climate, nice people – I think you'll like it.'

'To Turkmenistan?' Yana asked, moving nothing but her lips. It was even worse than she expected.

'It's a very responsible position, Yana Igorevna.' Rat-catcher's lips twisted in a superior smile. 'There's Caspian oil and you've got Iran nearby. You'll have the opportunity to demonstrate all of your talents.'

Yana squinted – this was beyond her. No one had the right to torture her this way.

'I've brought a resignation letter,' Yana said, opening her handbag.

'A resignation letter?' Rat-catcher asked. 'Yana, you know our rules – no one leaves us. And if they do, then they do so with their feet first.'

'Yes, I know,' Yana agreed. 'But I'll give it a try.' She took a small gun with a silencer out of her purse, threw up her hand and took aim at Rat-catcher. 'A new assignment, you say?'

Rat-catcher was still in his chair; his face had gone pale. Then he heavily swallowed, his Adam's apple moving.

'Yana, what are you doing?' Rat-catcher quietly mumbled, gripping the armrests of the chair. 'Don't do it. It's a stupid thing to do. I was joking – we can still make a deal.'

'I don't think so.' Yana shook her head. 'I'm sorry, Rat-catcher. I made a mistake, getting involved with you lot. Now I have to make up for it.' She raised the gun a little and fired, causing Rat-catcher to squeak. Then, pressing her lips together, she pulled the trigger a couple more times, the bullets, one after the other, dug into the body of the new Sovereign.

It was all over. Rat-catcher was lying with his body over the armrest of the chair and a thin trickle of blood running down from his mouth. Yana demonstratively blew into the silencer and smiled.

'You should have been more polite with me,' she said, looking at Rat-catcher. 'You can't even imagine what a woman is capable of, especially if you get her real angry. Bye!' Yana waved at the dead Sovereign, hid the gun in her handbag and left the office. She calmly walked down the hallway. On her way, she bumped into one of the Moscow officials, a short plump little man.

'He's busy right now,' Yana said, looking at the fat man with a smile. 'Wait for a half an hour, okay? He's got an important phone call.'

'Yes, Yana Igorevna,' the official agreed. 'Of course.'

'All the best,' Yana smiled again and headed for the stairs.

She calmly exited the house; no one stopped her. She got into her Mercedes, turned on the engine and smoothly drove out of the estate.

She had one more thing to do – it would be the last in this life. Having arrived at one of her apartments, Yana got behind the computer and e-mailed a few files she had prepared in advance. For safety, she used several e-mail addresses – she wanted to be sure that the files would reach their destination.

That's it. Yana left the apartment, locked the door and took the elevator down. Once outside, she stood there for a minute then got into the car and headed for the town exit.

The trip took about forty minutes. They could have stopped Yana at any point, but they didn't – she managed to leave the city without any problems. A thought flashed in her head – to leave, to disappear, but Yana dismissed it at once. It's stupid, pointless. Sure, she could hide – but what for? How do you live on, if you've got nothing left in this life?

She stopped on a narrow forest road; there was no point in going any further. Pine trees towered around her, a bright blue sky was peering through the tree tops. For some time Yana silently smoked; her gaze was unusually peaceful. Then she threw the cigarette butt out through the window and gave a tired sigh. She opened her handbag. Having retrieved the gun, she gently ran her hand along it then she quickly put the silencer top under her chin and pulled the trigger.

Epilogue

Maxim didn't think that he'd ever be able to go back to Rostov. But it happened as early as April the following year.

He was in for a surprise – both his house and his conservatory turned out to be intact. Even his plants were still alive; it turned out that Iris had hired a neighbor – an old lady – to take care of them. Maxim didn't expect such a gift from Iris and was truly grateful to her.

Perhaps, for the first time for the last few years, he could walk around the city without having anything to be afraid of – well, almost anything. The information sent by Yana was truly priceless: there was everything – names, contact information, posts of the Legion's officials, the entire architecture of the Legion, all the structures subordinate to the Legion. Having talked it over with colonel Marchenko, Boris handed him – of course, on certain terms – the received files. With such information in your hands you could feel like a god. Unsurprisingly, the local Legionaries couldn't stand the coordinated push of the special agencies and were forced to run away. Many preferred to leave the country altogether, rightfully assuming that it would be safer that way. In some regions, Legionaries were still holding on, trying to resist, but after the deaths of Dags and Rat-catcher, after the collapse of the Legion's structure, all of that was pointless.

Things were going quite well with Maxim's business too – it turned out that for the past few months his firm had only further strengthened its positions. After giving it some thought, Maxim decided to make the manager and the main workers of the firm partners, which guaranteed their interest in the job. That reduced his personal income, but it was worth it.

If everything was more than well with the business, then total uncertainty still reigned in Maxim's love life. Oxana clearly liked him; however, now Maxim himself preferred not to rush the events, afraid of being rejected again. Better let it happen on its own. He waited for Oxana's return to Rostov, hoping that then there'd finally be some clarity in their relationship. In order not to torment his soul, he tried not to think so much about it, preferring to fuss about with his plants or do magic research.

To Maxim's surprise, he was showing clear progress in magic. He had lucid dreams almost every night without having to apply any particular effort. There were also clear advances in the techniques of the real world; Maxim was getting better and better at understanding the laws governing the universe. Before, he couldn't even imagine that the real world would be so sensitive to his thoughts, his desires. All of that became a consequence of the purity Rada talked about. Stupid thoughts disappeared, as did stupid selfness. Maxim entrusted himself completely to the Spirit, acknowledging its power over him. It was a difficult thing to do, but Maxim managed to overcome himself. Everything was falling into place – to command, you had to learn how to submit. He, who puts himself on top of the world, makes a big mistake. Now Maxim knew how unnatural his former life had been, how little harmony and light it contained. He lived in the world – and didn't see it, didn't feel it. Now everything was different. Maxim realized with joy how harmonious his life was becoming.

That warm day in June Maxim, as usual, was working in his conservatory. He had just relocated one of his plants, when he heard someone softly knocking on the glass. He turned around – and saw Oxana.

'Oxana.' Maxim slowly got up, looking closely at the features of the face dear to him. Oxana smiled: Maxim smiled back and felt a weight lift from his chest. She came anyway.

'Hello,' Oxana said when Maxim opened the door of the conservatory. The young woman's gaze was kind and very warm.

'Hello,' Maxim replied. He wanted to embrace Oxana, kiss her, but restrained himself. 'Happy to see you.'

'And that's it?' Oxana grinned.

'If it was up to me, I would have kissed you all over. But I'm just afraid of hurting your feelings.'

'Don't be,' Oxana smiled, and was the first one to take a step towards him.

It was the longest and the most passionate kiss of his life. Finally, Maxim stepped away from Oxana, looked into her eyes and fell back to her lips. She didn't back away, and that seemed like a true miracle to Maxim.

'If you only knew how much I love you,' Maxim said, kissing the girl. 'If you only knew.'

'I know, Maxim. That's why I'm here,' Tears glistened in Oxana's eyes. She gave a guilty smile. 'Oh, I almost forgot – happy birthday.'

'Thank you.' Only then did Maxim remember that it was indeed his birthday tomorrow. 'I completely forgot.'

'But we didn't. Oh, here they come.'

Voices were coming from the outside. Maxim involuntarily stretched his neck, trying to get a sight of the visitors. A tall lilac bush was in the way, but he could make out Iris's loud voice right away. She wasn't alone; he could see Rada going down the path. After her came Iris and Danila walking next to each other. There was also Roman, Denis, Boris and Igor. The last ones to follow were Kostya and Mariana; they were quietly discussing something.

'Go on, say hello to your guests,' Oxana said. 'I got here a few minutes before them on purpose.'

'And just as luck would have it, I've got no food in the house,' Maxim mumbled.

'Well, we'll deal with that somehow,' Oxana said confidently. 'Besides, they won't stay long, only a couple of days.'

'And what about you?' he quietly asked the weighty question.

'Do you want me to stay?' Oxana inquired.

'I do.'

'Then I'll stay,' Oxana said and smiled. 'Go, or Iris will break your door. They don't know that you're here.'

'I'm going.' Maxim ran his hand along Oxana's hair, gave her a quick kiss and hurried into the house. He just knew very well that there was no door that could stop Iris.

[1] Resort town in Krasnodar Krai, Russia. Situated on the coast of the Black Sea.

[2] A region in the Caucasus, and an autonomous republic of Georgia.

[3] Joke: A big fellow comes to a construction site to look for work. They ask him – "What can you do?" – "I can dig" – "Anything else?" – "I can stop digging." – "Can you make a latter?" – "Yeah, I'll just have to dig for a long time." (tran.)

[4] Castaneda, Carlos. The Active Side of Infinity. A flyer is referred to as a predator "[…] it leaps through the air… It is a big shadow, impenetrably black, a black shadow that jumps through the air." (trans.)

[5] Russian style fruit dumplings (trans.)

[6] A 44-seat twin engined transport manufactured in the USSR 1959-1979 (tran.)

[7] Well-known Russian pasta dish – macaroni with fried minced meat and onion. (tran.)

[8] Soviet patriotic song (tran.)

[9] Medovúkha – an ancient Russian Pagan alcohol beverage, based on honey and very similar to mead. (tran.)

[10] 1 Peter 5:5

[11] Prèlest' – Russian word for lovely, used in the Russian Orthodox mystic tradition as to indicate a spiritual delusion, someone imagining her or himself to be close to God. (tran.)

The Author's Afterword

This book belongs to the genre of science fiction. However, not everything written here is of fantastic nature. Dream searchers do actually exist; you can find information on them on the internet. So that the reader will be able to sort out the realities, I should explain a few things.

First of all, you can divide dream searchers into two generations: the generation of the founders and those, who now continue this tradition. The searchers of the first generation almost never appear online; on open forums you can mostly meet the representatives of the second generation. However, the presence of two generations doesn't stop dream searchers from being a tight team of like-minded people. They are the people of knowledge, striving towards an understanding of the mystery of the universe. Their spirit is flawless. They are pure, honest and unselfish. That's what draws and will draw people to them.

When it comes to the practical side of the matter, the techniques mentioned in this book should not be viewed as a guide for action, but as information that will allow you to make your own conclusions. Familiarizing yourself with the techniques of dream searchers is best done in the real world – if you wish, you may find them on the Net. The description of the techniques offered in this book have passed through the author's prism of perception, and that means that in many ways, it reflects his own personal understanding of the topics touched upon. Consequently, the only objective of this book is to familiarize the reader with the world of dream searchers: the world that is wonderful and exciting but also dangerous. The tragic death of Sergey Izrigi in 2003, the leader of dream searchers, became a tragic confirmation of this. Nevertheless, dream searchers continue to exist – their movement is only growing wider. You too can join them – visit them, they will be happy to see you. On my part, I'd like to express my sincere gratitude to those who unselfishly shared and continue to share their knowledge – Sergey Izrigi, Tambov, Iveta, Imba, Ravenna, Doc, Spam and all of the searchers of the second generation.

Andrey Reutov
2005

BOOKS

O is a symbol of the world, of oneness and unity. In different cultures it also means the "eye," symbolizing knowledge and insight. We aim to publish books that are accessible, constructive and that challenge accepted opinion, both that of academia and the "moral majority."

Our books are available in all good English language bookstores worldwide. If you don't see the book on the shelves ask the bookstore to order it for you, quoting the ISBN number and title. Alternatively you can order online (all major online retail sites carry our titles) or contact the distributor in the relevant country, listed on the copyright page.

See our website www.o-books.net for a full list of over 500 titles, growing by 100 a year.

And tune in to myspiritradio.com for our book review radio show, hosted by June-Elleni Laine, where you can listen to the authors discussing their books.

mySpiritRadio